"Jenny . . . listen to me. It's not what you would have. I know. I understand. But you have stated to me that you could never love, never marry. Is that true?"

"Yes, yes, it is true," Jenny said.

"Very well then! If it is true and you believe me when I say that I do not ask you to love me, then why deny this marriage? I respect you, admire you, feel that you and you only out of all the women I have met could fill the post as Lady Waine. I must marry, so why deny me the opportunity of securing my fortune," argued his Lordship.

Jenny considered the logic of his proposal. "You must understand that . . . that I . . . oh do excuse my blunt speaking for there is no other way to put it. You have asked me to grace your life . . . do you realize, my lord, that if I should accept to do so, I would refuse to grace . . . to share . . . your bed?" she said, blushing furiously.

The Earl regarded her speculatively before replying. He wanted her, and had no intention of having a wife that would not admit him to her bedroom. Especially this chit who tantalized him with her every movement. Yet he had not gotten her this far just to scare her off. . . .

Fawcett Crest Books
by Claudette Williams:

SPRING GAMBIT

AFTER THE STORM

# AFTER THE STORM

_Claudette Williams_

A FAWCETT CREST BOOK

Fawcett Publications, Inc., Greenwich, Connecticut

*AFTER THE STORM*

A Fawcett Crest Original

Copyright © 1977 by Fawcett Publications, Inc.

ISBN 0-449-23081-3

Printed in the United States of America

10   9   8   7   6   5   4   3   2   1

For my brother Bobby

*Did ye not hear it? No; 'twas but the wind,*
*Or the car rattling o'er the stony street;*
*On with the dance! Let Joy be unconfined,*
*No sleep till morn, when Youth and Pleasure meet.*
*To chase the glowing hours with flying feet—*
*But Hark! that heavy sound breaks in once more,*
*As if the clouds its echo would repeat;*
*And nearer, clearer, deadlier than before!*
*Arm! Arm! it is—it is—the CANNON's opening*
*     roar!*

Lord Byron, 1816

The above stanza was written by Lord Byron to mark the Duchess of Richmond's ball on the eve of the Battle of Waterloo.

# Chapter One

The wind, no longer warm from the rays of the sun, bit at her face, causing her to blink her eyes. Long chestnut-colored hair whipped around her slender neck. She put one white delicate hand up and brushed the thick strands away as she stopped her determined steps. She brought her lowered dark eyes up and stared at a tall dark oak . . . their oak!

"Johnny," she whispered. "Oh, my John." There was a finality in the sound and she felt the old anguish steal over her, but this time the pain came dully and she found she could no longer cry.

Jenny dropped to her knees beside the weathered oak tree. It had been a year . . . a year since he had gone. One year since the Duchess of Richmond's ball and Waterloo!

For months she had been attempting to oust the memory of that terrible night, but now she wanted to recall every detail. She wanted to remember her John as he was, and then bid his memory farewell. Her hand capped her drawn brows and she closed her eyes. A sadness welled within her as she pictured his boyish face and she shook her head dolefully.

She recalled how Georgiana, the Duchess of Richmond's daughter, took her hand for support as they watched the fever of excited officers going off almost merrily to Waterloo! Even then—with those dreadful drums beating throughout Brussels—even then, they looked as though they were off to a parade.

Jenny dropped her head to her drawn knees as she forced herself to remember. Those drums, those awful drums beating wildly, calling their men to arms. The officers attending the Duchess of Richmond's ball left hurriedly, some actually going off to battle in their ball attire, and John had been among them.

Then the cannons began exploding the air and the English Beau Monde breathlessly awaited the outcome. The English gentry had flocked to Brussels that spring, for Napoleon had escaped, gathered an army, and begun to march. The Duke of Wellington, the English hero, had come to meet him. The English believed that Wellington would win when that meeting took place and wanted to be there to witness it. No one had anticipated the amount of blood it would take to fulfill their expectation. Thus it happened on June 18, 1815, that Wellington met Boney at Waterloo.

Jenny frowned and a tear made its slow progress down her cheek, for she still remembered the hideous deaths of those men . . . so many young men. She had gone out into the streets when the first carload of wounded trailed into the city. There she had remained with dozens of other Englishwomen, tending those they could. She had been exhausted, mostly from the pain of watching men, those weary young men, die. Her body ached, her heart felt shredded, and her mind—God, her mind screamed against such misery!

Then she looked up and saw Mac—Lieutenant William McMillan. He had greeted her quietly, his face distorted by pain. His left arm was covered with blood and dirt from a nasty wound and hung uselessly at his side. His right hand reached out for hers and gripped it tightly. "Never mind me, Jen. I . . . I don't know how to tell you . . . it's Johnny! He . . . he said to tell you . . . loved you . . . wants you to forget. . . ."

She saw the tears in Mac's eyes. She heard the words he was saying, and then all at once something tore through her. Some hidden beast from the realms of her subconscious loomed and swayed its omnipotent, blood-stained tentacles and Jenny screamed. A long heartbreaking scream before oblivion took pity.

Later that night she awakened and felt her bed in the dark and suddenly remembered.

Her screams brought her papa and Aunt Beth to her

side. She heard their words of comfort, but nothing they said had eased the torment of knowing John was dead.

The tears were flowing now steadily as she recalled that moment. "Enough, Jen . . . it is enough." She wiped her wet cheeks with a corner of her crumpled gown and stood up. "I came to say good-bye, John."

She stood transfixed before the tree they had called their own and traced the initials he had carved when they were children. She sighed heavily as she forced the horror of his death and the listless months that followed from her mind and turned to face the open fields of her beloved Devon.

Her papa and Aunt Beth had brought her home to Devon soon after Waterloo. They had hoped that her love of horses and her home would spark some animation back into her. However, this hope had yet to be fulfilled. Jenny Ashley found that the Grange reminded her all too much of her childhood sweetheart, and the depression that had taken hold of her had not let go.

She gave the tree one long last look, touching her fingers to her lips. "Understand, John, I shall always love you, but I *need* to forget the pain of losing you. Good-bye, love."

Jenny straightened her shoulders and turned resolutely to walk away from her past. The trials of the preceding months had left their etchings within her. She had found the quiet solitude of her beloved Devon landscape the only tonic that soothed her.

She crossed the open field with slow long strides and felt the overgrown grass brush against the muslin material of her old gown. The day had been tempered by the gray low clouds that hovered teasingly.

It was still midafternoon, and yet, because of the overcast sky, it appeared later. Jenny cast her eyes upward, frowned thoughtfully, and made the decision to take a shortcut across Farmer Cubbins' field. She reached the roadside fence and picked up her skirts, climbed nimbly up, sat on the aged gray wooden stocks, and then pushed herself forward onto the country dirt road.

She had been so engrossed with getting her skirts past the splintered rail and her feet over the ditch that lined the road that she hadn't noticed the rider coming around the bend in the road at what was certainly a reckless pace.

Her sudden descent onto the road caused the horse to rear and champ at his bit. This startled Jenny, and before she knew what had happened, she had released a screech, stepped forcefully backward, and landed herself in the very ditch she had tried to avoid.

## Chapter Two

Jenny heard a low male voice curse beneath his breath. She heard him dismount and within an instant felt herself pulled to her feet. A pair of startlingly blue eyes looked angrily down into her own large brown ones and said in a tone she had never heard before, "Well, well . . . at least it's a pretty wench that's detained me!"

Then, without another word, she found herself in his arms being ruthlessly kissed.

At first Jenny was too shocked to react, and when at length she made an effort to resist by pushing him away, she found that his arms held her in a vicelike grip. She was astonished, but when his lips would not release her own, she began to feel both anger and alarm. Suddenly a fighting spirit sprang to life within her and she allowed herself to relax a moment in his arms. As the scoundrel seemed to take this for an acquiescent show, his own grip relaxed.

Jenny had just enough time to carefully bring her foot into position to thrust it hard and forcefully into his shin. The man cried out with surprise and pain, releasing her and bending toward the source of his discomfort.

Jenny ran! She ran without looking back, though her skirts hampered her progress now and then by getting caught on a thistle bush. Finally, when she could run no more, she sighted the green lawns of Ashley Grange.

She leaned against a nearby tree, breathing hard and hurriedly glancing behind her. She thanked Providence that her assailant had not deemed it worthwhile to pursue her. Sucking in a long, delicious breath of air, Jenny proceeded toward her home at a more decorous pace.

Jenny entered the charming Tudor home through a side entrance that led past the kitchen quarters via a narrow dark corridor to the wide circular staircase. She blessed the fact that the kitchen staff was in a bustle over dinner and had not noted her disheveled appearance. The grand staircase was situated in the main hall, and Jenny held her breath as she approached, praying that Aunt Beth would not be about, for she had no wish to relay what had just occurred.

She shook her head, for she could well imagine what her father would say, and then there would be no solitary walks through the fields! Luckily she found the center hall deserted and made a swift dart up the steps and down the second-floor corridor to the safety of her own room. She closed the door behind her and stepped across the ample-sized room to her bed, plopping down with a sigh and giving herself up to speculation.

Jenny's lovely dark winged brows drew together. Why had the stranger done such a thing? Even in that short span of time she had noted that the man's dress and style were those of a gentleman . . . and his horse was a magnificent creature. "A gentleman? Ha!" said Jenny to her pillow. "Perhaps by birth, but not by action!"

Then suddenly she remembered his eyes—those deep blue eyes . . . they had looked so angry! She hoped his horse had not suffered a strained fetlock from the incident. Jenny sat up and went to her long wall mirror and gazed at her reflection. It was the first time in a long while that she had bothered to appraise herself. What she saw appalled her. No one could deny the glorious hue of her ripe chestnut-colored hair, but its luxuriant strands were at the moment strewn about in tangled disorder, making a web about her shoulders and down her back. Her face was pale and thin and there was little color in her high cheekbones. Her eyes appeared too large for her small face and her dress was old, dull, and crumpled.

"Oh, my goodness, Jenny!" she whispered to the girl in the mirror. "Look at you! It's no wonder you were accosted, for he . . . he probably took you for some serving wench." She noted with a grimace that her dress was not only old, but torn at the bodice, exposing the young fullness of her white breasts. It fitted too tightly at the waist, showing off to perfection the smallness of that same waist. "Tch, tch! Now don't you look like a dainty piece! Why I should have inspired a total stranger to such passion is beyond comprehension. Maybe he just goes about the countryside kissing girls in torn dresses."

The ridiculousness of this made her giggle. It was a strange sensation to hear herself laugh and she felt the tingle stretch through her body when she suddenly caught herself up and stopped short, sobering and returning to her bed.

She looked up to find her Aunt Beth's hazel eyes peeping in the doorway.

"May I come in, dear?" asked Aunt Beth hopefully, her plump cheeks flushed with pleasure.

"Certainly, Auntie, do!" said Jenny, smiling at the woman who had been mother, friend, and confidante for most of her life.

Aunt Beth bustled in, wreathed in smiles and mystery, and brought forth an enormous box. She rested the attractively wrapped package on the bed and looked at the astonished face of her niece with a sheepish grin. "Dear Jennifer, do not, pray, be angry with your foolish old aunt. Since you have refused to come to town with me and choose a few new gowns for the Season—for you must admit that yours are quite old and out of fashion—and my word, child, where you found that . . . that thing you are wearing is a mystery, for I should never have allowed it to be left in your closet had I known—"

"It was not in the closet, Auntie. It was in the trunk, an old dress that I used to wear quite a lot . . . when I was younger," said Jenny, frowning and remembering the last time she had worn it with Johnny.

"Well, that may be, but nonetheless you look a veritable ragamuffin!" Then, remembering the errand she had come on, Aunt Beth's warm face brightened. "Never mind that now. You see, actually, when I saw this . . . creation (for there is no other word for it), I could just picture you wearing it! Oh, dearest child, do not be put out with me, for I could not resist it, Jenny. It is just the right shade of pink for you. And my God, Jenny, what has happened to your hair?" rattled Aunt Beth, and then not waiting for an answer, continued, "I daresay you have been running about the woods again. Well, it doesn't matter if only you will put yourself to rights, for your papa is entertaining tonight, and we had hoped you. . . ." She let her voice trail off as she observed with delighted astonishment that Jenny had actually stood up and walked over to the package.

Jenny fingered the large silver bow that adorned the carton and a light young laugh came to her lips. This so affected her aunt that the plump woman immediately put her arms about the girl, thinking that this was the first time she had heard Jenny laugh in more than a year.

Jenny returned her aunt's bear hug. "Oh, Auntie, you sound so adorable rattling on in that fashion. Am I such an ogre that you needs must be afraid of me? It seems I have been rather a spoiled pet, haven't I? How awful for you and papa. Do not look like that, love, I have been all right now, quite all right, for some time past. Really, Auntie. Come, let us open this box and observe this creation of yours!"

"Oh, it isn't really *my* creation, Jenny. I cannot take credit for it . . . only for having the good sense to buy it."

This caused Jenny to chuckle again, but the gurgle of fun turned into an exclamation of enthusiasm when she lifted the froth of pink gauze from the box. Pulling it out, she pressed it to herself and scurried over to the wall mirror once again. As she scanned the image that met her eyes, she thought, I wonder what Blue-eyes would do if he saw you in this? However, this thought made her frown. Oh God, Jenny! What are you thinking? How can you? What kind of a girl are you anyway? "You do like it, dear . . . don't you?" asked Aunt Beth anxiously, quick to note the crease on Jenny's brow.

15

Jenny brought her attention back to her aunt. "Oh yes, Auntie, it is the most ravishing gown I have ever seen."

Aunt Beth regarded her niece thoughtfully, wondering happily what had passed to cause her darling Jenny's cheeks to blush with such becoming color. This was the first real spark of animation she had observed in her for quite some time, and she raised her eyes, giving quiet thanks to the forces that had been at work. Beth loved her niece almost as if she were her own daughter. She had lost her husband when she was still a young woman and before she had had any children of her own. Soon afterwards Jenny's own mother had died, and Beth came to stay, adopting Jenny as her own.

She and the Squire had lavished all their affection and attention upon Jennifer, petting and cosseting the child. They had watched her play with Johnny Dillingham; watched them grow together as children, for the lad had been only two years older than Jennifer. They had welcomed Johnny as their future son, and yet Beth had always worried over the matter, remarking pensively to her brother, "No one can deny that John Dillingham is a charming scamp, Alfred, least of all I . . . for you know I think the world of him. Yet . . . I have always felt he is a bit too dashing and irresponsible. Not the sort of qualities one looks for in a husband. And Jenny is just as daring as he. They will have no settling effect on each other. Then there is the fact that Jenny is still young. She has not been brought out for the London Season. Really, Alfred, she is going from the schoolroom into his arms . . . do you think it wise?"

The Squire had laughed at her, for he was well pleased with the match. His Jenny was marrying a fine lad and would not be moving out of his reach—what more could a loving father wish for? And so he told his sister. However, Aunt Beth had not been able to banish the thought that while Jennifer adored Johnny, it was not the same thing as being in love with a man, especially since Jenny had not known many men.

Aunt Beth broke her reverie and smiled tenderly at her niece. "You will look stunning tonight, dearest. Do not feel guilty, for I can see what is bothering you and

16

causing that frown. No one could expect you to mourn forever, and you know very well that Johnny would never have wished you to bury yourself alive!"

"I know, Auntie, I know. Do not worry, I shall be fine," said Jenny with a light sigh and an eye toward her window.

"I am certain you will be just fine. Just think, Jenny, soon we will be off to Brighton for the Season. There will be roût parties, assemblies—in no time at all you will forget all about . . . what you have been through. You will forget . . . Johnny, you know." As soon as the words were out, Beth realized it had been the wrong thing to say and she bit her lip.

*"No!* I will never forget him!" came Jenny's voice harsh and angry, angry with herself, for this was precisely what she had been trying to do. Yet when she heard the suggestion spoken by someone else, even someone as beloved as her Aunt Beth, it sounded so very faithless. She clutched her own hands helplessly. "Listen to me, Aunt Beth. I will come downstairs tonight, I will mingle with your guests, but I will never, never allow myself to . . . to fall in love with another man. I cannot do it. Please do not plan roûts and outings for me. I shall not go! I cannot go! It is not only because of Johnny's memory . . . but because I am afraid. Do you understand? I am afraid of the pain . . . I can never fall in love again."

Aunt Beth's frown darkened and she felt a pinch at her heart. "Yes, child. I understand all too well. It is the way of the Ashleys. Your father always shied away from remarriage, and I . . . I, too, was unable to find another to take my husband's place. However, we were older, much older, and we were wrong. We shut out the joys life could give, and you must not!"

"There is no joy, Aunt Beth, no joy that cannot be snatched away!" said Jenny bitterly.

"My dearest child, would you deny yourself the joys of the earth simply for fear that they will not last? Then why live . . . why go on? No, it is not natural. I know what Johnny was to you. We have not spoken—you have not allowed us to speak to you—but there are things that must be said. You had a marvelous relationship with Johnny. It

17

was a fairy tale . . . but it is at an end. I don't wish to be harsh, love, but he is dead! *You* are very much alive. You have a duty to that life . . . to your papa . . . to the people you have to meet yet," said Aunt Beth urgently.

"Auntie, Auntie," said Jenny, flinging her arms about her and choking on the words, "I do love you and Papa."

"Then you will attend tonight and be your old gay self!" responded her aunt, taking a firm approach.

"I . . . I will try. But as for the rest, don't ask me yet."

"No, we will leave the plans for the . . . rest to be discussed later. Now, young lady, go take your bath. I have asked Biddle to prepare it for you. Our guests will be arriving at seven."

Jenny looked at her aunt curiously. "Who is coming?"

Beth began to rattle off the names of the local gentry and finished blithely, "Oh . . . Sir Arthur and Lavinia will be here, with their house guest as well."

"Lavvy . . . Lavvy will be here? Oh, that is too wonderful! I hadn't realized they were back from London."

"Yes, indeed. They have been here for a week, but you have refused to listen to me whenever I suggested you take a ride over there for a nice chat."

"I . . . I don't think I quite understood that she was home," said Jenny sheepishly. "I hope she will not be cross with me."

"Well, I can't think why she should not be! Lavinia has been one of your dearest friends, and yet you have rejected her company, her condolences, and only answered one of her many sweet letters. It was positively atrocious behavior on your part, Jenny!" scolded her aunt.

"Yes, I have been rather horrid to all my friends . . . but Lavvy will forgive me," said Jenny softly.

"Yes, dear, I am quite sure she will and you will behave properly tonight . . . I know."

"You mentioned they have a house guest," said Jenny curiously.

Aunt Beth frowned thoughtfully but all she said was, "Hmmm . . . yes, the Earl of Waine. Your father and I have never really been well acquainted with him, and frankly, I was a bit surprised to find that he is visiting with the Digbys."

"Oh . . . why?" inquired Jenny, surprised.

"In truth, child, it is only gossip . . . yet one does wonder, for the Earl of Waine has achieved a deplorable reputation with regards to . . . er, women!"

Jenny's dark eyes opened wide. "Egad, Auntie, never say Sir Arthur is entertaining a rake? Why, that is beyond everything . . . especially with Lavvy so susceptible. She always had a penchant for scoundrels."

"That, dear, is what has me puzzled," said her aunt, frowning. "And I do wish you would refrain from using expressions such as 'egad.' "

"Faith! I wonder what's toward?" said Jenny, interested.

"Well, I imagine we shall find out soon enough. Do go take your bath, for the water was brought up ages ago and I do not want it to get cold before you have had a chance to get in." With that she turned and flurried out of the room, her matronly skirts rustling around her small plump body.

Jenny made her way to the dressing room, where she fingered the water and found it still scalding hot. As she undressed, she contemplated the months that had passed, and then her mind wandered to the time before she had lost Johnny.

Brussels had been so beautiful and titillating. The spring had been a profusion of color and exotic scents esconced the gay city. Her thoughts traveled back to one beautiful day. She had been waiting with Georgiana and Roland in the garden. They were going on a picnic, and then Mac had arrived with a note from John. She read it with a sigh, for Johnny was a member of Wellington's staff and this was not the first time a note had come around to advise her that he had been sent off somewhere with a dispatch.

She shrugged her shoulders, for it could not be helped. Johnny's note had apologized in his boyish manner, urging her not to fret and to attend the expedition with Mac in his stead. Georgy had put in her appeal to this and it had been arranged. Laughingly they had gone and she had enjoyed herself. Mac was the perfect companion; in fact, far more chivalrous than John was wont to be. Mac was as dark as John had been fair. His young cherubic countenance was gentle and his eyes were dark and penetrating.

She had teased Johnny many times about Mac's good looks, but he had only laughed, giving her shoulders a shake and saying knowingly, "Now, pea goose, you know your taste runs to yella-haired bucks like m'self." With which he planted a kiss upon her cherry lips as final proof.

She had sighed then, not as she sighed now. She lay back in the tub, relaxing in the soothing effects of the hot water, and after a while dozed off. A pair of startlingly blue eyes were suddenly looking angrily down into her own and what flashed across her unconscious was a kiss. A kiss that had burned her lips and aroused her mind. Suddenly she started up with shock and gasped to herself, "Jenny . . . what were you dreaming? . . ."

## Chapter Three

*They mourn, but smile at length; and smiling, mourn;*
*The tree will wither long before it fall;*
*The hull drives on, though mast and sail be torn;*
*And thus the heart will break, yet brokenly live on.*
                                        LORD BYRON, 1816

Several hours later Jenny approached the mirror, solemnly appraising herself. Her chestnut hair was piled on top of her well-shaped head and fell in gleaming torrents upon her shoulders. It caught the light and glistened tints of coppery hues so that the onlooker could not be sure there weren't bright new pennies afixed here and there to dazzle him.

Her winged dark brows were well defined and needed no blacking, nor did the lashes that rested now upon her flushed cheeks. Her dark eyes were large and enchanting in her small pointed face, hinting mischievously at her hidden personality. Her figure looked alluringly lovely in the pink froth that now encased it. The gown billowed gently around her to the floor, where matching pink slippers peeped out. The bodice of the gown was scooped and studded with sparkling diamonds. Yet gone was the spontaneous smile that had once characterized her. Gone was that joyful gurgle that had filled the Ashley house. Gone was the naughty, merry, and exciting creature, and in her place was a quiet, subdued damsel whose manner spoke of caution, of loss, and of fear.

However, this change had not subdued the wild glory of her appearance. Quite the contrary: what had once been a lovely scamp of a girl was now a regal and mysterious beauty. She had a maturity most girls her age had not achieved.

Many of the Ashleys' guests had already arrived, but Jenny had hung back in her room. She was feeling shy, dreading what would be her first social appearance since John's death. She fretted silently in the quiet of her room, wondering what people's reactions to her would be. They will say I have forgotten John, she thought morosely. They will think me faithless.

She moved restlessly about the room as in her mind these doldrums tossed fitfully upon themselves. 'Tis not that I am putting him out of my heart . . . only away from my thoughts. I must . . . I need to forget the loss of him, she pleaded inwardly with herself before whispering, "Oh, forgive me, John."

Then Aunt Beth was there, her blue silk gown softly framing her plump figure. She rustled musically about as she fussed over Jenny's person. Aunt Beth's eyes came to rest upon Jenny's face and an understanding passed between them. Her warm hand took up Jenny's and pressed it reassuringly. "How lovely you are, Jennifer. Your father will be that proud of you dear . . . do come." Beth's voice was soft and held a gentle coaxing quality that caused Jenny to smile in warm response. She gave over and allowed her aunt to tug at her trembling fingers and followed her to the staircase landing.

There could be no refusing, no going back now. She had given her word. Jenny descended the steps slowly, her aunt's hand still held tightly within her own. They walked demurely into the drawing room and stood for a moment. Jenny clutched her aunt's hand frantically for one frightened space in time and felt the pressure returned.

The room was well lit with tall tapers, showing to advantage the unusual ceiling. It had been done in the Adam style and was made of oval shapes filled with arabesques. There were damask hangings ornamenting the walls, and the carpet, which was centered in the room, had been specially woven to repeat the main design of the ceiling.

The drawing room was filled with richly dressed men and women, and though they did not glitter as they would in London, there was no mistaking their noble heritage.

Jenny scanned the room and relaxed, for the company, which was composed of people belonging to her father's intimate set, were all well known to her. She smiled and found that all eyes and lips were returning a gentle, concerned smile . . . and a welcome.

The Squire, looking tall and attractive in his cutaway coat of dark brown velvet and buff-colored breeches, came forward immediately. His dark eyes lit with affection. "Jenny, my babe, how enchanting you look. Come, child, and greet our guests."

One by one, she went through the cordial greetings until a squeal of delight came to her ears and she turned to find Lavinia Digby entering the drawing room. Jenny went forward at once, a welcome upon her lips, and the two friends embraced fondly. Sir Arthur Digby, a plump, balding man, looked kindly on and said something low to the younger gentleman at his side.

Jenny's gaze swept Lavinia's person and she exclaimed in surprised accents, "Lavvy . . . how modish and grown up you are! I am so very glad to see you again."

Lavinia Digby was a year younger than Jennifer Ashley and had just been presented during the London Season. Jenny found that the year had done quite a lot for her fair friend.

Lavinia was dressed in a white summer muslin that had been dampened to cling to her delicate form. She was a pert blonde with gray eyes and a naughty liveliness. Her complexion was smooth and creamy, and she was held to be quite a beauty. Her figure was slight, though tall, and her fondness for Jennifer was quite sincere.

They clasped hands and gazed at each other, gray eyes smiling at dark with full understanding. Lavinia said quietly, "Dearest Jen, how I have missed you, and quite forgive you for all the wrongs you have piled up."

Jenny laughed and pinched her friend's chin. "Ah, my Lavvy, haven't you always forgiven me?"

"Yes, and perhaps that is why you take advantage, minx!" replied Lavinia, giggling.

They stood back from each other, both remembering their manners, and Jenny turned to greet Sir Arthur, who had been patiently standing by. She held out her hand and they exchanged warm salutations before Sir Arthur motioned to the young gentleman standing beside him.

Jenny's eyes went up to gaze upon the stranger and she felt a gasp form in her throat. Horrified, she could not move, but stood staring with disbelief. He was perfectly composed, having had time to observe her, and seemed quite amused at the situation they had been thrown into.

She heard Sir Arthur say something about the Earl of Waine and mechanically put her hand into that of the stranger's. He bent over it lingeringly and she looked across at the eyes that rose to meet her own. Those lush blue eyes gazing so cynically amused at her. She heard him say in a mocking tone, "I believe, Sir, that Miss Ashley and I have already had the *pleasure* of a previous meeting."

Jennifer managed to stifle a choke and a militant sparkle came to her eyes. The gall, she thought, the barefaced gall of the man—to be so . . . so ungentlemanly as to place such emphasis on the word *pleasure*, knowing how I would feel!

"Indeed?" came the surprised reply from her father, who had made his way to the little group at the drawing room entrance in time to hear this last remark.

Jennifer blushed and managed, "Er . . . yes, we met quite by er . . . *accident* this afternoon."

"I see," responded the Squire lightly (but actually didn't).

Lavinia looked speculatively for a moment at Jennifer

23

but refrained from commenting. Taking Jenny's hand, she led her away to a corner of the room.

Jenny found it easy and enjoyable to listen to Lavvy's silly chatter. Lavinia, it seemed, was thrilled with London and the Beau Monde and they with her. All the *ton* were at her feet, and on and on she went until Jenny once again knew the warmth she had always felt for her flighty friend.

"Dearest Lavvy," said Jenny when Lavinia paused for breath, "you are such a love. How could you be anything but a success?"

Her friend laughed and embraced her once again. Dinner was announced and Jenny was led out by her father. Sir Arthur followed with Aunt Beth upon his arm. Jennifer noted with a flicker of interest that the Earl of Waine seemed very well pleased to be taking Lavvy into dinner.

The Earl was placed at the far end of the table and Jennifer was thankful that she had been spared the gruesome necessity of making polite conversation with this conceited rake. However, every now and then her eyes flitted across the length that separated them and she felt an odd pang, almost a twinge of annoyance, to see that he seemed to be having a marvelous time with Lavinia. She felt a strange heat flow through her veins as she recalled the brutal way he had misused her earlier that day. If Johnny were here, she thought, he would have called you out, sir! Her thoughts tumbled one on top of the other as she watched him flirt audaciously with Lavvy, and in her wrath she forgot for the first time to grieve over the thought of Johnny's name.

After dinner the ladies withdrew, leaving the men to linger over their port. Lavvy was called to by Aunt Beth and forced to sit in conversation with friends of her father's.

Jenny was grateful for a moment alone, and wandered off, opening the great glass doors that led into the garden. She stepped out, breathing in the cool early summer night's air. There was a strong scent of roses brought to her by the delicate breeze and she put her arms about themselves a moment and shut her eyes.

A deep male voice beside her caused her to open them almost at once and she was once again looking into those eyes! Those bright mocking blue eyes. Jennifer knew a sudden urge to slap his face as she gazed at him. One careless black lock, gleaming now in the moonlight, fell across his wide forehead as he bowed insolently before her. "Should I apologize to you, Miss Ashley? For in truth, I had no idea you were the Squire's daughter when I . . . er, came across you this afternoon."

"What difference does that make, my lord?" she snapped at him, her eyes sparkling.

He seemed to smirk. "A world of difference, my dear. I thought you were—and perhaps I should apologize for that as well—a serving girl, a mere country wench, though a very pretty one! Do you always run across fields and jump over fences unaccompanied?" he said, his eyes dancing.

"Yes! For our simple country men are gentlemen and would never stoop so low as to take advantage of a girl simply because she was alone, or because they thought her a peasant maid!" snapped Jenny, incensed.

"*Touché!*" said the Earl, leaning his shoulder against the stone wall and grinning. "This grows interesting."

Realizing that she had hit her mark, Jenny continued. "Even if I were only a poor country wench, as you referred to, only an insufferable, arrogant, despicable man would have behaved as you did. Why . . . if you had slapped me for almost causing you and your horse an injury, it would have been well deserved, for I had no business jumping into the road as I did. But I had to get past my skirts, you see . . . well, nevertheless you had no right to force a kiss on a defenseless female, regardless of her status!" she admonished on an austere note.

The Earl of Waine's sensitive lips quivered. "Aah, but you were not quite so defenseless . . . were you?" The grave tone of his voice did not tally with the merriment in his eyes and Jenny was quick to note this.

Her sense of humor was tickled. She had always been willing to laugh, even when a joke had been poked at her-

25

self. That willingness seemed to bubble within her as she began to appreciate the absurd situation she had been plunged into with this tall, mocking man.

Her dark eyes twinkled up at him. "Well, sir, you did deserve it, after all . . . you must admit that!"

"I will admit nothing of the sort, my lovely. Not if you do not admit to having deserved that . . . kiss," said the Earl, enjoying this play immensely.

Indignation soared within her breast at his flippancy. She felt a heat flow to her cheeks and knew herself to be blushing. She looked very stormy now, filled with a new and quite violent emotion. Emotion—something she had thought lost to her.

"Do you mean to tell me, my lord, that anything . . . anything at all—" she was seething—"led you to believe that . . . that *I* invited such action?"

The Earl threw back his thickly covered head and gave himself over to mirth. He was enjoying the chit's indignant fury. "No, child, it was that, or a spanking, and while I do most humbly beg your pardon for, shall we say, taking advantage of you—"

"*Oh yes! Do let us avoid quibbling!* Let us most emphatically saying *taking advantage!*" interrupted the militant miss.

"I cannot in truth say that I regret the action I took," continued the Earl blandly, ignoring the interruption.

Jenny's lips parted, but she was unable to find a suitable retort and settled the matter by glaring at him. Thus the Earl received a vision of brilliant dark eyes alight with fire, a fire that had suddenly sprung to life after a year's dormancy.

Jenny felt her body quiver with anger but her aunt's voice filtered through and she contained herself as she turned to answer her call. She found an odd reluctance to leave this arrogant man. There was more to be said, more lectures to spring at his brazen head. Not sorry, indeed!

She turned on her elegant heel, throwing the folds of her clinging pink gown behind her, and then, quite unladylike, stalked away.

The Earl of Waine stood a moment after he watched her go. A slow smile crept over his handsome countenance. He chuckled softly to himself and followed after a few moments.

Aunt Beth gave Jenny a searching look and thought that the child appeared to be in high spirits. She sighed with satisfaction. "Come, Jennifer, Lady March wants a word with you."

Jenny allowed herself to be carried off and sat beside the elderly white-haired matron who seemed determined to interest her in a dialogue of never-ending trivia. She found her eyes darting about the room and coming to rest on the Earl. She watched him, her temper still smoldering, but could not banish the thought that he was extremely good-looking. He stood well over six feet. His shoulders were broad, depicting the athlete, yet he wore his superbly cut clothes with unique elegance. His hair was black, and waved about his head in think long folds. His brows were black also, and seemed to tilt downward at the very tips. His mouth was well formed ... yet seemed to be continually sneering. And then there were those eyes. The deep blue eyes that had first caught her attention. They were framed with lashes as thick and dark as her own—and they curled, she thought with a grimace, as hers would not!

Yes, she thought, the arrogance comes from finding himself attractive to women. She estimated that he was in his late twenties, and there was an air of listlessness—or rather boredom—that hung about him that made her wonder. Suddenly she met those blue eyes, so outstanding in his deeply bronzed, rugged face ... and they laughed at her.

Insufferable, she thought and looked away.

Lavinia came to her and politely managed to extricate her from Lady March's side.

"Oh, Lavvy," Jenny breathed as they walked away. "Thank God, you have come, she was boring on and on and there was no escape. I shall thank Aunt for that tomorrow!" They laughed and found two empty chairs and sank down, eyeing each other happily.

Lavvy sobered and said quietly, "Jenny, before we go on, you know—of course, you know—how I have grieved for you. Johnny was my friend . . . indeed, we were all

27

dear friends. I had no wish to intrude, and you made it quite clear that you had no wish for my . . . my condolences, so I stayed away. However, Jen, I do not intend to now. Why, you should be in Brighton with me. We leave next week, and what a Season it will be! Jenny, you have no idea, for you were never presented. You became engaged, and entered society as a fianceé, not a debutante. I have made a hit, but you . . . you would be declared 'The Incomparable'!"

"Oh, Lavvy, what nonsense you do speak!" Jenny scoffed.

"Silly, silly Jenny. You do not realize what you look like. Why, your hair . . . it puts my yellow locks quite in the shade."

"How can you utter such falsehoods, Lavvy?" exclaimed Jenny, shocked and unbelieving. "My hair is brown . . . just dark brown."

Her friend shook her head. "Jenny, do you not realize, with every movement, your hair captures the light, shining a bright rich copper? Brown, indeed, you foolish child. It is magnificent. Your face is alive with beauty . . . your creamy complexion. Jenny, do you not know how ravishing you are? No, of course not, you would never listen to anyone but Johnny, and he would say naught but that you were a 'pretty pea goose.' Why even the Earl was quite astounded at your beauty, and he is a connoisseur, let me tell you!"

"Jenny shook her head, but looked at her friend intently. "Why is he here, Lavvy?"

Lavinia gave a low gurgle of laughter. "Oh, it is the most amusing thing. He is here to ask for my hand in marriage. However, he has not come up to scratch yet!"

"What?" ejaculated Jenny, horrified. "Never say so . . . oh, Lavvy!"

Lavinia looked a bit put out at her friend's reaction and a slight pout formed on her full lips. "Well, after all, I don't think you should be so surprised. I am not such a bad catch, Jenny. In fact, rather an excellent match for the Earl."

Jenny frowned. "No, no, Lavvy, you misunderstand. I do not think the Earl is good enough for *you*!"

Lavinia shrugged. "Well, as to that, he is considered by most to be the biggest marriage prize on the market that ever was. Just look at him—handsome, sophisticated, an Earl, and rich ... or at least he will be rich when he comes into his inheritance. That is why he is here!"

"I don't understand," said Jenny, puzzled.

"Dash it, Jen, haven't you heard anything about him? No, no, I suppose you haven't. The thing is the Earl would not marry if he did not have to. He has no choice in the matter. His inheritance is tied up in something known as entails or other ... which means in his case that it will not come into his hands until he marries, and he must marry before he is twenty-nine!"

"Faith!" exclaimed Jenny, putting a hand to her mouth and glancing involuntarily toward the Earl.

"Exactly so!" agreed Lavvy. "Shocking business, but there you are, and 'tis done all the time. You do know that, Jen, for when we were children you always said you would never marry for convenience, as do most of our set."

"Yes, but *you*, Lavvy ... do you mean to do so?" asked Jenny, truly shocked.

"Oh ... I don't know," said Lavvy, frowning, her gray eyes looking past Jenny into space. "I met the Earl in London, you know ... but he is not really my sort. In fact, I didn't really think I was his sort either. The thing is, as I have it from Father, the Earl is here because of his sister. He has been looking for an eligible bride these past few months and more and has only a month or so left him to find one. His sister advised him that she thought I would make a perfect match, and I suppose he agreed, for here he is. The strange thing is that he has been here all afternoon and not mentioned the matter to Papa. In fact, Papa is agog ... wondering when he means to."

"But you, Lavvy ... you would accept such an arrangement?"

Lavinia shrugged her white shoulders. "Oh, as to that ... I suppose so. There is really no one that I have a decided partiality for, and the Earl is the best social—and financial—match I could probably achieve."

"My dearest Lavvy, I cannot believe this of you. You, who have always been a romantic, wanting to marry for love, just as I had always wanted. How can you conceive of such . . . a cold alliance? It would be quite frightful."

"I have been thinking about, it, Jenny, and the thought of being married to a stranger is a frightening idea. But Jen, do you know what is worse? What if I were to marry the Earl and then meet someone perfectly eligible and fall in love with him?"

"Oh, Lavvy!"

"Precisely! Papa is not pushing me into it, you know, and in truth there are some things about the Earl that are not to my liking. For example, Jen, have you noticed how he seems to sneer?"

"Yes . . . and he always appears to be a bit bored," agreed Jenny.

"Yet . . . I would like to be Lady Waine, and run about being fashionable, and they do say that once a lady gives her husband a legal heir . . . the, er, other passions she may have are acceptable if she is discreet."

"Lavvy!" exclaimed Jenny.

"Don't be such a prude, Jen. All the ladies of the Beau Monde have lovers."

"I see," said Jenny quietly.

"Hush now! Here he comes," said Lavvy in a whisper.

Jenny raised her eyes to find him crossing the room toward them and her heart fluttered as she watched him approach.

He regarded them both quizzically. "Miss Digby, Miss Ashley . . . I would be honored if you would both accept an invitation to ride out with me in the morning and show me your lovely countryside."

Miss Digby smiled agreeably and answered before Jenny could utter the stark refusal forming on her lips.

"Oh, that would be fun. We could show you the Old Mill and have Cook prepare us some boxed lunches." She turned merry gray eyes to Jenny and an admonishing finger. "No, Jen! Do not look like that, for I see you wish to cry off, but I shan't let you. You must come, and you can ride Whisper!"

Jenny's eyes pleaded with Lavvy and her voice came hushed. "I . . . I can't ride him yet, Lavvy. It is too soon."

"Nonsense. You have put it off too long, Jen. That is why you are finding it so difficult now, and it isn't fair to Whisper . . . is it?" said Lavvy gently.

Jenny looked stricken. "Yes . . . yes, of course, Lavvy, you are right. But perhaps another day."

The Earl, an eyebrow cocked, had noted with interest this odd exchange of hushed words.

"Have done, girl!" came Lavvy's exasperated response. "Johnny would wish you to go, and go you shall! It is my duty to him as well as to you."

Partly from annoyance at Lavvy's reference to Johnny in the presence of the Earl, and partly from a deep and hidden desire to join them, Jenny capitulated. Without enthusiasm, she accepted.

The Earl regarded her through knit brows. There was a mystery about the child, an aura, and he was intrigued. He excused himself and went toward Sir Arthur, leaving the two girls to their chatter.

Damnation, he thought for the hundredth time that day. That cursed will. Certes, wasn't it just like Father to do such a thing. His father had died, seven years before, leaving him the title and an easy competence. The bulk of the fortune—which was not entailed with the estate, as the former Earl had made the fortune himself as a young man in India—was held in trust, in trust until Jason Waine married. However, if he, the oldest son, did not marry by the time his twenty-ninth birthday arrived, this fortune would fall into the hands of his half-brother Julian.

Both Jason and his sister Gwen had been angry and indignant upon hearing the conditions of this will. Gwen had since married, but nevertheless she remained extremely close to her twin brother and had no intention of allowing the money that was rightfully his go to that "other woman's son," as she always thought of Julian. There were moments when the present Earl, angry at having to secure himself an unwanted bride, had thrown up his hands and declared to her and to the world that he would do just as well without the money and continue to live within the confines of the penury his father had so

31

meagerly doled out. But the Earl was now in debt—gaming and trade debts. Clearly he had not been able to live within the limits of his "easy competence." His tastes were extravagant. He lived high because he was bored. He had had too much too early in life, and he was constantly incurring expenses from the weariness of ennui. He thought about the women in his life. They were all quite beautiful, but none was fit to carry his name. He had a pride of family and knew what was due the heritage of his name. Upon his sister's suggestion, he had written to Sir Arthur Digby, requesting that he be allowed the favor of a visit to further their acquaintance. He should have proposed his offer to Lavinia's father that afternoon, but having spent a few moments with the tiresome chit, he found himself reluctant to do so. He could not commit himself, for although Lavinia was undeniably pretty (he had ever a penchant for blondes), she was also undeniably flighty. She chattered too much and without sense about subjects that bored him. Had he been a younger man, perhaps her bubbling enthusiasm and ingenuous flirtation would have captured his interest, if not his heart, but he was not in the blush of his youth. Anyway, he had never found missish, dewy-eyed beauties to his taste. Not, even when he had first come to London and entered the gay world of the Beau Monde, he had never had a taste for that type of female. It was always the older, more sophisticated beauties who won his favor and his passion. He sighed, for these thoughts were pointless, he was running out of time. It appeared that he was trapped!

# Chapter Four

*BEHOLD HER, single in the field,*
*Yon solitary Highland Lass!*
*Reaping and singing by herself;*
*Stop here, or gently pass!*
        WILLIAM WORDSWORTH

The Earl of Waine sat back upon the cushioned seat in Sir Arthur's coach, regarding his host fixedly. Smiling wryly, he observed the discomfiture of this stately gentleman. Clearly Sir Arthur was waiting to hear what the Earl had to propose with regards to his only child. Sir Arthur hoped nothing would be said here and now with Lavinia seated beside him.

The Earl, however, was not thinking of his proposed nuptials. His mind was on the strange little piece he had met that afternoon, and then again this evening. He had thought Jennifer Ashley was a serving wench when he came across her earlier in the day. When he met her tonight, he thought her the most taking creature he had ever seen. He was determined to know more about the intriguing Miss Ashley, and saw before him the very people to enlighten him.

Jason Waine smiled coaxingly, saying in an offhand manner, "I noticed something strange about the Squire's daughter. Thought it odd in someone so young."

"Eh, what was that?" asked Sir Arthur cautiously.

"Call it a remoteness—no . . . something a bit more. Is there something wrong with the child? I got the impression she was recovering from a protracted illness."

Sir Arthur and his daughter exchanged glances before he answered quietly, "No, not an illness. You really could not call it that. Poor sweet girl. Such a good child. It pains me to see her so subdued, especially when I recall the kick-ups she and Lavvy were wont to throw." He sighed, shaking his head.

"Yes, Papa, I thought I'd die when I saw how quiet she

has become. Jenny was forever on the go, doing or saying something outrageous and capturing one's attention as well as one's heart. Now ... she seems to float away while you talk to her. Her mind wanders. She is just a faded version of what she was," said Lavinia dramatically.

"Faded?" said the Earl, frowning, feeling for no apparent reason a twinge of annoyance. "I would not describe Miss Ashley as faded in any way!"

Lavvy's brows came together. "No? But then, of course, you did not know her before. Do not misunderstand, my lord. Jenny is as beautiful now as she ever was ... perhaps more so in a new way. But she has changed drastically. Anyone who knew Jenny as she was a year ago—indeed, as I have known her all my life—would say so. Jenny had a spirit, a spirit that was wildly alive and just a bit mischievous. Why, 't wasn't more than two years ago Jen broke her arm in a fall and on a dare she took the phaeton out and raced Tom Brookes with her arm still in a splint. No, my lord ... she is not the same girl," replied Lavvy sadly.

"Why do you refer to last year as having been the turning point? What occurred to cause this change?" asked the Earl, intently curious and suddenly impatient to know.

"Waterloo!" said Lavinia gravely. "Waterloo happened to our Jenny. You see, Jen was engaged to be married to John Dillingham. He was a major in his regiment ... on Wellington's staff, you know. They became engaged, and as he was to be sent to Brussels, he arranged for the Squire to bring Jenny. They were having a wonderful time in Brussels ... everyone was, although I have often wondered how they could with Napoleon so near and on the verge, as it were, of such a stupendous attack. However, there they were, and John went off to Waterloo, but did not survive it. You cannot imagine, for you are not acquainted with Jenny, but though I was not with her, I know what she suffered. I won't go into details. Suffice it to say that she has had a very difficult time of it. Jenny and Johnny grew up together. His estate runs parallel to hers and they were constant companions. You rarely saw one without the other, for he was but two years older ... and they adored each other. I have been told that on the eve of Waterloo Jenny went out on the streets . . . a mere slip of a girl, but such was her spirit that she tended the wounded through the night and into the next day. She got the news from a friend . . . some Lieutenant. She collapsed when she heard . . . and has had a ghastly time of it." Lavvy sighed and gazed out the window. "I have always loved Jenny and thought I knew her well . . . yet even I did not know how deep her pain has gone and what it has cost her. She wouldn't see me this past year. She wouldn't see anyone . . . except for that same Lieutenant—I think his name is McMillan or something. It seems he was a friend of Johnny's and she lets him visit because she wants to hear about John. In fact, I was surprised that he was not here tonight. When I spoke with Aunt Beth, she mentioned that he was expected to come for a fortnight."

The Earl digested what he had heard in silence. He pressed a fist to his square chin and remembered the chit's eyes, those strange dark, sad eyes that had lit so brilliantly when she had lost herself to anger.

For one fleeting moment the Earl thought it might prove satisfying to banish that sadness from her eyes, and then quickly chided himself. What had he to do with some strange chit mourning a lost love? Bah! Foolishness!


"Jennifer . . . Jennifer?" called Aunt Beth as she looked around the half-closed door to Jenny's bedroom. There she found her niece all aflutter and looking quite breathtaking in a lovely riding habit of peacock blue.

"Oh, Auntie, do you think it will be too warm for this habit? I do hope not, for I can find nothing else to wear. Do you know, even this looks quite shabby!"

Her aunt hid her surprise quite admirably. Here was something new. Jenny was taking an interest in her garments. Just yesterday morning she had gone out in a torn dress without a thought for her appearance, and now here she was in a perfectly fashionable and lovely riding habit describing it as "shabby," Beth's brows drew together as she pondered the matter and then answered lightly, "Well, love, perhaps it is not the very latest mode, but I doubt that anyone could call it shabby. It will do nicely. As for the weather, I have just come from cutting the roses and it is a wonderfully airy breeze you shall be riding in. Just perfect for an outing and not the least hint of sultriness. Do you know, Jenny, there is a decided bloom in your cheeks . . . very becoming, child. It has been so very long since I have seen you look so enchanting. Now come along and stop worrying over the cut of your clothes. They are perfect. Lavinia and the Earl are waiting downstairs in the morning room for you, and Whisper has been sent for."

All at once Jenny felt her knees tremble. A dreaded ache crept into her throat as she thought of riding Whisper again.

Aunt Beth turned around and chided, "Tch, tch, Jennifer! Really, child, don't stand there and look as though you were about to be eaten. Your friend Lavvy is waiting, and though I don't approve of his Lordship, he is their guest and it simply isn't proper to keep them waiting."

The Earl's face suddenly loomed in her mind and she knew an eagerness to leave her room. Confound the man anyway, she thought, I'd much rather ride alone with Lavvy . . . and why should the thought of him cause such a commotion within me? Why? she asked herself. He is just a man, very like any other, with the exception that he is rude, arrogant . . . rakish. She turned off her thoughts and said out loud, annoyed with herself, "Oh pooh!"

"What's that, dear?" asked her aunt, turning around on the stair to look up at her.

Jenny grinned. "Nothing, love. Come, then, you are right, we must not keep Lavvy and his lordship waiting. That would never do."

Her aunt eyed her suspiciously, but took her arm and the two went downstairs together. A lackey brought her riding whip, which she placed in the crook of her arm. Then ambling toward the hall mirror, she settled her blue top hat on her chestnut curls. She pulled at the white silk gauze so that it settled on her shoulders. With a bounce, she turned and made her way across the hall where the morning room door was opened for her and she entered alone as Aunt Beth scurried off to another region of the house.

Jenny's chestnut hair was piled high beneath the top hat, but a fall of long, luscious curls cascaded down her shoulder, peeping from beneath the white silk scarf. She made a bewitching picture as she stepped across the room and took up Lavvy's gloved hand. With a slight tilt of her head, she greeted the Earl, her voice formal and cold.

She was astounded to find that her formality was met with an amused smirk. Good manners necessitated that she place her blue-kid-gloved hand in his own, and so she did, allowing him to bow over it. His blue eyes laughed at her and she felt a turbulence shake her as he placed his lips upon her gloved hand.

"I am sorry that I have kept you both waiting, and I shall not make any excuses for myself. Do let us go, as I understand that the horses are ready as well, and we should not keep them standing." she said hurriedly and swept them both a nervous smile before turning around and leading them out.

The Earl helped Lavvy mount her horse and turned to find Jenny still standing beside her own. She was stroking the white star upon the mare's nose and speaking softly to her. The Earl walked up beside Jenny, saying quietly in her ear, "I had a look at that mare of yours earlier. She is one of the finest animals I have ever seen."

"Thank you, my lord. She is rather special . . . and I fear I have been sadly neglecting her. I . . . trained her for both saddles, for as a child, I often rode in breeches."

The horse's ears twitched as though she sensed she was being praised and Jenny slipped her a lump of sugar.

The Earl assisted Jenny onto her horse and soon afterward three riders were on the drive and then into the woods.

They rode in single file until they reached the clearing path, where Jenny became flanked by Lavvy and the Earl.

"Jen, I was most surprised that Lieutenant McMillan was not present last evening. I had been under the impression that he would be visiting you this week," said Lavinia curiously.

"Yes. Regrettably, Mac—the lieutenant, that is—was delayed in Cornwall. His father is extremely ill."

"Oh, how terrible for him. Did you say Cornwall? My goodness, I would never have thought he came from there!" exclaimed Lavvy with surprise.

Jenny frowned and regarded her friend inquiringly. "Oh . . . I wasn't aware you were acquainted with the Lieutenant."

"Oh, as to that, I am not . . . at least not really. I was at a fête a month ago in London, and Lieutenant McMillan was a guest as well. It happened that we exchanged a few words and afterward I realized he was your Lieutenant McMillan. He is not very talkative, and though I tried blatantly to flirt with him—for he is ever so nice-looking—it did not take."

Jenny laughed. "You did not see him in Brussels! He was outrageously dalliant with the ladies there . . . but I suppose the war has changed him. What did you mean about his not appearing to be Cornish?"

"Oh . . . he seems far too gentle. One imagines all the Cornish to be rough and outspoken," replied Lavvy.

One would have thought that the Earl, having been left out of the conversation entirely, might by this time have experienced his usual ennui. However, it was not so. He had been sitting stiffly on his steed, taking in every word, watching every move of Jenny's hand, and the flicker of her eyes. He said softly, "It appears Miss Ashley has been smitten with a Cornish military man."

Jenny turned wide innocent eyes to him. "Smitten, my lord? Oh no! How remiss of us to exclude you from the gist of our conversation. We were speaking of a very dear friend of mine. Mac and I are very good friends . . . that is all." She was letting her thoughts stray once more, thinking of Johnny and promising herself never to fall in love again.

Lavinia grimaced at the Earl and called Jenny's attention back by pointing to the gate. "Do we open it or jump it, Jen?"

Jenny's eyes lit up with some of her old daredevilry. "Why, Lavvy . . . need you ask?" In a moment she was up and over and gaily inviting the others to follow, which they did.

The Earl bowed his head at Jen and remarked lightly on her excellent seat and Whisper's ability.

Lavvy laughed merrily. "Oh, no more, my lord. You will turn our Jenny's head, for she has trained Whisper herself. All the good manners of that mare should be attributed to Jenny's loving care."

Jenny smiled, acknowledging the compliment, and said softly, "Not all, Lavvy."

"Oh, to be sure, John had a hand in it, as he did in everything. But it was you that spent the time with her, and as I remember, 'twas you that taught her that nasty trick of throwing someone off her back at your command."

"What's this?" asked the Earl, interested.

"Oh, my odious friend here—" Lavinia waved her hand admonishingly at Jenny—"once infuriated me over some trifle argument, which ended by my advising her unwisely that anyone could ride Whisper as well as she. I then proceeded to attempt to prove my statement. Before I could ride off into the sunset, as all good heroines must do, Jen shouts, 'Drop, Whisper, drop!' and off I went, far too close to the sunset for comfort! There they stood, John and Jenny, whooping with laughter at my expense. That little incident did much for my humility, though I was unable to sit for quite a while."

The Earl chuckled appreciatively and looked at Jennifer, who smiled shyly back and said, "After all, Lavvy, you cannot deny that you deserved it."

"What is that to anything?" demanded Lavvy blithely.

"Oh, you must know that Miss Ashley believes in giving one his due!" said the Earl, grinning widely.

Jenny had the good grace to blush, and as this was entirely above Lavvy's understanding, she was quick to change the subject onto something she could take part in.

The Old Mill was reached and the box lunches opened, exposing several roast hens, boiled parsley potatoes, freshly baked buns, tomatoes, several sweetcakes, a bottle of port, and a container of lemonade for the ladies.

All this was soon devoured, as young people seem always to have large appetites. The afternoon was spent quite creditably, and when later that day the Earl and Lavinia said their good-byes, Jenny knew a reluctance to part from them.

She sighed, wondering whether the Earl would come up to scratch after all and propose to Lavinia that evening.

# Chapter Five

The Earl escorted Lavinia to her home, watched her scurry up the staircase, and turned, entering Sir Arthur's library. Here he sat for a long while in grave conversation with that relieved gentleman.

Shortly thereafter he called for his horse again and rode back to Ashley Grange. There Earl was shown into the study and stood, his hands clasped behind his back, his mind lost in serious thought. Ah, Jason, he said to himself, didn't Byron just say something to you—what was it—yes . . . "There, in a moment, we may plunge our years!" How true . . . how very true.

He looked up to find the Squire had entered and was extending his hand. Port was offered and accepted and the Earl tried to collect his thoughts during this passing of time. He had awakened that morning and known exactly what he was going to do. Lavinia was not for him. To be sure, she was lovely, but he knew that as his wife, she would lead him a dance he was not willing to participate in . . . not with a woman he would never love. No, the Digby girl would not do! However, his problem existed and increased with the passing of time. Marry he must, and so it was that Jason Waine chose another bride.

He had been attracted to Jenny the moment he had pulled her out of the ditch. He had suspected a depth within her, a passion he wanted to arouse. He found his ride out with her this morning had done much to strengthen this resolve. He liked her. He liked everything about her, and only one thing worried him; the continual reference to this McMillan. He believed that if a man must marry, then he should marry a female he could like and respect, and he found both these feelings prevalent whenever he thought of Jennifer Ashley.

The Squire heard him out with undisguised astonishment. When the Earl had finished his monologue of explanations and proposal, the Squire was unable to respond. Indeed, he was totally bereft of speech. Finally Sir Alfred Ashley found his voice. "She'll not have you, my lord!"

"But ... why not?" asked the Earl calmly, not in the least daunted by the Squire's attitude.

"You have only just met, and my daughter is just recovering from—damnation, man! This is the oddest bit of nonsense. You don't know each other!"

"I know enough of Jennifer to wish her to be Lady Waine, sir," replied the Earl.

"But you don't understand. Jenny was recently engaged to a young man who was killed at Waterloo. Jenny was ... very badly depressed. In fact, she has declared that she will never love again!" said the Squire irritably.

"That is only natural, sir. However, I am not asking Jennifer to love me, merely to marry me!"

The Squire's dark brows drew together and he shook his head. "But, my boy, my boy, what you are proposing is preposterous. You have not thought it out. Surely you would not throw away all chance of your future happiness by marrying a young girl who will probably never love you. Please excuse my frankness ... but I could not have it on my conscience if I were to allow you to do such a thing," said the Squire, truly horrified that such a handsome young man should be trying to arrange a marriage of convenience.

The Earl looked straight into the Squire's face. "I am nearly twenty-nine, sir, and very used to thinking things out for myself. My decision was not an easy one, but I *have* decided, sir. Are you objecting to me? Perhaps you have no wish to have me for a son-in-law?"

The Squire waved this away. He had, in fact, heard about the Earl's devil-may-care reputation with women.

He was well aware of his intimate association with the Prince of Wales, which was a mark against the Earl in the Squire's eyes. Then there was his friendship with that dandy Brummell, who had just fled the country to escape debtors' prison. However, these things did not make the lad objectionable, for there was no denying that he came from a fine family and would evidently be in a position to support a wife in luxury.

"No, no, my lord! I have no objection to your asking for my daughter's hand. However, even if I were to countenance such a scheme, Jenny would not! It is absurd. Until recently she has refused to see her friends, and she has advised us that she will not allow any young man to court her."

"But you, sir . . . do not object to me?" pursued the Earl, beginning to feel a twinge of annoyance, as he considered himself quite a catch.

"No, no . . . but I do give you warning. Jenny very likely will rebuff you, and she may not do it with aplomb! If she is a bit harsh, I beg that you will understand the circumstance is an unusual one."

The Earl smiled. "Rest easy, Squire Ashley. I shall not take anything your daughter says to me as a personal affront. I am fully cognizant of the probem here and realize all too well what she has been through. I think her loyalty to the memory of the lad she lost very admirable—indeed, it does her credit. I have already said that I need a wife, a suitable female to bear my name and allow me to inherit my father's vast holdings—holdings, I might add, that are my rightful heritage and which I do not intend to forfeit. Your daughter has impressed me, and I am certain we shall deal extremely well with each other."

The Squire shook his head and inquired whether the Earl wished to speak with Jennifer immediately.

"If it will not inconvenience any of you . . . yes, sir, I would," the Earl replied gravely.

The Squire finished off his drink. Here was a young man who knew his own mind, it seemed. He strode over to the bell rope, gave it a hard tug, and shook his head again.

A lackey appeared and was sent to fetch Jennifer. The

two gentlemen, in the quiet of the study, sat gazing silently at the Van Dyke paintings.

Jenny had gone out earlier, missing the Earl's arrival by only a moment or so. She had gone to her room, throwing off her riding habit in a disorderly rush, and just as hurriedly donned a white summer muslin, dotted throughout with red velvet. Her mind and soul were reeling with conflicting emotions and she only knew that she had to go out alone to think.

She flew out of the house and down the woodland path, tying her hair back with a red velvet ribbon and slowing down as she reached the thick of the sylvan setting that surrounded her.

Jenny's complexion shone with the exhilaration of exercise and high spirits. She sat down upon a fallen log and rested her chin upon bent hands, looking very much like a glorious poem painted into life.

She had said good-bye to their oak, yet she remembered the last time she had stopped there with Johnny. It had been cold then, for it was in the midst of February. She had worn her fur-lined cloak, she remembered, for the fur trim around the hood had been in his way as he bent to kiss her, and they had laughed. Then all at once he was telling her offhandedly that his regiment was leaving for Brussels.

She could see his face flushed with cold and excitement, and thought at the time that it was just like him to spring such dreadful news on her at a moment's notice. She looked away from him and bit her lip, recalling the last time. She had been at school in Worthing and he had posted down to see her, to tell her he was off for the Peninsular . . . in 1813. She had cried then and told him he was too young for such things. He had just turned nineteen and took umbrage, scolding her relentlessly. He had kissed her cheek in the end and was gone. Then, while she was still in school, she received a letter from him saying that they had defeated Boney at the Battle of Leipzig. Johnny's heroism had earned him a promotion and he returned to Devon in 1814, bearing the title of Major Dillingham. They had a wonderful year of joy, and then suddenly Napoleon had escaped and was recruiting an army. The Hundred Days' War began and Johnny rejoined his regiment.

She had not wanted him to. She had begged and hoped and pleaded with him not to rejoin, futilely. He had rejoined with an eagerness that had caused her to pout dolefully and accuse him of trying to get himself killed. It was then that he had proposed in that graceless way of his.

She remembered his glistening eyes as he asked her to follow the drum. It was the first time he had ever talked of love, and even then he had excused himself to her teasingly, saying that he knew she'd have him, but thought he'd do it up brown. Then all at once she was in his arms, with his tender kisses covering her face and his words pouring into her ears. Theirs had been a deep, fond friendship, easy and comfortable. He had never had a romantic turn, and she had never really expected it from him . . . yet she had always known one day she would end in his arms.

"The big clumsy wild blade," said Jenny softly to a squirrel chattering to his mate. She recalled how John had picked her up, twirled her about, and brought them both tumbling to the ground.

With a shake of her head, she brought herself forcefully out of her sweet pain and back to reality. I must stop this, she thought. I must stop thinking of what was . . . and concentrate on the life that lies ahead of me. I shall never love another but I shall mourn no more. . . .

Suddenly she remembered Mac. He had been so good to her, so patient. He had been there when she was battered and pitiful from heartache, and he had helped, asking nothing in return . . . nothing except the promise, that one promise. He had asked that she reenter society and allow herself to be courted. She could not!

She picked herself up and made her way toward home. She thought about the morning's ride. She had really enjoyed herself, though the Earl was as brazen as ever! Always dropping words that would remind her of that one stolen kiss. She touched her lips lightly and felt herself blush. She shook her head as the thought came to her that the Earl would be proposing to poor Lavvy. It occurred to her that he might even have kissed her lively friend by now. The thought tweaked at her nerves and for no apparent reason she felt a slight agitation.

A few minutes later she entered the house from the front doors and found there a lackey. He advised her that her father wished to speak with her in the study.

The Squire and Earl looked toward the study doors as they opened and Jenny glided in. They waited for the doors to be closed behind her and the Earl noted with a raised eyebrow the color in Jenny's cheeks and the smidgen of dirt her dress had picked up from the log.

"Father, I was told you wished to speak to me," she said, her eyes wide and noting with surprise that the Earl was present.

"Yes, dear . . . but we have a guest," said the Squire, motioning toward the Earl, who moved forward and took up her hand.

Bending over the white ungloved fingers, he said softly, bringing his blue eyes up to her face, "Out walking in the woods alone, my pretty? Tch, tch!"

She ignored this and greeted him cordially. "My lord, how nice to see you." Then, turning to her father, she said, "Papa? . . ."

"Dearest Jenny . . . come, be seated, child," her father replied, smiling fondly at her.

She took up a chair near the sofa and turned her head up expectantly. She was beginning to feel nervous. There was something in her father's tone, in the way he looked at her, that made her watchful.

"Jenny," said her father hesitatingly, "Jenny, his lordship would like a word with you in private. So if you please, dear, I shall excuse myself, as I do, in fact, have some writing to finish up."

Jenny's smile faltered. She did not relish the thought of being left alone with the Earl of Waine . . . this strange, quietly wild man who caused her hands to tremble.

Her father had already reached the door, but Jenny's small voice stopped him. "Papa? . . ."

His eyes seemed to stroke her. "It's all right, dear, I am sure his lordship will not detain you any longer than you wish."

A moment later he was gone, but Jenny's eyes were still on the closed door. The Earl of Waine bent his handsome head and said lightly, "I shan't eat you, Miss Ashley . . . really."

She turned and a bit of a nervous chuckle burst from her tight lips. "No, I don't suppose you could . . . with my father in the house."

He smiled warmly. "In that case, shall we go out?"

Jenny's eyes opened wide with surprise and the Earl laughed. "Not because I wish to harm you. Rather because the afternoon is still with us and the other night I noticed you had an exceptional rose garden on the grounds."

Jenny remembered that evening when they had exchanged rebukes and blushed. It seemed so very long ago. She stood up for answer and walked across the room to the double French white doors, opened them, and turned toward him, a challenge lighting up her dark eyes.

The Earl followed her onto the stone path and fell in step beside her. The path was surrounded on both sides by neatly cut flower beds sporting blooming tulips and budding lilies. The lawn was rich with the beginning of summer greenness and the sun stained a cloudless blue sky. They walked slowly, Jenny playing with the folds of her gown and carefully looking straight ahead, while the Earl moved easily, an amused smirk hovering about his mouth.

"Well, my lord, apparently you wish to speak to me, and as the rose garden is now within our sight, perhaps you will tell me what it is you want," said Jenny, sounding more nonchalant than she felt.

"Ah, but I had hoped you would sit beside me . . . there upon that very quaint bench, Miss Ashley," replied the Earl.

Jenny sighed, but sat down, turning to face him as he took up the place beside her. She raised a puzzled expression and felt a thrill rush through her as their eyes met.

"Now, Miss Ashley—Miss Ashley . . . how formal we are. Rather ridiculous when one considers how close we have been," said the Earl in a bantering tone.

Miss Ashley jumped to her feet, her eyes blazing and

her cheeks as red as the roses that bloomed behind her. "My lord, I regret that I . . . I will not be able to remain in your company if you insist on pursuing a . . . a line of conversation that I find particularly . . . despicable and revolting."

The Earl laughed and put out his hand, catching her wrist and gently coaxing her back onto her seat. "Forgive me, Miss Ashley . . . do be seated again and I shall try and refrain from . . . speaking of anything you might find . . . er, revolting."

Miss Ashley relented but sat straight up and gazed away from him, a set expression about her eyes and mouth.

The Earl's finger flicked his own nose and he moved forward on the bench. "Ah, child . . . please forgive me, but do let us dispense with the formalities. I should infinitely prefer to call you Jennifer, if you would allow it."

Jenny turned her eyes toward him suspiciously and a reluctant smile strayed to her lips. She sighed, as though defeated by his good humor. "Very well, my lord, though in truth I prefer to be called Jenny over Jennifer."

The Earl's lips twitched but he continued gravely. "Jenny, then!" He regarded her for a moment before continuing, noting that her hair made a wondrous frame for her piquant face, and her eyes seemed to hypnotize him with their depth and darkness. He said in a quite soft tone that the name Jenny suited her.

She frowned and pursed her cherry lips. "Do you think so? I have always thought so . . . though I cannot say I really like the name. I would much rather have been a Clarice . . . or an Arabella."

He shook his head. "No, Jenny, you are out there. You are most definitely a Jennifer."

She sighed sadly. "I suppose so, but do let us get to the issue at hand. I fear we have sidetracked from your purpose and I am most curious to know what it is."

"My purpose," said the Earl with a rueful smile. "I think first I had better start by informing you a little of my circumstances. . . ."

"But . . . why?" asked Jenny, surprised.

"After I have done so, I think you will have that answer," said the Earl, a slight frown hovering about his blue eyes.

"Well then, my lord, do proceed."

"Bear with me, child. I will start with my father's death. It took place seven years ago and I came into the title, the estate that carries the family name, several properties in the north, and a small competence. However, the bulk of the fortune was kept in trust for me until I married. On top of this entailment was another ... that being the stipulation that if I did not marry by the time I had attained the ripe old age of twenty-nine, the fortune would go to my half-brother. According to my trustees, I must find a suitable wife and tie the knot in order to inherit what is rightfully mine. The thing is, I will be twenty-nine next month."

Jenny smiled naively. "Really. . . ? Next month? I shall be twenty in August."

His lips twitched but he continued in the same grave strain. "However, you must see, because of the conditions of my father's strange will, that I now have a problem."

"Oh yes, that is quite clear, for I have some of this from Lavvy, you understand. I must say I am surprised that Lavvy has refused your offer ... apparently she has, although she led me to believe that she had quite made up her mind to take the match. Though, to be honest, I am quite pleased she did not. You would not have dealt well together, my lord," said Jenny knowingly.

His lordship's eyes danced and his mouth quivered, but he controlled himself. "I am afraid you are under a misapprehension, Jenny. I have not asked Miss Digby to be my wife, nor do I intend to, for I most certainly agree with you ... she and I would not suit!"

Jenny felt a strange sensation float through her body and a disproportionate sense of relief swept her. "I ... gather then that there is no one for whom you have a decided preference or attachment, my lord?"

"No. I have never found a woman who could engage my affections on a permanent basis. Frankly, the young ladies who have been presented to me this past year have either bored me to distraction with giggles and silence, or have been—well, never mind that now. I have never fallen in love, and apparently will not be allowed the time to do so, as my inheritance will be forfeit if I am not married by the end of the coming month. My sister has tried to find me a suitable bride, but has not met with success. However, I think that I have found one."

Oddly enough this announcement caused a twisting sensation in the center of Jenny's stomach. Why should she care whom the Earl married, she thought crossly. If he had found some girl to fill his requirements, what was it to her? Yet, her voice faltered when she spoke, "Oh . . . you have found some . . . one?"

The Earl's deep blue eyes regarded her intently. "I would be honored, Jenny, if you would consent to be my wife."

Jenny gasped and one hand went to her heart. Her eyes blinked and she moved backward in her seat. Her hand found its way to her burning cheek and she looked away from him. Her thoughts were a-jumble, beating at her mind. Did you hear him, girl? she asked herself. Did you hear the arrogance of the man? He has actually asked you to be his wife! Not for love of you—that would be understood, forgiven—but for convenience!

Her eyes began to fill with tears as she recalled how different this proposal was from her first . . . from her John. Here was this brazen, dashing rake offering his name . . . not his love.

She tried building a wall of anger against him with these thoughts, but strangely enough, found that she could not. Instead, reason seemed to push its weight between her mind and heart, forcing her to look at the situation logically. The Earl had come to Devon to ask Levinia to be his bride. For some inexplicable reason, he had asked her instead. He had been honest with her, offering no false pretext for his proposal, no false promises. She managed to turn a controlled but pale face to his lordship and said sadly, a hint of deeper emotion in her voice, "I . . . I cannot accept your very flattering proposal. I want you to understand, my lord, that it is not you, though I . . . I do not think I would suit you, yet that is not my reason. I cannot marry anyone—not anyone—because I have noth-

49

ing to give. My heart has gone into the grave . . . I have none to give."

"I have not asked for your heart, Jenny . . . only your hand," said the Earl gently.

"How . . . how can you propose such a horrid thing? You offer no love . . . you ask for none. What manner of life do you extend to me, my lord? What to yourself?"

"A good one, Jenny. It is not unusual for beings such as we to form a marriage of convenience. Jenny, you say you can never love again. I accept. Why should you waste your life away? As my bride, you will enjoy being a Countess, presiding over your own household. You will be spared the fawning of young bucks courting you . . . offering their love when you want none of them. I ask you to marry me, knowing full well that you say you can never love again, and do not ask you to do so."

She wrung her hands. "My dear sir, you wish to make me your wife, knowing all this?"

"I do!" he said firmly. His eyes searched her face and for a moment his mind rebelled. For a split second he wanted to say, "No, Jennifer, I want you to want me . . . I want you to love." However, he subdued this impulse and waited.

"I cannot, my lord," said Jennifer on a final note.

"Is there nothing I can say to change your decision, Jenny? You do know you needn't fear me . . . I would never harm you or ill-treat you."

"Again . . . I can only say that I regret it is not in me . . . to accept, my lord."

The Earl of Waine stood to his more than six feet and Jenny gazed into his bronze handsome face. He bowed over her hand, turned abruptly, and began to walk away.

Jenny watched his broad back and her eyes overflowed with tears. "My Lord!" she cried.

He turned around immediately and strode toward her, stopping directly in front of her. "Jenny . . . Jenny, listen to me. It's not what you would have—I know, I understand—but you have stated to me that you could never love . . . never marry. Is that true?"

"Yes, yes, it is true," said Jenny, the tears flowing freely down her cheek.

"Very well then! If it is true and you believe me when I say that I do not ask you to love me, then why deny this marriage? I respect you . . . admire you, feel that you and *you* only—out of all the women I have met—could fill the post as Lady Waine. *And I must marry*, so why deny me the opportunity of securing my fortune," argued his lordship.

"But consider, my lord. It would be so unfair of me to allow this absurd compromise . . . for it is not a marriage, not in my eyes. You are entitled to find a wife who will love you and . . . and give you children. I can do neither!" pleaded Jenny.

The Earl hesitated, his eyes flickered and narrowed slightly, but he sat down beside her, taking her hand in a reassuring manner. "Jenny, do but listen to me, child. I have no time left to me to do the thing you say. I must marry, and I wish with all my heart and being that you, Jennifer Ashley, will accept the . . . compromise I have offered you. I will not make any demands upon you, and in return expect none to be made upon me. I have several estates—at least, I will have after I am wed—and you may choose which one you wish to reside at. I will stay on in my London flat . . . so you will not find me in your way. As to children, this is not the time to discuss such a matter. I ask you again, Jenny . . . please, child, do me the honor of becoming my bride and gracing my life?"

She glanced up at him and was conscious of his magnetism and felt a sudden need for his strength. His eyes seemed to penetrate her soul and a thrill, a titillating motion, trembled in her, something she knew not what seemed to penetrate her being, and she only knew she had never felt quite this way before.

"You . . . you put the matter of children aside . . . yet it is all important, my lord. You must understand that . . . that I—oh, do excuse my blunt speaking, for there is no other way to put it. You have asked me to grace your life. Do you realize, my lord, that if I should accept to do so, I would refuse to grace . . . to share your bed?" she said, blushing furiously.

The Earl regarded her speculatively before replying. He wanted the chit, and had no intention of having a wife

51

who would not admit him to her bedroom ... especially this chit, who tantalized him with her every movement, with her dark sad eyes. This was certainly a marriage of convenience, one that would not interfere with his regular habits, for the Earl had no intention of abstaining from his haunts, some of which included several lovely fancy pieces. However, as long as he must marry, he saw no reason why he should not have children as well. In fact, somewhere in the recesses of his mind, he actually wished for them. Yet he had not gotten Jenny this far just to scare her off. Not wishing to lose any ground, he made a hasty decision and said slowly, his voice low and grave, "Jenny, I promise you, child, that I will never force my attentions on you. I wish you to carry my name and beg you to rest easy. I will not force my way into your privacy.

Jenny looked away and a sob escaped her lips. Well then, Jen, she thought, here is your chance for escape. No roûts ... no beaus presented to you ... no hateful courting ... no love! Just as you wish. You will have your own home ... your freedom ... and you will be making this man happy. And you cannot do that for any other. "Then, my lord, I accept your very flattering proposal."

Thus there in a moment, each had, indeed, plunged their years!

## Chapter Six

*Sweet Love of Youth, forgive if I forget thee,*
*While the World's tide is bearing me along;*
*Other desires and other hopes beset me,*
*Hopes which obscure, but cannot do thee wrong!*
EMILY BRONTË

The Earl of Waine brought her trembling hand to his lips and placed a light kiss upon it.

"Shall I walk you back to the house and ring for your papa? He should hear our news immediately, for I imagine he is anxious on your behalf."

"No! Please, my lord, I believe that he will be ... greatly shocked and perhaps it would be better if I told him ... by myself," she said hastily.

"As you wish, Jenny," he said lightly, wishing he could kiss her lovely lips. I . . . shall leave you, then, until later."

She watched him go and shook her head. What have I done? she asked herself. Oh, dear God, what have I done? She only knew that when he had turned and started to leave her earlier, she found she could not let him go! She had no idea why ... she only knew that something inside of her had called him back and allowed him to convince her to take this course.

"You have thrown away all chance of future happiness," she said out loud, "Oh, my word ... what will Mac say? He will be so shocked, so disappointed in you, Jen."

Then her thoughts returned to the Earl. She thought about his arrogant swashbuckling walk, about his self-assurance, about the lushness of his blue eyes and the way they had of resting hypnotically on her. Her mind felt tortured with conflicting emotions. She was attracted to the Earl, she was aware of this humiliating fact and ridden by guilt over it. Something else nagged at her—fear! She had no wish to fall in love again, especially with this overbearing, faithless rake. She had discovered too early that love can be wrenched unmercifully from one in a split second. She had no wish to experience that sort of pain again. She looked up from her cogitations to find her father regarding her tenderly, compassionately, and she felt a sudden terror. How could she ever explain away what she had done?

"Jennifer, my babe, I can see you are upset. You needn't be. His lordship understands the strain his proposal has put upon you."

"But, Papa, you do not understand," said Jenny, shaking her head and frowning.

"Of course I do, and so does the Earl," said the Squire, interrupting her. "We spoke at length about his absurd scheme and he assured me that he would not take umbrage at your rebuff. Whatever you may have said, rest assured that he has not taken insult."

"Oh, Papa ... wait, you do not understand! How can I tell you? Oh, Papa, what you will think? I ... I did not refuse the Earl's ... flattering offer," said Jenny, as though she were dropping eggs.

"What?" ejaculated the Squire, astonished. "Never say you have accepted him? Jenny, my dearest child, how can this be? You have only just met him! I do not believe it!"

Jenny buried her face in his large buckskin-covered chest and found that although she wanted to do so, she could not cry. She said in a barely audible voice, "Yes, Papa, it is true ... I am going to marry the Earl."

The Squire's expression was one of deep consternation and he put his daughter from him and regarded her fixedly. "No, Jennifer ... you cannot tell me you have fallen in love with him. It is impossible. Why, just yesterday you declared that particular feat was beyond you. The Earl is nine years your senior ... and he is marrying for all the wrong reasons. Your aunt and I have planned such a festive Season for you, darling. You should meet so many young lads, much better suited to you—"

Suddenly Jenny knew that she must convince her father she was doing what she wanted and she said in a solemn voice, "I ... I do not want to meet young, gay lads, Papa ... I want to marry the Earl."

Sir Alfred Ashley felt at a loss. He had given the Earl his consent to approach his daughter because he had been certain Jenny would refuse. It was not that the Earl was not suitable, for his family name was among the *haut ton,* his was an old established house, his fortune would be extensive, and Jenny would make a lovely Countess. But something was wrong. He knew not what ... but something was not as it should be. Why had Jenny accepted the blasted man's offer? Why?

He turned his reflections off and his eyes tried to penetrate Jenny's calm exterior. "Jennifer, this is not what I wanted for you," he said, his voice breaking on the last word.

She threw her arms about him and pleaded. "Papa ... dearest friend ... it is really want I want. For many good reasons of my own. I shall be happy ... you needn't worry. And to prove it, I shall post down to you every month and stay until you throw me out. Really, Papa, just think, your little girl will be a Countess in charge of several thriving estates with horses and phaetons and ... many things."

"You have all those things now, Jennifer ... you needn't marry for money," said her father sadly.

"Oh, ridiculous Papa ... of course, I needn't marry for money. But it is gratifying to know that my marriage will keep me in the style you have taught me to appreciate," she said, smiling.

He returned the smile and patted her hand. "It is just that I want you to be sure, child."

"I am sure. And really, Papa, though he is not John, I am well pleased with him," she said on a truly convincing note.

She observed that her father's troubled countenance relaxed slightly. "Well, then ... please, Jen, your aunt will be anxious to know, and in truth, I should like to speak with her in private. Do you mind being left to yourself?"

"No, Papa. In fact, I should like to stroll about alone for a while," she said softly and watched him walk hastily toward the house. "Poor Papa," she said to herself, "I have confused you so."

She meandered about the gardens, her eyes taking in all the details of her beloved domain. How beautiful my home is, she thought. How can I leave it and go with some stranger ... a man I hardly know, a man who has, by his own actions, shown himself to be selfish, brazen ... a rake? Did he not steal a kiss before he knew your name? Did he not later laugh about it as though 'twere a trifling? Well, 'tis of no importance any longer, I will marry him ... but he will be nothing to me, nothing more than a shelter from love. He is the escape I need.

She plumped herself down on the dry green grass and stared into the bed of yellow tulips. I wonder what his home is like ... whether there are such lovely gardens. In fact, I wonder where his home is. Dear me, Jen, she thought with a rueful grimace, you haven't even found out how far away you shall be from Devon! What have you done, girl?

Aunt Beth adjusted the lace trim on her cream-colored muslin afternoon dress and brought her hazel eyes up to her brother's puzzled brow. She had received the news with less surprise than he had, sitting back in her chair and saying nothing as she considered the matter.

The Squire seemed irritated with her attitude and said in a testy tone, "Well, when the devil are you going to say something, Beth?"

"I don't barge into things, Alfred. After all these years, I should think you would know that. I have given the matter my careful consideration and my first comment is that it is not all that astounding. Had a notion something was afoot, though I couldn't quite put my finger on it, and in truth, never thought the Earl would move that quickly."

"Confound it, Beth, how can you say you knew something was in the air is beyond me!" said the Squire peevishly.

She smiled complacently at her brother. "Poor dear, I daresay you would have noted it as well if you hadn't had your nose into that new machinery you received this week. It is really quite understandable. The Earl, you see, had come to ask for Lavinia's hand. I realized the moment I observed them last evening that he would never go through with it. Lavinia is far too excitable. She lacks the smallest grain of sense, and I am sure an experienced man such as the Earl must have recognized that in a trice. Then all at once I discovered that Jenny had met the Earl by accident earlier yesterday. It began to make sense—her sudden interest in clothes, her decision to come to the dinner party. It was quite apparent to me that the Earl was intrigued with our Jenny. Have you noticed, Alfred, how men seem always to take to Jennifer? Even Mac, who has declared himself a hardened bachelor, has a decided tenderness for her."

"That, my dear, does not signify. We are speaking of Jenny's accepting the Earl's offer. I, too, find it quite understandable that men should fall in love with Jenny—one has only to look at her—but, Beth, *she* has accepted to marry *him*!"

"I do not find that impossible to believe," said Aunt Beth blandly.

"You do not?" shouted the Squire, incensed. "Pray tell, why not?"

"I have already explained that Jenny seemed to take a sudden interest in her appearance after she met the Earl. She then accepted to ride Whisper and go on a picnic, did she not?"

"Confound it, Beth, it ain't the same thing. The girl goes on a picnic with as handsome a man as I have yet to see ... that, m'dear is one thing! It is not reasonable that she should accept to marry him after knowing him less than two days. Devil a bit! John took an entire year after they had come of age to ask her to be his wife!"

"Yes, that is true. John did not sweep her off her feet. It was gradual and natural. This is swift and altogether different and probably just the thing she needed."

"Devil is in it that I can't resign myself to it," said the Squire sadly.

"Dearest Alfred, Jenny has always had her head squarely on her shoulders. She has always known what she wanted and whether it was right or wrong for her. There was no changing her mind once 'twas made up. I expect she thinks she has good reasons for this oddly hurried marriage, and I believe that it shall all work out in the end."

"Do you, Beth? Well ... since there is little we can do about it, 'tis best we think of it in those terms," replied her brother gravely.

"Hmm ... yes, dear. And by the by, I met the Earl just as he was leaving and asked him to dinner. He was very happy to accept my invitation."

"Faith, Beth, is there nothing you cannot attend to with placidity?" said the Squire with an amused twinkle in his dark eyes.

"Yes ... the marriage arrangement and settlement. I do think it would be better if you discussed them *after* we dined, though I believe his lordship will attempt to discuss them with you upon his return here."

"Quite right. Perhaps they may change their minds after dinner," said the Squire hopefully.

Aunt Beth laughed. "I do not see why a good dinner should do anything to alter their decision, Alfred."

The Squire regarded his sister fondly. "Do you know, Beth, though I live to be age wise, I will never cease to be amazed by your wondrous spirit. Ah well, I only hope my child does not regret this day's work . . . for it is one time her papa won't be able to wipe it all away and make it better."

"I think, Alfred, that Jennifer has already learned that there are things that one can never wipe away."

## Chapter Seven

The Earl of Waine smoothly tooled his horse through the fermentation of clanking wheels, shouting street peddlers, and crying beggars reaching with their eyes as well as their hands. It was already past noon and London's heart beat painfully to the throb of life.

The Earl's accustomed eyes swept past these ordinary scenes and his ears half shut out the noise. However, the sight of a street urchin's bare bleeding feet and hopeless large dark eyes caused him to halt his horse. He reached into his pocket, produced a coin, and threw it to the boy, who whelped something incoherent and scrambled for the money. The Earl felt for the hundredth time a sense of helplessness and guilt. He watched the urchin running away, darting his head back and forth as though he feared his treasure would be lifted from him. Jason Waine winced as he thought of the child's suffering and gently urged his horse to proceed.

The scent of poor sewage and horse manure receded as the poorer quarters of London were left behind. Just as the scent improved, so did the appearance of the homes, taking on first a respectable, and then an elegant semblance.

Duke Street was reached at last and the Earl dismounted in front of his lodgings. He tied the reins to his post and mounted the steps to his front door. There he was met by his butler, an estimable individual of mature years.

"Good afternoon, my lord."

"Yes, Dobbs, and so it is. Have my horse taken to the stables and my phaeton prepared and brought by my tiger in one hour. I want a hot bath and shall be in the library . . . call me when it is ready."

"Very good, sir," replied the butler.

Jason Waine removed his gloves and hat and placed them on a mahogany wall table and made for his library, while his butler proceeded to relay his orders to a waiting footman.

His eyes swept the room and noted with some satisfaction that all had been maintained as he had left it. One could not detect that each and every ornament and table piece had been removed for its daily dusting, so accurately had each been returned to its place.

Ah well, thought the Earl, with a woman about, that will soon be changed! She'll be wanting to rearrange all the furniture . . . though she need not visit this particular establishment. Well, to work, old fellow!

He situated himself at the Regency desk he had recently purchased and scribed the wedding announcement that had been agreed on by the Squire and himself yesterday evening.

A smile planted itself upon the Earl's handsome face as he recalled last evening and Jenny's dark eyes. He had not been able to resist teasing her at every opportunity and an easy camaraderie sprang up, alleviating the natural tensions that had pushed their way into the air.

Jason Waine sealed the envelope containing the wedding announcement and sauntered back to the hall, unceremoniously calling out for Dobbs, who appeared from a side door.

"Ah, there you are. Have this taken round to the

*Gazette* immediately. I am going up to take my bath . . . I am not at home if anyone should call."

"Yes, my lord . . . but the bath is still being prepared."

"Quite all right, Dobbs. It will be ready by the time I get these riding clothes off." With which his lordship mounted the narrow stairs that led to his modest bedroom.

The Earl's lodgings were far inferior to those of many of his intimates, as they contained only a small library, parlor, and dining room on the first floor, with the kitchen and servant quarters below stairs. The second floor housed only two bedrooms and one room with a marble bathtub. The ground floor only received running water. Hot and cold water alike had to be carried upstairs.

There were other irksome things that nagged at the Earl, for though he was able to make do with a small house and small staff, he had a love for horses and had many times to forgo an excellent buy because it was beyond his means—means that by right should have been available. Then there was the fact that his ability to increase his financial position was limited by the pittance he was given. At first he had defiantly declared to the trustees that he would manage with the pin money they doled out rather than marry. However, as the years progressed and his debts rose to greater heights, he realized that it would not be wise to adhere to this declaration. His tradesmen's bills had increased to alarming proportions. And his gaming debts had all to be paid. Since he was a man of honor, gaming debts were his first obligation, and he had no intention of going the way of his dear friend Beau Brummell and fleeing to France!

No, he would not follow Brummell's lead. Yet hadn't Lord Byron married a year and half ago—influenced by his need for money? "Good God!" exclaimed the Earl, thinking of the disaster that had followed. Yet, Annabella Milbanke had been a maid of an odd cut . . . his Jenny was not made of such frigid, heartless stuff!

Similar thoughts revolved in the Earl's haunted mind as he tooled his team of beautifully matched bays through the busy streets to his sister's home.

It was already three in the afternoon when he arrived

at Berkeley Square and pulled up to an imposing three-story brick building. He jumped down nimbly from his seat and placed the reins in his tiger's hand. The young boy took these up and smiled naughtily at the Earl, for he was a favorite of his lordship's and allowed some license. "Where shall I drive 'em, m'lord?"

"Go round the park twice, lad, and then come back for me. I want you here within the hour. And if you scratch my yellow wheels, there will be the devil to pay!" The Earl grinned.

He skipped up the six steps to the double doors of his sister's spacious townhouse, and raised his hand to the knocker just as one of the doors was opened wide.

The retainer at the other side of the door smiled warmly and excused himself. "I thought I heard your voice, my lord. Her ladyship will be that pleased, for she has been walking about with your name on her lips these three days."

The Earl grinned at the butler, for they were well acquainted, and Jason Waine dropped his black top hat onto the dark round table situated in the center of the richly tiled hall.

"Where is she, old boy?" asked the Earl amicably.

"In the morning room, my lord."

The Earl dismissed the retainer with his eyes and crossed the wide hall to the yellow-painted double doors. These opened into the room and his grin broadened as his eyes found his sister seated at a dainty Oriental desk situated between yards and yards of yellow drapery.

"Gwen . . . what a picture you are!"

His twin sister screeched with delight and nearly toppled her chair as she jumped to her feet. With extended hands, she made her way across the room toward him.

Gwen Henley was the Earl's twin, and while they were not identical, there was a remarkable likeness and a deep bond between them. Her hair was as black as his own and she wore its long tresses wound around her head in shining bands. She was a tall and elegant woman enswathed at the moment in a fashionable morning dress of maize muslin. Like the Earl's, her eyes were blue, though she often remarked with a shake of her head that hers lacked his deep lush color.

"Jason, Jason, you naughty boy . . . what can this mean, your coming back so soon? I had not expected you until later in the week."

"What is this? I have it on very good authority that you have been wishing to hear from me these three days, and here you are, wishing me away. Tch, tch, faithless twin!" teased the Earl.

"Now, you know exactly what I am talking about, so don't dally with me, Jason! I have been on edge these past three days because I wanted to know what was happening out there in the country with Lavinia . . . and now that you have returned, I fear that all has not gone well."

"Indeed, my love, all has gone very well! Better than we could have hoped for," said the Earl mischievously. He seated himself, leaning his shoulders into the silk-printed sofa back and crossing his buff-colored legs.

"Jason, tell me . . . oh tell me at once," commanded his sister, planting herself beside him.

He brushed an imaginery speck off his black shining hessians and brought his blue eyes up to hers.

The double doors of the morning room were flung open with abandonment and a child of no more than four years came dashing into the room, his gray-haired nanny in hot pursuit.

"Uncle Jason, I saw you, I saw you from the window!" cried the boy joyously.

Uncle Jason ruffled the child's dark curls and assisted the boy in his frantic effort to climb into his lap.

"I did it!" exclaimed the child proudly. "Want to see me do it again?"

"Not now, love," replied his mama. "Your uncle and I have something to discuss. Whatever you want him to see, he can see later."

"Now . . . please, Mama, now!" pleaded the boy.

"What is it you want me to see, Master Henley?" asked his uncle dutifully.

"I killed the dragon . . . with the sword you brought me! I killed him dead eight or five times!" replied Master Henley.

"Did you, by God?" exclaimed the Earl with a show of proper awe. "And did you save the fair damsel, my lad?" "Oh no, Uncle Jason," retorted the boy, shocked. "Damsels are girls. *I* don't save girls! Just treasures and maybe horses and things!"

The Earl and Lady Gwen laughed and the boy had his head ruffled again, an act allowed only to his very favorite people, and as his uncle was numbered among these fortunate creatures, the violation was forgiven.

"That will change, Robin my lad!" replied the Earl with a grin.

"Well, Uncle Jason, are you coming?" asked the boy, sticking to the issue tenaciously.

"No, Robin, your uncle will have to see that particular slaying at another time."

"Can I whisper something to you, Uncle?"

"I think you had better, lad," replied the Earl.

The boy proceeded to do so, directly into his uncle's ear, but nevertheless loud enough for all to hear. "Maybe, if you come up soon, the Yogurt Ogre will be there . . . and 'cause he is bad, you can help me catch him."

"The Yogurt Ogre?" asked the Earl, opening his eyes wide.

"Uh-huh!"

"Very well . . . anyone with such a title must be caught and questioned thoroughly, I quite agree."

Having thus been gratified by his uncle, the boy allowed his nanny to lead him out of the room, turning at the doorway and admonishing a finger at his beloved uncle not to forget about the Ogre.

Laughing, the Earl turned to face his sister. "Yogurt Ogre?"

"Yes. Nanny makes yogurt and gives it to him when he has a tummyache. Or at least she tried, for he didn't really like it until she concocted this tale about a Yogurt Ogre who goes about the country concealing himself and snatching away the children's yogurt. After that, he couldn't eat it fast enough."

The Earl chuckled over the vision this produced and exclaimed merrily, "Lord, Gwen, he could have stayed a bit longer. I really enjoy playing with him. Poor little tot, sending him off like that."

"I know . . . I am a selfish wretch, and so I am, but he shall have you all to himself later. Now, I want to hear your news. When are you to be married? Will it be in Devon? Oh, never say you have brought Lavinia and her papa to town?"

The Earl made a deprecatory cough and a bemused expression flitted across his face. "No, I have not brought the Digbys here. Why on earth would I do such an odd thing?" Then not waiting for a retort: "I am to be married next week—Friday, in fact—and the wedding will take place in Devon. However, the bride is . . . er, not Lavinia Digby!" His eyes twinkled mischievously at his sister's astonished face.

"What?" ejaculated Lady Gwen, sitting bolt upright. Then one hand tugged at the kerchief resting in her sleeve. Pulling it out, she waved it at him and then clutched it with both hands. "Oh, Jason, have you done something dreadful and insulted the Digbys? For if you have I shall . . . I shall do something terrible to you . . . I warrant you, Jason!"

"I have not insulted the Digbys. I have merely decided that Lavinia and I would not deal well together and avoided the subject of marriage while I was a guest in their home."

"Jason? . . . Jason, whatever can you mean?" inquired his sister, amazed.

"What do I mean? Simply that I am to be married next week, but not to the fair Lavinia," replied the Earl, his eyes dancing.

"Oh, for heaven's sake, Jason, how can you? Tell me at once whom it is you are marrying."

The Earl chuckled and then stood up, clasping his hands behind his back and moving toward Lady Gwen's writing table. He turned once again to face her. Resting his long body against the desk and folding his arms, he said lightly, "I am betrothed to Miss Jennifer Ashley of Ashley Grange."

The Earl had little time to analyze the stirring within his body that his own words had caused, for his sister jumped to her feet and whittled the distance between them to a fraction of an inch.

With her elegant white hand upon his blue sleeve, she scanned his features and then gasped, "Oh, my faith, Jason, you are in earnest!"

"Well, and why shouldn't I be?" asked the Earl with a bemused frown.

For answer his sister gaped at him open-mouthed, all at once at a loss for speech.

"Gwen!" He chuckled. "I can fully appreciate your . . . surprise at this piece of unexpected news, but tch, tch, sis of mine, do close your pretty mouth if you are *not* going to say anything."

"You . . . you cannot marry Jenny Ashley!" trilled Gwen agitatedly, her cheeks taking on color.

The Earl's good humor began to drain. "I have no idea what should prompt you to utter such a ridiculous thing, and at the moment I really do not care, for what is more to the point is that you referred to Miss Ashley as Jenny! I was not aware that you were acquainted with the child."

"Of course, I know her. Oh, Jason, what have you done? I sent you to Devon to offer for that little bouncing fair-haired chit—you must admit you had ever a penchant for yellow-haired creatures! Oh pray, Jason, however did you come across Jenny? Never mind that . . . you must find a way to cry off. Of all the most vexing situations. . . ."

"Cry off? Are you mad?" replied her brother, frowning darkly. "Why on earth, Gwen, should I do such an ungentlemanly thing . . . as if I would!"

"Jason, you do not understand—"

"I certainly do not, and I think, my darling sister, that you must now take a chair and explain what all this"—he waved his hand in the air—"hysteria is about."

Gwen ignored his command and remained standing, pulling at the handkerchief in her fist. "Jason, you have no idea—and it is such a long, odd tale that I am not sure you will understand it when it has been told. Could you not just believe me if I tell you that Jenny is not for you? My dearest twin, she will never be a biddable wife!"

The Earl felt a twinge of irritation and his response

was brusque when it came after some pause and penetrating eye contact. "Nevertheless, Gwen, I should like to hear this uncomprehensible narrative of yours."

His sister gave him her graceful back and took the hand-painted Oriental chair nestled behind its matching desk before beginning her story. "You must remember that George and I fell in with the *ton* and took up residence in Brussels last spring . . . though *you* would not, you insisted on remaining behind with poor Byron and John Cam—"

"Gwen, would you mind getting on with it? I am fully aware of why I remained behind the flock and with whom the idle hours were passed."

"Well, indeed, Jason, you needn't be so testy! It was in Brussels, you see, that I met Jenny. Though there is a difference in our age, and she was single, we struck up a close friendship. Why, I was wont to meet her everywhere. She was engaged to some young boy—a major, attached to Wellington's staff, you know. Oh, Jason, don't you see, it is not that I don't approve of Jenny . . . I do, in every way she is exactly the girl I have always dreamed of having for a sister. She is a beauty . . . a diamond of the first water . . . far superior to the Digby chit.

"Yet, Jason, I still hold, this will not do! Wait," she said, holding out her hand for she could see he was about to bring down a tirade on her head, "just a moment and I will explain my meaning. I had—still have—a tremendous fondness for Jenny. She was the gayest, most marvelous creature, forever laughing and urging her companions to laugh with her. Oh, indeed, she would make you a truly regal Countess, Jason . . . and still I say you cannot marry her!"

"I grow impatient with you, Gwen! Thus far you have only increased my conviction that I have made the correct choice—"

"La, Jason! Do let me continue," interrupted his sister hastily. "Now, where was I? Ah yes . . . I assume you are aware already that she lost her young major to the Battle of Waterloo? Hmmm, yes, I see that you have been told something about him. Well . . . we returned to

London shortly before the battle took place . . . missed Lady Richmond's ball because my dearest George did not wish to have Robin and me exposed, although we were certain Wellington would deal with Napoleon. I have always felt that George regretted missing that one . . . however, that is neither here nor there, and I see you are getting angry again. The thing is—and I tell you this to your head—that you cannot do this dreadful thing to my dearest Jenny!"

The Earl of Waine stood up to his full height, quite impressive a figure, even to his rather tall sister, and frowned darkly down at her,

"Do you realize, Gwen, that as much as I love you, the desire to choke you is becoming increasingly uncontrollable?"

"Oh dear, you still do not understand? I shall have to be somewhat more explicit."

"Yes, my sister, if I am ever to be free to join my nephew and catch that Ogre of his!"

"Well, then! You, Jason, are making a marriage of convenience. It is a common thing, though I had never wished such a thing for you. But then, you were always such a stickler, and it must be done, we are both agreed on that point. To even consider the fact that the estate, your estate, would pass to *that* woman's son is . . . is inconceivable. . . ."

"Gwen, we are not in agreement on that point. My father made a disagreeable will, and I need the financial freedom our estate would allow me. Yet I have always been fond of Julian, and when the estate is turned over to me, I shall *not* do to my half-brother what my father has done to us both. Julian and I are now both living on a pittance. When the estate is legally mine, I intend to endow Julian with what I believe should be his."

Gwen waved his words away impatiently. "But, Jason, that young popinjay would not do so for you,"

"Gwen, please, love, we do not agree on this issue and I cannot be governed by what others would or would not do. I have my own set of rules and my own code of honor, in addition to the code of honor upheld by any

67

true gentleman. Now, if you would please explain why I cannot do this, as you so uniquely phrased it, to Jenny!"

"Yes ... yes, of course. You want a marriage of convenience. The Digby chit understands these things. With her as your wife, you would be free to go your own way ... discreetly, and she would have no hesitation to follow suit—that is, as soon as she bestowed upon you a legal heir. Lavinia is full of naughty notions, fun, and ... easier ways. Jason, did you not realize that Jenny is not made up for that sort of life? I can only assume that if Jenny Ashley has accepted your proposal, she has done so because she has fallen in love with you. It's no wonder, too ... a tall handsome Earl sweeps down, wins her heart and her hand. I cannot allow you to hurt the child, for she is naught but a child. She will not understand when you carry on with your little birds. She will wither, Jason. She will not be able to carry on an intrigue of her own to divert her mind. Why, just look how she buried herself in the country when she lost her major. I have heard from mutual friends of the sort of pain she underwent. Jason, she is not the girl for such a marriage!"

The Earl of Waine's lush blue eyes narrowed. He sucked in his lower lip and decided that he would have to be frank with his anxious sister, for there was simply no mistaking her sincerity in the matter.

"Gwen, you are under a misapprehension! I will tell you briefly that Miss Ashley—Jenny—has agreed to marry me ... but not to love me!"

"What?" ejaculated his sister. " 'Tis impossible!"

"In fact, Gwen, she has told me to my face that she will not share my bed. She has been admirably honest in explaining that she had given her heart to this major, and that when he died, so did her ability to hope for the normal way of life—a husband ... children! Oh yes, Gwen, she has made it perfectly plain that when she marries me, it will be to escape her relations' efforts to put her back into society, where young men might court her. She has no wish to be loved and no wish to love any man. I have chosen this unique female because I found her exquisitely beautiful, delicately regal, mature beyond her years ... and because while I still wish to continue my pleasurable pastimes, I have no particular desire to have my wife's name bandied about with those of my acquaintances. If I must have a wife, I want one who will do me credit! Jenny has denied me some of a husband's rights and will therefore excuse my faithlessness . . . and even so, I will do everything in my power to make sure my excursions never come to her ears or cause her embarrassment. I respect and like the girl and have no intention of allowing her to be hurt."

Gwen Henley sat back against the handpainted chair. Her fine brows were drawn. "But . . . but, Jason, you will eventually want an heir . . . you are so fond of children. Yet you say. . . ."

The Earl of Waine's sensitive mouth quivered and his eyes danced. "Eventually, my sister, I will beget an heir! I have no wish to force myself upon my future bride, and I doubt that I shall have to! I am sufficiently experienced in the art of seduction—indeed, I pride myself upon the subject. I have no qualms on that head. Jenny is young and I am not thought to be an ugly brute. I am perfectly willing to bide my time and choose the right moment."

"You are disgusting! Of all the mannish, vainest—planning the seduction of your own wife!" retorted his sister.

"Eh? . . . seduction . . . what's this? What's this?" came a jolly voice from the doorway.

The twins looked up to see a tall, rather substantial gentleman with ginger-colored hair falling in a bushy shag about his head. His face was ruggedly attractive and he had the look of a man who enjoys the outdoors. His smile was wide and genuine.

"George, my love," said his wife happily as her eyes lit upon his large form.

"'Pon my soul, George, you do fill that doorway! You've put on five pounds since I've last clapped eyes on you!" said Jason, beaming.

Sir George Henley and the Earl of Waine's friendship had started at Cambridge. The Earl had been vastly pleased when his friend had married his only sister some six years ago. They grinned at each other as Sir George came across the room, brushing past the Earl to plant an affectionate kiss upon his wife's waiting cheek.

Sir George was athletic but he had a large man's appetite, which he rarely curbed. He was beginning to develop a bit of a paunch, which he now rubbed good-naturedly in response to his friend's remark. However, he was not one to be diverted, and he quickly brought matters back to the point that had caught his interest. "What the devil do you mean speaking of seduction to my wife, Jason?"

The Earl laughed. "It was necessary, George, upon my honor 'twas! Need a few pointers!"

The Earl immediately received a rap across his knuckles from his indignant sister.

"Indeed?" said George, chuckling. "Don't think she could help you there!"

"George!" snapped his wife with outraged shock, putting up her chin at the insult.

"Well, dear, stands to reason that any woman as lovely as you are doesn't have to resort to seduction to get what she wants," her husband replied quickly, giving her a tender glance that caused her to blush contentedly.

"Wish me happy, George. I am to be married next week," said the Earl lightly.

His friend's sandy-hued brows drew together. "I wish you all the joys that the right kind of marriage can bring, Jason."

"Ah, my George disapproves," said the Earl with a mocking smile.

"You've only to cast your eyes about to see what marriages of convenience bring. Look at Lady Caro and poor William Lamb forever trying to brush away the mess she leaves behind. What of our own Byron with that ... that creature he married. ..."

"Poor dear Byron ... and Augusta. As a sister, I feel for her. Why, imagine how ridiculous to call a deep affection for one's sister ... that horrid word, I can't even say it!"

"Damnation! Are they saying it still?" demanded the Earl, flushing. "I thought John Hobhouse had got that treacherous creature who has the audacity to carry Byron's name to state that Byron and Augusta has not committed incest."

"Oh, to be sure the magnanimous lady did indeed so

state something of the kind in moderate tones, but society must find some evil great enough to excuse her flight. After all, everyone seems to think that good is ranged on Lady Byron's side and bad on Lord Byron's."

"Just my point, Jason!" said George Henley, shaking his head. "There was merry young Byron, but eight and twenty, hailed the Lion of the Day, smashed down by the wrong marriage. I could cite you hundreds more—"

"Please do not, George, my nerves are already beginning to throb!" said Jason, chuckling. "I could, of course, chuck my debts to the wind and fly to France as the Beau did? . . ."

"You very well cannot!" replied his sister."And if you are to be of any help to the Beau, you *must* inherit. Which reminds me, George, I had prepared a packet for Lady Jersey to take with her to Calais for our poor Brummell. Did you enclose the draft you spoke of?"

"No, love . . . some of the Beau's friends at Watier's took up a collection and I included my draft with their packet."

"I shall miss him so . . . we all shall, and it vexes me to no end when I think that it all could have been avoided if only he had apologized to Prinny!" said Gwen sadly.

"No use pining over it, Gwen. Beau Brummell never retracted anything. He is too proud. When he dug into Prinny back in thirteen, he signed his financial doom. He'd been in debt for years . . . the only thing that staved off debtors' prison was his association with the Prince, and now and then a lucky winning at the table. His disastrous losses this year brought it all down around him . . . and there was naught any one of us could do to put a halt to his vagaries," said her husband, frowning and screwing up his lips.

"At any rate, my dear ones, *my* life is not likely to take a different route if I do not get my hands on my estate, and as Jennifer Ashley is not likely to accuse *me* of incest, I intend on being married next week without further argument!" said the Earl with a note of finality.

His sister sighed but his brother-in-law took up his hand and gave it a hearty shake. "Very well, you have our felicitations!"

The Earl smiled warmly. "Good. I want you to be my best man, George! My future bride has requested that we keep the wedding party to a minimum, which is perfectly in keeping with my inclination. We will be traveling immediately after the wedding breakfast to Waine Castle, as per the stipulations of that bothersome will!"

"All right then, we can continue on to Brighton. Would have already been there if it hadn't been for your delaying the choosing of a bride, you horrid man!" said Gwen. Then with a sigh: "Oh, Papa! How could such a reasonable and loving father have done this to his first-born son?"

Her husband frowned thoughtfully. "Have a notion that he thought Jason was a frippery fellow that needed taming. In fact, the old Earl once said something of the sort to me when Jase and I were rusticating at Waine . . . after the scandal with Lady Willbough, you know. Jason, a mere young buck, climbing into that pretty lady's bed and getting caught! That was a rare kick-up, Jason! Should have let Lord Willbough pink you—only fair, considering—but no, you had to run the fellow through!"

"Faith, that was a frightful time! I thought Jason would have to flee the country. I was so thankful that Henry Willbough pulled through, but you know, George, he was and is a nasty man! He only challenged Jason because he thought he was a mere stripling boy who didn't stand a chance. From what I understand, he is fully aware that the large nursery that bear his name was not fathered by him. In fact, they are called the Willbough miscellany!"

Her brother laughed out loud but voiced his agreement with George's supposition. "Indeed, George, I started out rather bad, a wight given over to the calls of flesh! So he meant to curb me with a wife. Poor Papa, for the truth is, time has done it for him, and if I'm not a damn sight luckier than most husbands—excepting you——a wife might set me back again!"

Suddenly Gwen grew strangely grave. "Have you written our . . . 'beloved' stepmother, Jason?"

"No . . . I shall do so in the morning."

She nodded and then said, derision distorting her mouth, "She will be pleased, don't you think?"

He chuckled. "She will get over it."

"Jason, you will be careful . . . please . . . when you arrive at Waine Castle?" she said compellingly.

"Silly Gwen, you are not going to let those old suspicions spring up again! All right . . . you may be easy I shall keep my blue eyes open at all times!" he replied.


# Chapter Eight


Jenny reined in Whisper and spoke something into his ears. She reached behind her neck, gathered her wayward dark tresses, and retied them with the red ribbon that had fallen loose.

It was a glorious morning. The sun shone down upon a pattern of fields whose cornstalks were beginning to reach toward the sky. She had ridden past the fields, past the meadows of colorful wild flowers, toward Blackdown Hills for this sight. Soon she would be leaving all this!

"Faith, Whisper, how can I bear it? I love Devon . . . I love its meadows, its combs of trees and hidden springs. I love its moors, its plain of wild ponies. . . . Oh, Whisper, there is no other place in the world like Ashley Grange and Devon."

Last evening had been dreamlike. She had felt divorced from most of its proceedings. She had been midly astonished to find that her aunt made no objection to her hasty engagement. Contrary to her expectations, Aunt Beth seemed on the whole fairly excited by the news.

The Earl arrived after what she felt was just a few minutes. He had explained that he could not, under the circumstances, spend the night at the Digby's and would be taking leave of her shortly after dinner.

They strolled about the grounds and Jenny felt a sense of pleasure that she was able to discuss intelligently the subjects he seemed interested in.

Conversation at dinner had been surprisingly delightful. The Earl had put himself to the task of setting everyone at their ease. He did so with charming adroitness and Jenny was conscious of a stirring of admiration. He amused them with the more innocent exploits from his foolish youth, and before long they were all in the way of easy discourse.

A breeze stroked Jenny's soft clear cheeks and she sighed. "Easy, my darling," she said gently to her mare, for Whisper was growing restless and pawing the dark, rich earth.

Jenny slipped off her mare's back easily and led her horse onto the tall green carpet that skirted the wide riding path. She sat down and gathered her knees up beneath her riding skirt of blue linen.

She scanned the slope before her, smiling at the waving buttercups, and for no reason at all remembered the scent of the wisteria bushes that lined one of the many garden paths on the Grange. They had gone walking after dinner. There was a moon out and its mysterious rays had flitted across the lovely purple blooms. A gentle breeze had teased her senses with the exotic perfume of the wisteria, and she had known a moment of contentment there . . . with the Earl.

Then a blast had ended it all, for the Earl reminded her of their coming nuptials. "Jenny? . . . I have gone over the wedding arrangements with your papa, but all that he and I could settle with any certainty was the 'marriage settlement.' As far as the final date is concerned, I must have your approval," he said mildly, as though he would make little of it.

"I—I see. When exactly did you . . . wish the marriage to take place," she answered, feeling as though her entire body was on fire.

"Friday next. I know it is a bit soon, but I feel that a delay would be—in our case—somewhat pointless."

"Y-es, I can appreciate your reasoning. Very well, then, Friday next. But, my lord, I must insist that the wedding take place here in Devon and that our family minister handle the ceremony."

"Agreed," he replied, smiling and taking up her soft hand in both of his.

She withdrew it gently and lowered her eyes. "Also, I would prefer a small wedding party."

Unreasonably, he felt irritated by the reversion of her hand. He was piqued, for he had meant only to be kind and her aloofness nettled his ego. He clasped his ungloved hands behind his back, fingering the emerald ring he wore on his right pinky. "As you wish," he said in a quiet voice. "I will keep my own set to a minimum, though I expect your father will be inviting quite a group."

She chuckled. "Poor Papa is so bewildered that he will leave the entire thing up to my aunt, and Aunt Beth will do as I ask and keep the guest list limited."

He chuckled. "That sounds very much the spoiled child, Miss Ashley."

"And so I am, my lord," she said mischievously.

"I see I shall have a time with you. Which reminds me, my little bride . . . if you must go off for strolls through the pastures in torn peasant dresses, kindly do so with your maid in attendance!" he said, grinning.

Jenny put up her chin defiantly. "I will not! When I stroll, my lord, I often forget to keep my pace down, which means at times I run, skip, and hop! I will not be hampered by a whining female, which my aunt's maid would be if she had to follow."

He laughed and flicked her nose and Jenny noticed an odd expression in his deep blue eyes. "Then beware, miss, the next time your assailant may take the precaution of safeguarding himself from that dangerous little foot of yours."

A confusion mastered her and showed in her eyes, causing him to chuckle appreciatively. He led her back toward the house, saying something commonplace to set her back at her ease. When they had reached the glass doors, he stopped and once again took up her hand. This time he held it firmly when she attempted to extract it. With a set purpose, he raised it to his lips and pressed a light kiss upon the white knuckles before releasing it.

"Good night, my Jenny. I shall be here Friday next," he said.

She looked startled. "Don't ... don't you come in, my lord?"

"Thank you, no, child. I have already bid your relations adieu, for I have a bit of a ride tonight and must get started."

"Faith, my lord ... never say you are riding to London tonight?"

He chuckled. "I am pressed for time, but no, not that pressed. I will ride for three hours or so and then stop at an inn along the way."

"I see. But your hat, gloves, my lord?"

"They are with your footman. If you would be so kind as to have him bring them to me at the stables, I shall go have one of the livery boys saddle my horse."

"Very well, then, I bid you goodnight and safe journey," she said shyly.

"Fare thee well, my bride. Friday next," he said softly.

Jenny disappeared behind the doors and went directly to the hall to instruct the footman in the Earl's wishes.

She then skipped lightly up the staircase and into her own room, feeling a wondrous excitement pulsating within her. She chided herself that the thought of being the Earl's wife caused her heart to flutter. She was aware of the turbulance of emotions within her breast, and the fact that the Earl generated these feelings annoyed her. She was irked with herself. Her sense of faithfulness to Johnny felt jarred and threatened.

She had said she was marrying the Earl to escape the torture of being loved ... and loving. Yet, something nagged at her, a guilty, prickly sensation that haunted her innermost thoughts and made her shout *no* ....

Whisper bent her graceful neck and nibbled at the grass directly behind Jenny's back, his nose bumping her slightly.

Abruptly she swept her deep musings away. "Enough ... I have thought enough. What is to be, will be. Ah, Whisper, your mistress is so profound today." She stroked her mare's nose. "At least you, Whisper, will be coming with me ... at least that much of Devon will be mine."

Jenny had ridden out that morning north into the region known as Blackdown Hills. Ashley Grange was situated just within the southern border of Devon, between the

76

villages of Chard, which lay in the Somerset County, and Cullompton in Devon. The hills swooped around their land like the profile of a large jolly man cracking a smile, and in that smile sat the home she had known all her life.

She rode Whisper home slowly, gazing at every familiar scene as though she were encasing it in glass and filing it away for future need. By the time she had reached her home, it was past noon and the house seemed to be in an unusual stir.

Little could go on in Ashley Grange without the servant's detection, especially where Jenny was concerned.

Nearly the entire Ashely staff had served the Ashley name for many years, or had seen their parents and relatives do so. They had always been treated fairly, paid well, and taken care of in their old age, and they felt a deep-rooted loyalty toward the Squire and his family.

Jenny had gained their hearts as a child and they had followed her progress in the effort of living with both interest and sincere care. They had sighed happily with her joys; they had wept with her, and now, they worried with her. The whispers were rife and the head shakings inevitable, for they sensed all was not as it should be. Jenny did not have the look of a maid struck with sudden love . . . and if 'twere not love, then what?

Jenny noticed something undulating in their expressions when they cast their concerned eyes upon her. No announcement had as yet been made to the staff, but she was fully aware that they all knew, and moreover, that they were not wholly approving.

This irritated her. Jenny had the inevitable nature of a girl who has been spoiled all her life, that being the perverseness of needing to have her own way. She was able to make up her mind about anything, almost in an instant, and once she had done so, she had to follow it through. She had made a decision, and whether that decision was right, wrong, good, or bad, she wanted the full support of the people she loved.

A parlor maid carrying a tray of silver that shone blindingly and yet was about to be polished passed Jenny in the central hall. She smiled at the mistress, who was some ten years her junior, but her eyes held pity and Jenny cocked a brow.

This was really too much, Jenny thought. She knew the staff was sincere, and ordinarily she excused the huge amount of liberties this caring urged them to take, but *pity* for a decision that she had made was something she would not allow, and so she would show them!

She summoned the butler in a tone that caused his eyes to flicker ever so slightly.

"I want the staff assembled here in the hall immediately. Every one of them . . . unless they are in the process of executing something for my aunt or father."

"Yes, miss, at once," he replied and turned to do her bidding, wondering what she was about.

Jenny's foot did a little dance on the marble floor, and her pearl teeth assaulted her lower lip as she waited. Finding that it was taking a bit longer than she had anticipated, she sat down upon the Gothic wooden bench that ornamented the hall, and thought that while it was a work of art, it certainly was not meant for comfort.

At last the harried retainer reappeared, leading a neat double line of wide-eyed servants.

Jenny stood up, but did not smile at them, which caused their eyes to stiffen in position, as their mistress was not wont to look so severe.

"I have asked you all here because I felt that there is something I should advise you of immediately. Originally I was willing to leave it to my father, but as he will be away until dinner and I feel the matter needs immediate attention, I have decided to give you my happy news at once. I am sure, though I can't imagine how you come by your information, that you are all aware that I am to be married to the Earl of Waine. It is with pleasure that I confirm your . . . information. We are to be married next Friday. I know that you were not able to wish me joy earlier, because you had not the official announcement. However . . . now you do!" said Jenny blandly with her chin just a little in the air and her eyes beginning to dance as she took in their expressions.

The butler led what turned out to be a chorus of congratulations. Jenny accepted their good wishes and allowed them to return to their duties.

With a slow smile beginning to quiver, she turned and started to make her way toward the stairs when she was recalled.

"Miss Ashley, please forgive me," said the butler hastily. "I had forgotten that a letter has arrived for you."

Jenny picked up the envelope from the proffered silver salver and thanked him. Instead of proceeding upstairs, she turned on the ball of her foot and walked slowly toward the library, gazing at the name on the envelope.

She broke the carnelian seal and closed her eyes, sinking into the comfortable sofa her aunt had recently installed in this room.

"Mac!" she said softly, opening the folded paper and reading slowly. It was indeed from the Lieutenant. He was writing to advise her that his father was still ill and he could not leave Cornwall yet. He asked that she forgive him . . . and he begged her to go out and not bury herself in the house.

She read his closing sentences over again:

> I don't ask that you dance, Jen. I don't ask that you sing. I ask that you listen to the music, watch the sun rise, and let them make you smile. I can't bear to see you lose yourself, and in fact, shan't let you!
>
> I miss you terribly and you will have to watch out, little miss, for when I arrive this time, I expect you to properly entertain your guest. I want to be shown the countryside, and taken to the local festivities . . . and I want to hear your laugh!
>
> I am affectionately yours,
> Mac

Jenny put the letter in her lap and covered her eyes with the palms of both hands. Mac, she thought, how the deuce am I to tell you? How can I write that I'm not dancing, I'm not singing, but I'm going to acquire a husband . . . or more aptly, just a new name!"

She dropped her hands and stood up and moved

toward the window. How am I to tell you, Mac? You will be so shocked. Oh, dearest friend, whatever will you think of me?

She drew a long breath and made up her mind. It must be done, and now. Sitting down at her father's writing desk, she shook her head once more before dipping the pen into the inkwell, and knew an odd sense of relief that she was *writing* her news to Mack instead of facing him with the words.


The news of Jenny's engagement swept the countryside as fast and almost as stupendously as had the news of the Battle of Waterloo a year ago. Gifts and letters of congratulations started to pour into the Ashley home. Domestic tranquility became a thing of the past, as Jenny and Aunt Beth rushed to and from the dressmaker's, and they were bombarded by visitors, some genuinely happy for Jenny, some curious to know more of the sudden engagement, and some a little of both.

On the third day after the event, Lavinia swirled down upon them and nearly burst with satisfaction at finding Jenny alone in the rose arbor.

"You sly little miss!" crowed Lavinia, baiting, "I just can't believe it, and yet I must, for I see that it is true ... for you are blushing, Jenny Ashley. Isn't that just like you. You were always one to go and do the most outrageous thing, and then blush beet red when faced with it!"

"Oh, Lavvy, it is not exactly as you are thinking!" cried Jenny, really very distressed.

"And what am I thinking?" asked Lavinia, putting her hands on her hips and tilting her fair head.

"Sure now, Lavvy m'darling, and how would I be knowing what it 'tis going round that scatterbrain of yours," trilled Jenny, firing up and giving her tease for tease.

Lavvy laughed loudly and then sighed. "Now that is my old Jenny. 'Tis good to have ye back again," she replied, picking up the dialect.

Then all at once they fell into each other's arms and gave themselves over to the wondrous release of mirth.

Wiping their eyes, they sank upon a stone garden

bench. Lavinia tugged at Jenny's hand, urging her to face her.

"What I want to know is . . . everything!" demanded Lavvy.

"I am sure you do, but for now, all I shall tell you is what you already know. I accepted to marry the Earl and will do so on Friday, and I would be so happy, Lavvy, if you would consent to be my maid of honor."

"Consent? I would never forgive you if you had neglected to ask me, you . . . you odious thing! What do you mean you won't tell me anything?"

"Just what I said, Lavvy . . . for, in truth, there is naught to tell. The Earl asked, and I was pleased to accept."

"Love at first sight . . . 'tis a wonderous thing, I'm sure . . . but is it?" asked Lavvy, cocking an eyebrow. "I see you are blushing. But do you know, Jenny, I think he is just for you. Knew it the moment I watched you two together. I thought, He's taken with my Jenny . . . and what's more, he makes her eyes light up!"

"Oh no, no, Lavvy . . . I . . ." said Jenny, faltering.

However, Lavvy did not halt her romantic wanderings. She had already drawn the conclusion that the Earl and her best friend had fallen in love at first sight. It was, for her, the only possible answer to this sudden decision of Jenny's to get married to Jason Waine.

"Poor Mac—the Lieutenant, I mean," said Lavinia, coming down from her musings with a sigh.

"Why 'poor Mac'?" asked Jenny, frowning.

"Well . . . don't tell me he won't be surprised," said Lavvy reasonably.

"Yes, he certainly will be," agreed Jenny, the frown darkening.

"Not only surprised . . . disappointed as well, for he was probably expecting to walk down that aisle with you himself."

"What?" ejaculated Jenny. "Lavvy, your romantic notions have slipped away with you. Mac has never ever felt that way about me. We have been friends—very good friends—and *he* has no need to marry for any purpose other than satisfying his heart."

"Sure 'n' that's what 'ee would be doing, m'darlin'," said Lavvy, grinning.

"Now stop it, Lavvy. That is not funny, and how you can utter such nonsense is beyond me! You have never even seen us together!" retorted Jenny.

"That's true ... yet he spoke of you with such reverence," said Lavvy.

"Just as I speak of him," replied Jenny. "You can be rather silly at times, Lavvy. Mac has never shown that sort of interest in me—not even in Brussels when we spent so much time together ... when John was away."

"Well, I could be wrong. It was that I flirted with him in vain, and thought that when he didn't respond to me ..." said Lavvy pouting.

Jenny laughed. "Silly chit! Mac likes older women. Noticed it in Brussels. Most of his flirts are ladies he can't be trapped into marriage with. He has often told me that he wouldn't be happy as a married man ... likes to be on the go."

"All right, then, I shall concede. Now do take me inside and feed me, Jenny. I haven't had a bite since morning and I smelled gooseberry pie when I came through the house."

Jenny laughed. "Very well, then. Come along ... though gooseberry pie is very fattening and I want you looking your best on Friday."

"Odious girl ... for you must know I planned on having two slices, and it's really too bad that women don't wear corsets so that they could eat more. Now, don't laugh ... really, Jen, these clinging fashions worn on bare skin may be fine for slim figures like yours, but we more full-figured girls. ..." She allowed her voice to trail off as she moved her hands over her delicately thin body, for Lavvy was one of those maids who eat all they wish and still remain whispery and elegant.

They laughed and joined hands as they reentered the house. The Squire and Aunt Beth were meandering past the gardens on one of their constitutionals and they heard the merry laughter of the girls.

"That ... is the warmest sound I know," said the Squire.

"Yes, it is good to hear it again," replied his sister.

"May it thrive. And Beth, how will we go on in this big house without her?"

She patted his hand. "Jenny will be getting married and going away for a while, but I expect that we shall be seeing her quite a lot in the future . . . and soon you shall be playing with your grandchild upon your knee."

The thought made the Squire smile, but he shook his head sadly. "Know the only thing I regretted in not re-marrying, Beth? I am the last of the direct line. The Grange, after going from father to son for one hundred and fifty years, will do so no longer."

"Don't fret it, dear. It will still go to an Ashley, and it is the name that matters."

"I suppose . . . yet, there is something to be said about one's duty, you know. When I was younger and had the chance to remarry, I wouldn't hear of it . . . and now I am old and have no son."

"Ha! What does that signify? You might have married, without love, and not had a boy! What, then, of duty? A loveless marriage, and the estate would still have gone to an Ashley cousin."

"Do you know, Beth, that you have a way of laconi-cally spouting logic that is not to be denied, that inevi-tably cures my ills and still urges me to dispute with you!"

They heard a shriek of laughter again as Lavinia and Jenny found still another topic that brought them joy, and the Squire smiled contentedly.


# Chapter Nine

*Pause Not; The time is past! Every voice cries, Away!*
PERCY BYSSHE SHELLY, 1814


Although most of the *ton* had deserted the sultry London atmosphere early in May for Brighton, there were still quite a few whom the Earl was able to wile away the days with.

In Brighton, the Prince Regent noted with a sigh that

still one more of his younger intimates had collided with fate, as the *Gazette* was distributed in this, *the* coastal resort that the Regent had raised to stardom some twenty years before.

The Earl received a bombardment of congratulatory mail from his friends and distant relatives, as well as a good many somewhat remorseful notes from ladies who feared their connection might, upon his marriage, be terminated.

The Earl's first reaction upon receiving such sad entreaties was to write the most favored of these females and assure her that their very enjoyable relations would in no way be affected by his upcoming nuptials. However, when he seated himself at his writing desk, picked up his pen, and dipped it into the inkwell, he found that the words that flowed before his eyes were callous and somehow disrespectful to Jenny.

A deep frown inserted its presence upon him. This is ludicrous, he thought. There is no need for me to assure these ladies of anything! They will be available when I want them, and there is no need for me to participate in a correspondence that can only cause embarrassment to my future wife. For he was well acquainted with the wiles and petty cruelties engaged in by some of the gossip mongers, and he had no intention of allowing Jenny to be hurt in such a fashion.

This was something new, this forethought for someone he barely knew, and it weighed heavily. He had no wish for Jenny to be unhappy. He genuinely believed that, in time, he and Jenny could have a very comfortable and friendly relationship. He never doubted his ability to break down her barrier and enter her bedroom, and what was more to the point, he wanted her to be the mother of his children. The thought of having children caused the frown to disappear. Jason Waine wanted Jenny for his bride, his lover, and the mother of his children . . . and Jason Waine wanted to retain the freedom he had enjoyed as a bachelor.

Oddly enough, though the Earl went merrily about with his cronies to the theatre, to Vauxhall Gardens, and to White's, he did not at first visit the latest of his interests.

However, a note from this particular pretty arrived just before he was preparing for his return trip to Devon. He flapped the note gently against his fingers, picked up his hat and cane, and went out on the quiet street. It was close onto seven in the evening, but not quite dark. He meandered down the length of Duke Street, crossed the busy traffic at Oxford, and made his way to Seymour. This particular female had already cost the Earl a great deal, he thought ruefully, but he did not yet feel he was ready to part with her. She was a lovely fair-haired actress of little talent and less style, yet she was well able to please and rarely expected him to spend more than an hour with her, which was all he was willing to give her of his time.

He gave the knocker of her front door a lazy pull and a parlor maid opened the door. The girl, a plain, inexperienced miss, dropped a curtsy to this, her mistress's protector, and advised him that her mistress was awaiting him upstairs.

The Earl's eyes found the stairs, and suddenly he felt inexplicably bored. He felt all at once that this routine was more than he could take, and he sighed for his lack of desire.

"If you would be so kind, tell your mistress that I wish to speak with——"

He was interrupted by an incomprehensible sound from the top of the stairs. "Jason ... darling, my sweet pet," said Aurora Davies with a shake of her fair curls.

Her bright blue eyes glittered invitingly, though, in truth, she was not in love with the Earl. She liked him very well, but had recently had a better offer from a royal Duke, who was also in a position to further her career.

"Aurora, you are, as always, enchanting. Do come down so that we need not speak with all these steps between us," said the Earl lightly.

"Come down?" asked the lady, somewhat startled.

"Er . . . yes."

"Are you all right, Jason?" asked the lady, picking up her skirts of transparent muslin and descending toward him.

He waited for her to reach his side and then put his

strong arm about her waist and smiled down into her face. She allowed him to lead her to one of the two rooms that made up the first floor of her small residence. It was a small front parlor, comfortably if not altogether richly decorated, for the Earl had not been able to afford more on his income. He led her to a gray velvet sofa and pulled her down beside him.

Her dark red-painted lips teased him for a kiss and he embraced her long and hard. However, he found the familiar experience less satisfying than it had been in the past.

The lady happily did not notice his lack of ardor and smiled inquiringly at his hesitant attitude.

"Aurora, I have something to tell you."

"Yes, love," replied the lady, not wholly interested.

"When I left you last week, it was not on business as I had allowed you to suppose."

"No . . . was it not? But then, Jason, I have no hold on you," said the lady amicably.

He regarded her penetratingly for a moment, half suspicioning that she had been busy while he was away. His feelings were not in any conceivable way attached to Miss Davies; however, he did not like the notion that a lady under his protection might be entertaining in the home he provided for her. " 'Tis true, Aurora, you have no hold on me whatsoever. However, I am afraid that I must tell you that I am to be married and will be out of town for approximately one month."

"La, Jason . . . how marvelous for you. I do wish you both happy," said the lady.

"You do?" asked Jason, surprised, his pride slightly nettled.

"Bless me! Of course, I do. What's more, Jason, it comes at precisely the right moment, for now we shall be parting on the best of terms."

"Parting?" asked Jason.

"Yes, love. You see . . . the Duke of York has made me quite an attractive offer. . . ."

"I see," said the Earl dryly.

"No, you do not. I have played fair with you, Jason. Now, don't go thinking I've bestowed my favors where they don't belong. I don't play that way with a right 'un. No . . . I ain't that sort. We had an understanding, and I've lived up to it, but now it's time we kissed good-bye."

"And so it is, Aurora," said the Earl, grinning involuntarily. "You have been a grand old girl, and you shall do a vast deal better with York!"

"I'd liefer by far do better with you, Jason. You know the Duke lacks your manners, your face, and those great strong arms . . . but I won't be young all my life. Why, I'm nearly twenty-five, and I have to build some sort of a nest egg for the future. You understand now, don't you, love?"

The Earl kissed her hand. "I wish you luck, Aurora, and I bid thee farewell."

He stood up and started to take his leave of her. Miss Davies' blue eyes opened wide. "But, Jason, ain't you going to stay a while? I haven't left your house yet . . . and you haven't tied the knot, so what's to stop us?"

His warm smile lit up his face. "Now, Aurora, it would never do to prolong the agony of parting."

"Aw, go on now, love. Stay but a while," she said coaxingly.

For answer he dropped a kiss upon her waiting lips and then was gone in an instant.

He walked into the darkness of the night and made his way to Oxford, where he hailed a passing hackney. Strangely enough, he felt an overwhelming sense of relief. He could have convinced her to remain under his roof, for he would soon be rich, but his pride and lack of inclination prohibited this, and he left feeling free and clean of conscience. "White's at St. James," he advised the driver curtly before disappearing into the carriage.

He watched the passing scenery as the carriage made its way past the fashionable residences of Mayfair, past the highest kicks of fashion displayed in the shops along Bond Street; Picadilly was crossed and the hackney pulled up to the curbing in front of a brick building with a modern protruding window, better known as the Bow Window, from which the members of White's Club now and then ogled any passing female so unwise as to risk her reputation by walking by.

He paid the hackney, entered the club, and was hailed by his few friends still remaining in London.

Only one conscious thought returned to disturb the pleasures of winning at faro: The Earl could not shake the fact that he had felt guilty at being with Aurora. He had felt guilty and he had felt a need for Jenny's dark eyes.

Jenny paced across the flowered design of the woven rug that stretched across the oak flooring of her attractive bedroom.

Her aunt's maid, Biddle—whom Jenny had long ago dubbed Biddy—came hustling into the room after knocking and received a welcome from its nervous occupant.

"Dearest Biddy . . . here, let me help you," said Jenny, coming forward to relieve the elderly maid of some of her burden. "Never say you carried all those bandboxes upstairs by yourself?" she exclaimed under the weight of some of them. She dropped the boxes upon the bed and motioned for Biddy to follow suit, which she did thankfully.

"Oh no, miss. One of the lads from the dress shop helped me. I gave him a coin and sent him on his way."

"I see," said Jenny before turning her attention to the boxes and lifting off one of the white and gold lids.

"Gracious me!" exclaimed Biddle at sight of an adorable yellow twilled bonnet. "If that isn't the loveliest shade of yellow. Oh, miss, you will look simply grand."

"Thank you, Biddy. Would you like to see some of the other things Aunt and I have bought?"

"Oh and I would, miss. But 'tis that busy we are below stairs . . . what with the wedding breakfast to prepare and the labeling of the gifts. Oh, and your aunt asked me to remind you that thank-you notes for them must be started on, if you are ever to get done."

"Of course, I shall get myself together and come down and do so."

She watched the gray-haired woman disappear and sank down upon her mauve quilt.

It was true, the house was in a turmoil of excitement. It was the first wedding to take place since her Aunt Beth's, many years ago. There was much reminiscing among those of the staff who had been present, and their earlier doubts seemed by now to have been dispelled.

Jenny herself was boiling with mixed emotions. She felt her young heart bursting with the weight of dread, anticipation . . . and something she could not fathom. Her emotions left her confused and short-tempered.

She had thought she was pleased that the Earl had left on the same day of his proposal. At first, she had breathed a sigh of relief that she would not see him until the day of the wedding. Now, she wished with all her heart that he were back.

She wanted to speak with him. She wanted to know more of his family, their relative positions. She wanted to . . . hear his voice and see his face. Jenny told herself that this was only natural. After all, she would be carrying his name and would, of course, have to entertain his family from time to time. Therefore, there was nothing in it if she wanted to speak to him about them. It was only natural that she should want his company now . . . for, she told herself, as husband and wife they should be friends, even if they could be nothing more!

Then she thought of the wedding and felt a tremble shake her bones. She brushed it aside. With determination, she stood and went to do the necessary duty of writing thank-you notes.

Later that day Jenny escaped the house and made her way to the rose arbor, a favorite thinking spot. She had no sooner plopped herself down when a footstep on the winding path brought her head up. With a disappointed sigh she welcomed her aunt, for she had been hoping the Earl would surprise her by arriving earlier than he had indicated.

"Hello, dear. May I intrude on your thoughts for a while. There is something I wish to discuss with you."

"Of course, Auntie," replied Jenny at once, realizing that soon she would be living away from this marvelous woman, this beloved sweet woman, who had always been there when she was needed.

"Very well, then, child, I wish you to attend to what I

am saying with a little more patience than you are wont to have, for I may say something to set up your bristles."

"But whatever do you mean?" asked Jenny surprised.

"It is because ... because—oh dear, this is somewhat more difficult for me than I had expected. This discussion was not necessary before when you were engaged to John, simply because ... he was a young man with whom you were on easy terms. There would have been little embarrassment for you on your wedding night, as I expect he was not worldly ... and ..."

As her aunt faltered for words, Jenny blushed, knowing all too well what she was talking around. She had no wish for her aunt to know the sort of bargain she and the Earl had struck up and squirmed upon the garden bench.

"Dear, dear," pursued her aunt valiantly, "the thing is, Jennifer, that the Earl of Waine has a reputation for ... for a ..."

"A rake," said Jenny, grinning suddenly at her aunt's confusion.

"Well, not precisely. Let us call it an appreciation of women that leads him to ... to ... dally with attractive females in a fashion that is rather open."

"And why not, Aunt? After all, he was not married," said Jenny.

"No, of course he was not. However, his past experiences may be mentioned and I would not want you shocked ... but that is not what I really wanted to prepare you for." She took a long breath. "Jenny, men of his stamp ... often stray. It is to be hoped that his love for you, and his happy home, will keep him from doing so. However—"

"Oh, Aunt, I beg of you, do not worry yourself over the matter. I am not a green girl. After a season in Brussels, a girl could not walk away unaware of how life goes on among most of our set," said Jenny, interrupting hastily.

"Yes, but I know how possessive you are, Jenny, and I want you prepared. Not all men are like your papa, for I don't believe he ever glanced at another woman while your

90

mama was alive ... or for that matter, like my own dear husband. Your John would never have bothered himself with any other females, for he often expressed the commendable notion that you were the only girl worth passing the time with. However, the Earl's reputation—"

"Oh, Auntie, it is nothing to me if he strays now and then, though I should not like him to go about doing it before the world," said Jenny, wishing her aunt would drop the subject.

Aunt Beth regarded her niece with some trepidation. "Well ... I am relieved to find that you are aware of such a possibility. However, I am not at all pleased with your attitude."

"You are the sweetest creature, Aunt Beth, and I do love you ... but this is something I must handle in my own way and in my own time. The Earl has asked me to marry him, I have accepted. The future is ahead, and you have prepared me ... so rest easy, I shall not be shocked."

Her aunt had been dismissed and was too well acquainted with Jennifer to miss the look in her niece's eyes. She would get no further with Jenny today.

Jenny released a sigh as her aunt returned to the house. This was becoming sticky, and once again, she knew an irritation of nerves.


Wednesday morning brought forth two elegant coaches, some luggage, a few servants, Sir George and Lady Gwen, and the Earl. They made their way toward Salisbury, where they would be spending the night before continuing to an inn near the Ashley estate.

The journey took them nearly eight hours, as they made slow progress and took frequent rests in order to spare the horses.

Dinner had been ordered in the Salisbury Inn's private dining parlor; Lady Gwen looked up from her roast duck and considered her brother.

"I must say, Jason, I find this very irregular! Why we should not go directly to Ashley Grange tomorrow and spend the night with them is more than I can fathom. I would like to spend some time with Jenny before you whisk her off on Friday."

"I have my reasons," replied her brother blandly.

"Dreadful creature! I know you have your reasons ... undoubtedly they are good ones. What I want is to know what they are," replied his sister, glaring.

"Poor little Robin," said her brother for answer.

"Why 'poor little Robin?' " exclaimed his sister, annoyed.

"Why 'poor little Robin'?" agreed her husband.

"Sending him off to Brighton. I would think he would have enjoyed my wedding," said the Earl.

"Ah yes, I agree with Jason that was a paltry thing to do to the little chap," said Sir George.

"Faith, you can't really mean that I should have dragged the boy one hundred miles to Ashley Grange and then another hundred to Brighton! 'Tis bad enough that *we* have to undergo such an ordeal," exclaimed Gwen, with a shake of her shining black curls.

"She's right there!" said her husband, ever ready to agree with logic.

"Never said she wasn't ... but in either case, the lad loses out," said the Earl, happy to see that his sister's thoughts had now taken a new direction.

"Poor little chap!" said her husband, much struck with this aspect of the discussion.

"Indeed, yes, George ... but you do agree that the pleasure of going to his uncle's wedding would have been dispelled by the tortures of such a long journey in an uncomfortable coach?" said Gwen.

"Uncomfortable coach?" said her husband. "Now, Gwen, that is doing it rather too brown! When I purchased that little job for you last month, you declared it was the finest thing you had ever set your eyes on."

"And so it is, George," said Lady Gwen quickly, "but I don't suppose anything would be comfortable after eight hours ... and we still have some traveling to do tomorrow."

This debate continued for some time, and the Earl relaxed in his chair, saying little until he saw it waning, at which time he added a piece of fuel and withdrew to observe its effects.

Friday finally arrived and brought the two parties together at Ashley Grange.

The Earl and the Henleys arrived with barely an hour to spare before the wedding, and therefore Jenny was not downstairs to greet them. Aunt Beth and the Squire made them comfortable, exchanged surprised greetings with Lady Gwen, whom they had met in Brussels, but had not realized was the Earl's sister.

"My . . . but there is a remarkable likeness when you stand beside each other!" exclaimed Aunt Beth.

"May I go up to Jenny? I do so want to speak with her before the ceremony," said Gwen excitedly.

"Of course, she will be so pleased," replied Beth, still awed by the fact that Lady Gwen was the Earl's sister.

A knock sounded on Jenny's door and she turned from the long mirror, picked up her cascading train of white organza, and invited the intruder of her musings to enter.

For a moment Jenny remained unmoving, her dark eyes focusing on Lady Gwen's features. Of course, she thought. That is why his face has always seemed so familiar. I have always felt something when I looked upon him. "Gwen . . . I . . . I can't believe it. I was not aware that you were the Earl's sister . . . he never mentioned your name," said Jenny, rushing to put her arms about the tall, graceful woman.

"Horrid creature that he is, did he not tell you that he had a twin sister?"

"No, only that he had a sister . . . and I neglected to ask any details."

"Dearest Jenny, you look superb! White suits you . . . where is your veil?"

Jenny pointed to the vanity table where the crown of silk roses and lace reposed.

"Oh, how lovely." She turned and then reappraised Jenny admiringly.

Jenny's wedding dress was sleeveless. The bodice was heart-shaped and embroidered with pearls. There were pearl swags that connected the front and back of the dress across her bare arms. The waist was fitted and billowed out into a wide bell-shaped skirt, caught up at the hem in cascading swags, from which Jenny's dainty feet peeped.

Jenny's chestnut hair was piled up on her head in glorious grecian curls. Copper fire glittered among the white silk rosebuds pinned throughout the curls. Her complexion was rosy and her dark eyes shone.

Gwen took up Jenny's white-silk-covered hands and pressed them lightly. "You are radiant, my dear . . . and I wish you happiness. But are you certain this is what you want?"

"Gwen?" exclaimed Jenny, surprised. "He is your brother!"

"My brother, yes, and I adore him and want the best for him . . . but you are such an innocent—"

"Stop it! I may be innocent but I am not blind. I have my eyes open. Your brother was honest with me . . . and I with him. The subject is not open to debate. No, I will not withdraw my hand from his. I am not such a one as that!"

"No," said Gwen quietly. "No, you are not, and I cannot tell you how pleased I am that you are to be my sister."

They embraced each other and then Gwen clasped her hands anxiously. "It is too bad that you are not going abroad for your honeymoon . . . it would have been so much more pleasant for you," she said with a troubled frown.

"Oh, I . . . I really don't wish to," said Jenny.

"No? You do realize that you and Jason will not be alone at Waine Castle?" said Gwen gravely.

"Er . . . why yes, I seem to recollect something Jason said about his brother—"

"Half-brother," corrected Gwen. "It may not be altogether . . . enjoyable for you, and I believe the place is not what it was."

"Oh? Haven't you been there—for you speak as if you haven't seen your home in ages."

Gwen smiled. "I left for my aunt's in London some six years ago . . . for the Season, you know. My aunt presented me, though it was really a waste of time, as I had already decided to marry my dearest George long before, but that is another story for another time. Here, I do go on, and *you* are probably nervous as a kitten."

"No, I like to hear you talk, actually. It takes my restlessness and temporarily shelves it."

They were interrupted by Biddy at that moment as she came into the room without knocking, exclaimed something about her rudeness at having interrupted her mistress while she had a visitor, and began to withdraw when Jenny's chuckling voice called her back.

"It's just that your aunt says we shall be late, miss. I'm to dress your hair with the wedding veil and escort you to your papa's waiting carriage. The Earl will be meeting us at the church."

Gwen excused herself and went below stairs to meet her husband and anxious brother.

Jenny was led down the rear stairs and ushered into the coach, where she found her harassed papa and her calm aunt. All at once, she burst into tears.

"My babe, what is it? Just say the word and I shall turn the coach around and you shall not marry the lad. Darling, you need not if you don't wish to. Don't fret. Papa will handle it all."

"No, Papa . . . it's not that I want to back out," sobbed Jenny.

Her aunt dabbed at her cheek and clucked her tongue. "You will end up looking a mess, dear."

This caused a small hysterical titter to escape Jenny's lips and Aunt Beth said coolly, "There now, that's better. I believe I did the very same thing when I was about to be married. You were in the other coach, Alfred, with Mama . . . and I cried into Papa's coat so that my tears stained the material."

"Did you?" asked Jenny, while her father looked dubious.

"Of course. 'Tis a big step for a girl to leave the people and home she loves and feels secure in. 'Tis a wild adventure, marriage. You will be fine, dear."

The parish church was reached and Jenny was shepherded into a small antechamber, where she found Lavinia in pink silk and flutters. They held each other tightly

95

and then all at once the moment came. She heard the organ, heard someone singing, felt Lavvy proudly holding her long white train. A room filled with some thirty people hazed before her eyes as she moved slowly down the aisle, flowers in hand.

She saw the minister, Bible before him, and thought she would not make it, could not go through with it. Then her eyes found Jason Waine. He stood there, slightly to one side in his cutaway of ivory superfine, looking tall and handsome. His waistcoat was of white silk, embroidered with blue. His ivory knee breeches showed his well-defined and athletic legs. His black hair was combed with its usual studied carelessness and framed his face in thick gleaming waves to his neckline. His lush blue eyes were glittering in his deeply bronzed handsome face. She saw him gaze at her and her knees crumbled beneath her. She felt as though she would have fallen to the floor had not her father supported her arm.

She walked beside her papa what seemed an infinite distance toward the Earl; she felt her hand placed upon the Earl's waiting arm. She barely noticed the tall, jolly man standing beside the Earl until the minister was asking for the ring.

Jason Waine had been waiting for this moment with a great deal of restlessness. His days in London had left him feeling lonely in some inexplicable way. He found his dreams filled with a pair of dark, sad eyes, and was reminded of a kiss that he had stolen. He now stood holding his breath as he watched his bride approach and thought she was the loveliest thing on earth. He smelled the scent of spring when she was near him. His blue eyes twinkled at her reassuringly and she felt them say, "We are friends—remember," and she felt her anxiety ebb.

She repeated words almost dumbly, and then the minister said something about a ring. The large, grinning man at the Earl's side produced a gold ring studded with diamonds and she felt the Earl slip it onto her finger.

She heard the minister instruct Jason to kiss her, and swallowed hard as the Earl bent toward her, a gentle smile on his lips ... and then they were on hers, softly and quickly, almost too quickly, withdrawn.

She felt a surge of heat rush through her veins. She knew a wild longing to drop into his arms and escape this hot, crowded room. She was burned by the nearness of him, burned in a way that was new and horrifying to her, and she knew she had never experienced this emotion when she had been with Johnny. There was little time to reflect upon the strangeness of this, for all at once they were running down the aisle and rose petal leaves were being flung joyously at them. They heard the sound of laughter as people shouted congratulations. Then, just as suddenly, she was beside the Earl in the quiet of his elegant coach and they were alone.

The Earl of Waine looked down at the woman beside him and smiled. "Well, Lady Waine."

She managed to return his amicable smile and ignored the thumping of her heart. "Well, my lord?"

He laughed and relaxed back against the seat. "It is to breakfast, hearty congratulations from our well-wishers, and then, my girl, we shall be off for Waine Castle. Are you afraid?"

"In truth, 'afraid' is not precisely the correct word. 'Anxious' would describe my feelings more appropriately, my lord."

He chuckled and took her chin in his gloved hand. "My dearest and most lovely wife . . . can you not find it in your heart to address me as Jason?"

"I am sorry. Jason then. Do you know that you are a horrid individual?" said Jenny, remembering a grievance and once more falling into the easy friendship they had established before his departure from Ashley.

"It's always been plain as pikestaff to me, though I have taken pains to hide the fact from you. However, did you manage to uncover me?" teased the Earl.

"Really, my lo—Jason! Why did you not tell me that Gwen Henley was your sister?"

"Oh, in truth, it slipped my mind," said the Earl honestly.

"Slipped your mind?" asked Jenny incredulously.

"Well, Jen, you must admit, darling, that I had the devil of a time getting you to accept my very handsome proposal of marriage, and then . . . you did not ask who my sister was, you know."

"Yes, that is very true. But I must tell you, Jason, that it is very agreeable of you to have Gwen for your sister. We are great friends."

"At last my lovely sister has been of some use to me." The Earl grinned. "I thought that was something that would never come to pass."

"Oh, she is perfectly right in calling you odious. You are!" His bride laughed.

"Ah, but you shall not say so when I have told you that I have obtained the best of lady's maids and sent her to await your arrival at Waine Castle," said the Earl with mock austerity.

"Why, Jason, how bright of you to do so. How did you know that I have no maid of my own?" asked Jenny.

"Your aunt advised me, actually. Said you've been sharing some dear creature with the odd name of Biddy. Mentioned the circumstance to Gwen, for she is very good in these matters, you know. Found me just the sort of girl you'll need, and I sent her with my valet and luggage on ahead."

They had arrived once again at the Grange, and the Earl jumped nimbly down from his coach and reached up for his bride. They were immediately enveloped in a crowd of merry people and heralded into the house.

Jenny's eyes scanned the room and thanked Providence that the Dillingham's had been away and unable to attend the wedding. That would have been a meeting she could not have faced with equanimity.

Lavinia's silly chatter and Gwen's attentions helped her through the tenseness of the hour, and she found she was able to relax and enjoy her own wedding party to some extent. Then she felt her elbow touched and found the Earl's blue eyes glittering mischievously at her. "I must tell you, madam, that while I relish the sight of you in your bride raiments, I must ask you to . . . er, remove them."

Jenny's eyes opened wide before she realized the Earl was once again teasing her.

He laughed at her expression and said with mock gravity, "Lady Waine, how can you misconstrue my innocent meaning? I am asking you to go and change into your traveling clothes, for while I am told a mail coach can span the distance between East Devon and Dover in twenty hours, I am quite certain we will not! Their horses don't live above five years, and you and I care too much about our animals to treat them so badly."

Jenny's face fell. "No, of course we must pace them ... but so soon, my lord? Must we leave so soon?"

He suddenly knew an urge to please her, to wipe the anxious look from her eyes, but he knew, too, that the rope must be cut. "I am afraid so, child. We should leave immediately if we are going to maintain any sort of a schedule. Don't want to be traveling the coast road in the evenings, which is what I fear we will be doing if we allow any more time to elapse."

"Oh ... why is that, my lord?"

"Jenny, I shall very likely wring your neck if you pursue in this lamentable habit of calling me 'my lord,' " said Jason amusedly.

"I forgot," said Jenny simply. "But, Jason, do tell me why you don't wish to travel at night. Are you not familiar with the road ... for I have an excellent guide I can bring al—"

His laugh interrupted her. "My dearest child, I have traveled the road so often I could do so without the benefit of vision. It is because I don't wish to expose you to the terrors of being attacked by highwaymen."

"Highwaymen? Oh, how exciting!" exclaimed Jenny.

"There is nothing exciting about having a pistol pointed at your head and your jewels torn off your neck," said the Earl dryly.

"How poor-spirited of you, Jason. There is no need for such gloomy suppositions. We could, of course, capture the dreadful creatures and rid the road of their scourge," said Jenny, laughing.

The Earl had a sudden urge to catch her up, contained it, and said softly, "If you are going to have a hand in this courageous act, I suggest you retire to your room and adorn yourself with the proper garments for such delivery."

She chuckled appreciatively and called for Lavinia to join her. Gwen raced after them and the three young ladies fell in together. Lavvy and Gwen seemed to speak at the same time and Jenny was grateful for their diverting company.

She had been putting on something of a bravado, but deep inside Jen was beginning to feel a sense of uneasiness. What if the Earl should not keep his promise ... what if he should try and force himself upon her? He might mistake her show of friendship, he might ... Oh no, Jen, he would not. You know that he will respect your wishes, she told herself.

Lavvy worked on the troublesome buttons of Jenny's wedding gown. It was slipped off and thrown carefully aside a great deal quicker than it had earlier been donned. A bright yellow muslin traveling suit was produced with a pale maize ruffled blouse and brown kid boots. These were smoothed on and the new yellow bonnet placed rakishly upon her dark curls. Then a cherry was slit and placed upon her lips for color.

Gwen pinched her cheek and repeated her wishes for happiness, saying once again that she was jubilant to have such a sister.

Jenny regarded her wistfully. "Gwen ... could you not come to Waine with us?"

Lavvy opened her gray eyes and blinked incredulously. "Jenny, what a zany you are. How can you want company on your honeymoon?"

Jenny blushed. "Well ... it is not an average honeymoon, Lavvy, for I understand Jason's brother will be at the Castle ... and I would so love to have everyone there. We could organize all sorts of things together."

"Jenny dear, George and I cannot possibly come, for our son was sent on to Brighton, where he will be waiting for our arrival. And ... I don't get along with my stepmother," said Gwen, her eyes taking on a cold expression.

"Oh," said Jenny, downcast. "Oh dear, I have just had a fearful thought—what if I don't get along with your stepmother?"

Gwen sneered. "Then you shall ask her to leave your home."

"Oh Gwen, I could not do that. After all, it is her home as well."

"It is not!" hissed Gwen, her eyes glittering. "She was left the dower house, but because she is too tight-fisted to move in and maintain her own staff, she has remained in Jason's house. Waine Castle was left to Jason without the entailments. Its maintanance is paid for out of the estate, and *that* woman and her son have been living off Jason's good nature."

"My goodness, Gwen . . . what has she done to you to make you so bitter?" asked Jenny, surprised at Gwen's hardness.

"It is nothing that should be troubling you on your wedding day," said Gwen, smiling again. "Come, let us hurry, for if I know Jason, he will be in a fidget."

Jenny's aunt entered the room then and Jenny fell into her comfortable arms. She felt seized with a terror—how could she leave her aunt, her father, and her home for some strange man she called her husband, but could never be wife to, and for some strange household?

Her aunt spoke softly to her and eased her with soothing words. "Remember, child, this is your home always. We are here whenever you want, and if you don't write regularly, you shall find us at your doorstep. A circumstance your father advises me will probably happen much sooner than you wish."

"Oh, how can you say so? I will always want you with me!" exclaimed Jenny.

They hugged each other tightly for a long moment. Jenny knew a longing to stay with an impatience to be off. She was torn between the need for what was, and the need and desire for adventure.

She was led downstairs by her aunt, with Gwen and Lavvy making up a silent train behind her. They descended the steps slowly to find the Squire's anxious eyes upon them. Jenny rushed into his arms and assured him quietly that he was her dearest love. He held his daughter tenderly, and a tear moved silently down his rugged cheek.

Jenny then found herself overwhelmed by the guests and bade them each in turn a fond farewell. The Earl managed to get his arm about his bride and steer her toward his waiting carriage, and once again, she felt she was gliding dangerously through a dream.

# Chapter Ten

She stood a moment while the Earl issued instructions to his drivers, and gazed at the coach of blazing black and gold. The sun shone brightly on the luggage piled on top and she noted gratefully that either the Earl or her papa had remembered to have Whisper tethered to the rear of the coach. A footman rushed toward the door, which boasted the Earl's coat of arms, and pulled it open for her. She went in slowly and situated herself for the long ride.

The Earl jumped spritely in beside her and she felt the coach begin to move. She was able to appreciate the thick luxurious upholstery, which was well designed and comfortable. She sank onto the cushioned seat with a deep sigh and gazed out the window. She wanted to sit and silently study the scenes.

Jason Waine sensed this and allowed her to lose herself to thought, watching her out of the corner of his eye.

They passed out of the Ashley gates and made their way to the post road, passing the Dillingham estate on the way. She thought of Johnny. You are Lady Waine and you are going to Waine Castle. Never will you be Lady Dillingham, she thought, but without bitterness. She told it to herself as though she needed to drum the fact in and make it less like a fantasy.

The Earl was undergoing some very strange emotions himself. He had watched her descend her stairs and thought her figure alluring. He knew an overwhelming desire to be alone with his bride. Now that he was, his intuition cautioned him. He had to remind himself not to frighten her.

He had known many women—widows, opera singers, other men's wives, Drury Lane actresses—all lovely, and most of them had satisfied his physical needs. He had watched his friends fall in love, watched them marry, though few marriages had fostered in him a good opinion of the state of matrimony. There were, of course, some love matches that seemed to perpetuate; his sister's was one. Yet *he* had never fallen in love. When he was a young man, he had formed a deep infatuation with Lady Jersey, who was a good deal older and wiser. They had been lovers and were now good friends. Apart from her, he could think of no woman who had inspired any real affection.

A great many caps had been flung his way, and he always managed to meander his way through. Some of the blushing virgins put in his path had teased his interest for short durations, but never before had he set out to win a chaste girl's heart. He found that for no logical reason Jenny tickled his soul.

He had liked her right off. He respected her and felt drawn to the sadness in the recesses of her eyes. He wanted her in every way a man could want a woman, but treaded carefully, for he was all too aware that she was skittish, ready to bolt at the first sign of romance.

It was some time before either of the two individuals bemusing their lot came out of their thoughts, each with a different purpose in mind

Jenny was the first to speak and her tone indicated that she was determined to be friends with the man who sat beside her. "Tell me, my lord—I mean Jason, and ask that you excuse my lapses, I find it difficult to think of you in any other terms—but tell me about your home, your family . . . for I really know so very little."

A mirthless laugh escaped his lips, which seemed to curl. "They, my dear, are a motly crew. However, you will not be expected to bear with them if they misbehave, as Gwen has predicted to me."

"What do you mean?"

"If Gwen were allowed to have her way, she would have our stepmother and my brother Julian cleared out of Waine by tonight. However, I should not like to do such a thing, unless we were given no choice."

"No, what a perfectly terrible thing that would be if we swept down on them and shooed them out of their home," said Jenny sincerely.

"Undoubtedly. Now, then, you are aware that I have a stepmother, a brother—or half-brother, as Gwen insists. There are also my wards, the Wendall boys. They were the sons of my father's closest friend over at Dean. When Peter Wendall of Dean died they were no more than babies—their mother had died during a premature birth sometime before that. Their estate is run by trustees. However, my father was named guardian and they came to stay. I lost my father shortly thereafter and their guardianship reverted to me.

"There is, too, a young governess, a local girl who tends to them and lives, of course, at Waine Castle. In addition to this menagerie, I have a cousin, Howard Waine, though he does not live in the Castle. He has bought a small cottage on Waine lands and acts as my agent—a damn good one, I might add."

"Well, I think it sounds very nice, all those people. It would be so gloomy to live in a large castle all by oneself, after all," said Jenny.

He smiled at her. "Lord, Jen, there is no need for you to live at Waine. We must spend a month there under the conditions of the will. However ... afterward, you may come to the Waine townhouse in London, or take up residence at one of my estates, either at Bath or any other of your choosing."

"My goodness ... so many homes. What can you possibly do with all those?"

"Not all of them are adorned with homes. Most of our estates are farmed. Only in London, Bath, and Dover do we have permanent residences. However, there is no reason why I could not build you a home anywhere you choose."

Jenny laughed. "You are very generous, Jason, and if you will excuse my frank speaking, I think it very odd of your father to draw up such a strange will. Why did he not just leave everything to you outright, with a reasonable portion to your brother?"

Jason scowled a moment. "In truth, Jenny, 'tis a bit complicated. According to English law and tradition, the estate goes to the first-born son of the house. However, if the estate is not previously entailed, the bequeather may determine how the estate should be divided, by leaving a will.

"To understand my father's reasoning in this matter, you would have to know more about his life ... our life together."

"Could you not tell me about it?" asked Jenny curiously.

"I suppose so, Jenny ... though it is not exactly the thing one should tell his bride upon their wedding day."

"I don't mind ... really, I want to know."

"My father, Gwen, and I were very close. An odd circumstance considering the fact that Gwen and I were not the result of a love match. Far from it, in fact. My father had been forced by family duty to marry an heiress to bolster the Waine estates. That was when my father was a young man in need of financial assistance to stave off the loss of the Castle. My mother was in love with him. She came from an excellent family and would bring him not only a great deal of money, but lands as well. They married. It did not take long for my mother's love to turn to hatred, for Papa was not in love with her ... and she discovered it in the cruelest of ways when she found him with one of the serving girls.

"By that time a year had past and we were born, Gwen and I. My mother took up residence in another part of the house. Both parents doted on us. We were everything to our mother, who seemed to grow old before her time ... for she was ill. We were six when she took to her bed. By the time we were seven, we had learned the meaning of the word 'mistress' and knew that our father kept one in town. She was a local beauty—what a beauty—but she had little else. She was the daughter of the town's only innkeeper. Soon after we discovered her, we discovered that we had a half-brother, for she had given our father a son . . . Julian."

He smiled ruefully at Jenny's wide-eyed astonishment. "Yes, my poor innocent, such things do occur to stagger the mind. There was Julian, my father's by-blow . . . and my mother knew. I don't know how she learned of it . . . perhaps the gossip mongers could not refrain from reinserting the knife into an old wound. At any rate, it didn't matter, for it was too late. My mother was twenty-nine and she was dying."

"Oh, Jason . . . oh, how dreadful for you and Gwen," said Jenny compassionately.

"Dreadful? Yes, I suppose then it was. You see, the sad thing was I never really liked my mother. I always felt she was . . . mean-spirited, that she had given up. But Gwen adored her. For Gwen, it was nearly the end of the world. She died then, complaining all the while of stomach ailments . . . there was nought anyone could do for her. And he waited only six months before bringing Lillian home. I was tolerant, you see, toward this beautiful woman they called my papa's mistress, but Gwen . . . oh, how she hated her! Papa married her and brought her home just six months after we lost Mother, and for Gwen that was too much. Julian was just an infant, but Gwen despised him. I thought he was an innocent and should be treated as such, and because Gwen was wont to listen to me in those days, she allowed her hatred to center on Lillian instead. Papa adopted Julian, of course, so that he would carry our name.

"Then Gwen discovered something and got the notion into her head that 'twas Lillian that had poisoned Mother and caused her death."

"What . . . but how could she?" ejaculated Jenny, shocked.

"You see, we had gone into town and Gwen had overheard some of the tattle mongers going at it. It seems Lillian had been seen visiting the Castle several times during the week before, and on the day that mother died. Gwen rushed home and examined the cook in her audacious little manner. I can recall how awed I was by Gwen's mastery. The cook confirmed to us that Lillian, who was now Lady of the Manor, so to speak, had indeed been in the Castle, and had, in fact, visited the kitchen."

"Oh my God!" breathed Jenny.

"Oh no, my love! It turned out to be all nonsense, for we went to the doctor, who reiterated that our mother had died of consumption and not poison."

"Well, then, was Gwen convinced?"

"Not she. Accused the doctor of making an invalid death certificate. Imagine that—for Gwen and I were no more than eight by then. She stood there and told him to his face that he had not checked for poison and simply assumed that our mother's long illness had been the cause of her death."

"What did he say?"

"What could he say? He answered that there was no need for such a test, as the late Lady Waine had died of consumption and not at the hand of a murderer ... or murderess. Gwen had to drop the issue—we were only children—but she never dropped it from her heart or mind. It even caused a rift between Papa and her for a while."

"Oh, Jason, how ghastly for you both."

"That was some twenty years ago. Julian is now nearly a man and Gwen a happily married woman. She left Waine, you know ... just after Papa's death. Went to stay with relatives in London ... we have them, you know, loads of 'em. She married George, who is, luckily, my closest friend, and all ends well."

Suddenly Jenny felt a chill rush through her and impulsively she took the Earl's hand. "Jason ... do you believe it was consumption?"

The Earl frowned. "I have often asked myself that very question. Lillian is many things—none of which I admire—but a murderess? No, I don't think so."

He felt her hand in his and thrilled to it. Wishing to retain her hand, he continued his mesmerizing account. "Lillian lived on the outskirts of Dover, while we lived further west ... for the Castle is situated west of Dover, toward Folkstone. That she should take rides to Waine, allow everyone to know she was there, obviously visit the kitchen, if she was going to send poison to my mother seems ludicrous, does it not?"

"No, not if she was your father's mistress and knew your mother never left her room. People would just think she had come to see your papa."

"They would think that, because that is precisely what she had come to do. Look, Jenny, don't misunderstand me. I have more reasons than I care to mention for loathing my stepmother. I try to contain these because they are not altogether just. There is something you should know. Lillian loved my father. She gained little more than worldly comforts by marrying him, as she was not accepted socially. While he was alive, people were barely civil to her. After she lost him, they were downright rude. I have said that she is many things—'tis true—but she needs a friend. I don't want to influence you against her. It is not fair, and the Lord knows, fate has not been altogether fair to Lillian Waine."

"Fate, perhaps, has not been, Jason ... but you have, and are," said Jenny, seeing a side of him she had not heretofore been aware of.

He laughed and tweeked her chin. "So, and that is exactly how my wife should feel about me."

She stiffened at once. She would have to be careful or she would be giving the Earl the wrong impression. She turned her gaze toward the changing sky and felt a slight dismay as a drizzle spattered gently against the windowpane. She watched the sky turn gray as the coach rumbled onward into Somerset County. It was well past noon when they reached Yeovil and stopped at a quaint thatched-roof inn. Tulips decorated the window boxes and scores of red and yellow tulips protruded around the building in near flower beds.

The Earl jumped out of the carriage and instructed his drivers to water the horses and enjoy their repast before turning to assist Jenny. He held her waist a moment and his blue eyes sought her own, but she kept her gaze downward.

"Thank you," said the Earl in an amused tone.

"For what, my lord?" asked Jenny, surprised.

"I could not help but notice that you were admiring my hessians." He lowered his voice. "It's the champagne," he confided. "My valet mixes it with blacking."

She realized he was hoaxing her and laughed. "I have heard that the Beau was wont to do so."

"He was . . . and I hope still is in his French surroundings. I do, in fact, indulge in the practice myself."

She took a good look at his boots for the first time. "Ah, you must, for they do, indeed, shine to perfection."

"Now that we have thoroughly exhausted the topic of my exquisite boots, would you take my arm, madam, and perhaps this country inn will be able to satisfy your palate."

"I am not really hungry, but I am glad we stopped here, Jason. It's so lovely."

They were ushered into a private parlor by a landlord who foresaw a promising tip.

A bottle of port was brought forth, with lemonade for the lady. This was followed by apples and cheese, for the luncheon was not quite ready. When it appeared, Jenny's appetite apparently awakened, for she fell upon the roast hens, boiled potatoes, sliced tongue, cauliflower, fresh bread, and butter with enthusiasm.

The Earl smiled to see her eat and waited for her to sit back with a contented sigh before allowing their plates to be removed.

It seemed to Jenny that they never lacked conversation, which was something she had worried about before the wedding. She supposed the feeling that came over her of having known him a long time was due to the fact that she had been friends with his twin sister and he was in many ways much like Gwen.

Cakes and tea were brought in, and while the Earl sipped his wine, his wife nibbled at the sweets and downed her hot tea, keeping up a lively banter all the while, for she discovered that the Earl was a friend of her favorite young poet, Lord Byron.

"I have always admired his style—so forthright and outspoken. To write with such clear vision and honesty . . . well, he must be a remarkable person. I cannot believe that a man who has written with such depth and beauty could have committed the alleged misdeeds the crowds seem to believe he has."

"My naive darling, Byron and I were at Cambridge together and I must admit that he was ever a devil! Had this pet bear that he actually brought to classes! Claimed the creature was sitting in for his degree! Then ... he had an eye for beauty and never could resist a woman. Though truth is, Byron was no chaser! No, Byron is no saint ... but he is no worse than any of us. 'Twas that wife of his. You see, she tried to convert the poor fellow to her quiet ways. He had ever a lively sense of humor ... and she has none whatsoever! In leaving him, she had committed a social solecism and one that needed defending. When the rumors—rumors borne of silence—when they sprang up, she did not admit them to be truth, but saw a way to save her reputation at the expense of his, which she felt was already tainted. Thus truth was belied with silence ... her silence!

"Byron was in debt and his heiress of a wife had not inherited. She had given birth to a child and the Byrons were being dunned daily. It is my opinion that she wanted the financial security she had with her parents. She achieved that."

"But, did she not love Byron?" asked Jenny, horrified.

"At first, yes. Later, no, I don't think so ... or at least, not enough. You see, he hadn't treated her with the romance displayed in his poetry. And I think she always thought she could change his loose ways and was put out that she could not!"

"But to accuse him and his sister of ..." Jenny faltered, shaking her head.

"*She* did not! John Cam Hobhouse got, in fact, a sworn statement that she was leaving Byron for some hidden reason of her own and *not* because of incest, sodomy, or even infidelity." The Earl sighed. "When I think of how Byron begged her to return to him—'Call the dogs off, Bella, and come home,' he said."

"I wonder why she did leave him, then?" said Jenny curiously.

"Do you know, I doubt that even Byron really knows."

" 'Tis odd, I think ... I am so glad he is still writing. His *Childe Harold*, third and forth cantos, are glorious!"

"I regret, Jen, we must again be on our way," said the Earl, standing up.

She sighed and stood up, giving him her hand, which he linked through his arm before leading her out.

An hour later found them ambling down an inadequate road toward Shaftesbury. They had crossed the bridge over the River Stour, past farm meadows rich with their early summer crops. Jenny gazed at the passing scenes, thinking that next to her own dear Devon, Somerset was perhaps one of the loveliest counties that England could boast.

She let go a laugh as she watched a lamb playing in the tall grass, and the Earl smiled at her sounds. She pointed out the cattle with their newborns grazing quietly on buttercups. They passed quaint buildings of weathered stone, strewn about the orchard fields ablaze with the promise of fruit to come.

This country road was a particularly hilly route, which made slow going, so it was past seven when they reached the sleepy village of Shaftesbury. The only inn was at the very edge of the town, and they made their way toward it.

Jennifer was taken up to her room, which she was well satisfied with. She washed and straightened her hair before returning to the Earl below. He, too, had gone to his quarters and refreshed himself before coming down to dinner. Jenny knew a sense of comfort in his presence when he finally entered the dining parlor to find her already seated.

The dinner was passed pleasantly. He offered a toast to their marriage and Jenny accepted to drink the warm dark wine. Without meaning to, she stretched her arms and let go a yawn.

"My poor child, this has been a long day for you. Let me escort you to your room."

"You don't mind?" asked Jenny shyly.

"Mind? Of course not. We have another long trip tomorrow and you should get your rest, for we start out early."

He strolled with her down the corridor, up the narrow steps to the first floor, and stopped before her door.

This was his wedding night, he thought dolefully, and he wasn't likely to receive even a kiss.

In this he was incorrect, though, for Jenny lifted herself to her toes and planted an amicable kiss upon his bronze cheek. "Thank you, my lord, for your kindness and consideration. Good night."

Then she was gone, and a dark oak door stood between them. The Earl of Waine heaved a sigh of remorse and made his way to his room.

## Chapter Eleven

*The Wanderer would not heed me;*
*Its Kiss grew warmer still;*
*Oh come—it sighed so sweetly;*
*I'll win thee 'gainst thy will!*
                                EMILY BRONTË

In spite of the wine and the need to sleep, try as she would, Jenny was not able to. Thus it was that she awoke at eight the next morning, just a bit heavy-eyed. She rang for the girl who had helped her undress the night before when she discovered that the buttons to her blouse were unreachable to her own hand.

She changed her garments for a lovely traveling gown of blue muslin, covered with bouquets of embroidered yellow and white daisies. This pretty gown had a blue bonnet to match and a transparent shawl, which she folded over her arm, noting that she probably would not need it.

She found the Earl in the dining parlor with eggs and bacon on a plate before him.

"Jenny, had I known you would be up by now, I would have waited before ordering for myself."

"Oh please, Jason, don't even think about it, really. I

am not hungry. I rarely have more than toast and coffee for breakfast."

"Did you sleep well?" queried the Earl, recalling his own restless night.

"Not really. I suppose it was the excitement of the day," said Jenny, suddenly blushing.

The Earl felt an unreasonable amount of joy in hearing that his wife had slept little better than himself, but refrained from so stating. Instead he expressed the suitable amount of sympathy and poured her coffee.

Several games of piquet whiled away the hours of tedious travel. A quick lunch was taken at a passable country inn, and then they were once again on the road.

Jenny yawned, feeling that she could no longer keep her eyes open, and turned apologetically to the Earl. "Would you mind, Jason, if I slept for a while?"

"Mind? Of course not, child. You get some sleep and don't worry, I shall wake you when we stop for tea."

He had the urge to ruffle her hair, which she had allowed to fall in long luxuriant waves upon her shoulders and back, but restrained himself.

She gave him a grateful smile and cuddled into her corner of the coach, pulling the rug up to her waist and placing her head against the cushioned sideboard. Within moments she had fallen asleep and appeared to Jason like an angel.

The Earl watched his bride as she slept and was conscious of an odd sensation, one he did not wish to contemplate. He shook his head and pulled a face as he watched her bump and roll in sleep with the movements of the carriage. She is going to have a stiff neck, he thought. Gently and deftly he eased her toward himself, depositing her head upon his lap. He reached across and pulled the rug back over her. He placed his hand lightly on her shoulder to steady her and then forced himself to look away from her face.

He gazed at the passing scenery with disinterest and it wasn't long before his blue eyes returned to Jenny. She thrilled him. He found her childlike innocence strangely tantalizing. He wanted to possess her and was convinced that soon he would. He was winning her confidence. He was sure of it, had sensed it when they stood together at the altar and again yesterday when she had placed her hand in his. Then, last night, she had kissed his cheek. He was sure that he could arouse her and knew that soon he would have to try.

His finger moved lightly across her white shoulder and he reveled in the vision he had of awakening her passions. Lord, he thought, his eyes appraising her, following the line of her neck to the fullness of her young, supple breasts bursting provocatively from the confines of her gown. She is the most exquisite creature I have ever viewed, he thought, frowning, but this was not precisely true. Jason Waine had known countless beauties, and though Jenny was indeed lovely, there had been some he had known who had surpassed her. Yet he felt with all his being that none compared to her.

She stirred in his arms and her dark lashes fluttered. She heard his deep male voice tell her softly to return to sleep. She closed her eyes, but she was now fully awake and realized with a start that she was stretched out like a child in the arms of this man.

Jenny opened her eyes to find him looking down at her, his own blue orbs filled with a strange light. She moved and raised herself up with a shy exclamation. "Oh, excuse me, my lord! How uncomfortable for you. I am very sorry."

"Don't be, Lady Waine. You were precisely where I wanted you to be," said the Earl teasingly.

She blushed rose pink and averted her eyes, which caused him to chuckle. She watched him stretch out his legs and open the window. He called to the driver to halt the carriage and then turned back to Jenny.

"If you don't mind, Jen, I think I'll ride on ahead and have the inn prepare some tea."

She smiled her acquiescence and watched him saddle his roan and ride out of sight. The thought occurred to her that he was the handsomest man she had ever seen. "That is it, Jen," she said softly to herself. "That is the key word—*man*! He is a man and you are but a girl ... and Johnny was a boy."

She gazed at the tall grass playing with the breeze and opened the window to catch some of the sweet aroma.

The day had turned chilly, but compared to the stuffiness of the coach, Jenny found it delightfully inviting. The coach seemed to be slowing, although she could not make out any building on either side of the carriage. She felt the tilt of the carriage as the driver swung onto a winding driveway and she peeped out of her side window. She had not been able to catch sight of the posting house because it had been almost totally hidden from view by a long row of rhododendron trees. They were in full bloom, and Jenny's eyes opened wide with admiration at the lush purple flowers. The coach pulled up in front of the impressive building of mellowed gray stone and Jenny saw the Earl come across the flagstone steps. He opened the carriage door and reached out his hand. "I have ordered our tea and biscuits to be brought out to us in the garden. They have a very lovely view just to the side and a lily pond that I think you might like."

She gave him her hand and jumped easily down to the pebbled ground, thinking that she had a very thoughtful husband, still unaware that the Earl was wooing her.

Tea was passed in harmony and once again they were on the road. Jenny heaved a sigh, for she was becoming restless in the coach and impatient to arrive at their destination. She turned and was surprised to find the Earl had tilted his hat over his eyes and raised his long, well-formed legs to the seat before him. It appeared to Jenny that he had every intention of going to sleep.

Jenny, though kind hearted, was spoiled, and up until now, even the Earl had indulged her. She suddenly felt ruffled by his disinterest.

"Are you . . . are you going to sleep, my lord?" Indicating by her tone that she did not wish him to. She was bored and wanted him to keep her occupied with his easy conversation.

The Earl did not move and he did not open his eyes but conceded, "It appears that way."

She felt piqued by his mocking tone. "Oh! But . . . I did so want to talk with you," she said wistfully and waited.

The Earl did not respond to this and had every appearance of having already fallen asleep, but Jenny pursued. "However, if you would *rather* sleep. . . ." She allowed her voice to trail off and pulled a face, returning her eyes to the fields.

A few minutes passed and she regarded him again before saying in a whisper, "Are you asleep, my lord?"

"Yes," came his lordship's firm response.

Jenny put her chin up and stared at him while the coach rumbled on. A few more moments passed. Jenny allowed her chin to drop and ventured, "Well, I do not think it very sporting of you to sleep when I . . . when I most particularly wanted to speak with you!"

The Earl did not feel it incumbent upon himself to reply.

"At least when I was tired, I had the good manners to ask you if you minded if I slept," challenged Lady Waine.

This challenge went ignored.

"I can see you are going to be most disagreeable and so I will not speak to you any longer!" threatened Lady Waine, glaring at her husband.

His lordship retained his comfortable-looking position and seemed to all practical purposes to be actually asleep.

Jenny was made of stern fiber and so persisted. "I can, of course, talk to you . . . and you needn't answer. There are a great many things I would like you to answer, but as you feel disinclined to converse with me at the moment, you needn't, of course. After all, if you insist upon being odious, and rude, I shall put off my questions until later and instead begin by telling you all the things you have been impatiently waiting to hear.

"Where shall I start? Ah, yes . . . I've got it. We will start with my infancy. You will never credit it, my lord, but do you know that when I was an infant I was quite wrinkled and had a lamentable habit of drooling upon anyone kind enough to pick me up?" There was a sauciness in her tone that caught his sense of humor and he raised his twinkling eyes to her face.

"Detestable brat, I would say!" responded his lordship, returning his face beneath his top hat.

"I was much worse than that, my lord, for as I grew

116

older, I had a dreadful habit of kicking my feet when I heard the word *no*."

"Reprehensible, indeed," said his lordship, not looking at her.

"You odious man, at least look at me when you insult me," cried Jenny, playfully jabbing at his arm with her small white fist.

"Knattish as well!" countered the Earl, grinning beneath the darkness of his hat.

"Oh, knattish am I?" ejaculated his wife, bent now on displaying her strength. She grabbed the lapels of his elegant buckskin riding jacket and gave him a shake.

At that, he put his hat aside and in one movement sat up and took strong hold of her small white hands, disengaging them from his coat. He smiled down into her impish countenance and said in a low tone, "Now that, my lady, I will not allow! For wrinkling my coat you shall have to pay a forfeit."

All at once and very much like the first time, she found herself ensconced in his arms. His lips were like fire on hers, demanding ... compelling her to respond. She felt her veins light up with a burning sensation that ran through her body. Jenny knew an urge to heave all to the winds and melt against him. His lips were possessive and hard, bruising her mouth with his desire. She put one trembling hand to his chest and pushed at it.

He released her at once, but his eyes were still upon her and she could sense the anger he felt, observed it by the set lines of his mouth. Her own gentle eyes fell before his and she said softly, "Please, my lord ... do not do such a thing again."

He did not apologize, but turned away from her without a word and she no longer tried to dissuade him from sleeping. She sat huddled in her corner of the coach while he slept, and gazed unseeing on the green pastures.

The smell of salt was in the air, and she knew they would soon be reaching Southampton. They had been driving in a southerly direction since they left Salisbury, as the Earl wanted to connect with the coast road and follow it to Dover.

117

The sun was beginning to set, and Jenny closed her eyes, hoping for sleep to shut out her confusion.

The Earl was angry, but not with his wife. He was angry with himself for his lack of control. He knew that he had frightened her at a time when he wanted to win her with tenderness. They had become close. He had sensed it and reveled in it . . . for without that closeness, he would never be able to win Jenny's heart. He realized that unless he had her heart, he would never be admitted to her bedroom, and he was beginning to want that more than he thought possible.

He had fallen into a restless, troubled sleep and awoke to find Jenny gazing out upon the stars. With a pang of guilt, he thought that she must be filled now with anxiety and he hastened to alleviate her fears.

"Are you tired, child," he asked gently.

Jenny was so relieved to find that he was no longer displeased with her that she smiled gratefully across at him and shook her head.

The Earl cursed himself inwardly for causing her to feel so alone, and reached up to the glass-covered oil lamp that was mounted to the side wall of the coach. He lighted it and said easily, "Ah, that is better."

"Thank you, my lord," said Jenny shyly.

"I would suggest we return to our games of piquet, but I doubt that we could read the cards in this dim light," said the Earl, attempting to dispel the tenseness between them.

"Will it be much longer before we reach Southampton?" Jenny asked in a tone that pulled at his heart.

The Earl looked out the window but could not recall precisely where they were. However, he returned an answer that he thought it would not be much longer.

Indeed, five minutes later they had pulled up at an extremely small inn. The Earl jumped to his feet and scanned the place, which was not lit very well. He turned to Jenny with a frown. "This place seems a bit inadequate, Jenny. We could drive on into the village and locate something better."

"No . . . I am far too fatigued, my lord, and hungry too," replied Jenny, not wanting to travel anymore.

"Very well," said the Earl, turning to his drivers and advising them to bed the horses down and to procure any refreshment they wished, as they were staying the night. The Earl had an excellent reputation among the people who had the good fortune to work for him. In spite of his meager circumstances in the past, he paid high wages and always threw in extras. In return, his people were extremely loyal.

The Earl led his weary wife into the dark hall of the inn. By this time, the innkeeper came hurrying out, bowing and apologizing. His daughter, who apparently lived down the road with her husband—a farmer the innkeeper seemed very proud to have as a son-in-law—was about to give birth to her first child. As a result, his wife had rushed to her side and was not available. The innkeeper's son, who took care of the stables, had ridden to town to fetch the doctor. Even so, he explained that he would be most happy to attend to their needs.

It has been previously stated that Jenny was kindhearted. It often happened that she was so to a fault. Immediately she took command, saying briskly, "My good man, do you mean there is only your wife to look after your daughter whilst she is in labor?"

"Yes, m'lady. Her husband, Tom, he be out of town buying supplies. Left this morning and won't be back till tomorrow. . . ."

"Good gracious! Are you sure the doctor will be available?" exclaimed Jenny.

"Why, I . . . I don't rightly know . . . but my son will fetch him if he be anywhere in Southampton."

"Very well then, this is what you shall do if your son is unable to find him. I have had some experience in the matter, as my aunt and I on two occasions delivered a servant's child when our doctor was away. In the event that the doctor cannot be found, I would be happy to assist your wife."

The innkeeper bowed with humility. "You are very good, m'lady."

Jason Waine eyed his wife with secret admiration. It occurred to him that among all the women of his acquaintance, not one of them would have known how to perform such a thing, and most certainly would not have offered their services after a long day on the road.

The innkeeper ushered them into the only dining parlor he had, which was public, but at the moment unoccupied. He apologized that all his wife had prepared was some mutton stew and fresh bread, and went to procure same.

Jenny wanted to wash her hands, but not wishing to disturb the harried innkeeper, made her way to the kitchen, where she found him bustling about in a frenzied haste. She pumped the water into a basin, while he protested. She laughed over his protests and proceeded to wash her hands and face in the cold fresh water.

She returned to the table to find the Earl thumping it with his hand. "Where the deuce have you been? I leave you for a moment and the next thing I know you are gone," said the Earl, who had gone to advise his drivers that they would have to attend to the horses themselves and then come to the kitchen for their victuals.

"I went to the kitchen to pump some water into the basin," said Jenny, smiling.

"Jenny!" exploded the Earl angrily. "Really, child, you did not!"

"I imagine you are thinking of the proprieties, my lord. I assure you I was not!"

"Obviously!" said the Earl testily.

"Oh pooh! It was a question of catering to society, which dictates that a lady does not pump her own wash water, or catering to my needs. I needed a wash, and obviously the poor man out there had his hands full."

"My dear girl, you could have waited until his hands were less burdened," replied the Earl, beginning to appreciate his wife's position.

"Yes, I could have waited, but you see I am spoiled and impatient. I wanted to wash my hands and face *then*. The pump and the basin were within easy reach, and my hands have not suffered unduly . . . have they?" said she, naughtily putting them out for inspection.

He pulled a face and commanded her to sit down. She thought it wise to do so. They glared at each other and then suddenly burst out laughing.

"Very well then. If my wife can pump her own water, I

suppose I can fetch my own wine." He got to his feet and sauntered across the room to the wine rack behind the counter. He chose an acceptable year of brandy and two glasses, and set them on the table. He poured the dark liquid and offered it to his bride. "I think we will need this."

She took the proffered glass and sipped timidly, for she was unused to drinking.

Presently the innkeeper appeared, his thin worn face flushed and his dangling white apron stained with the results of his achievement.

He hovered about while the Earl and his lady tasted the mutton stew, and breathed a sigh of relieved contentment when he was informed by their expressions and accompanied compliments that the mutton stew was extraordinarily tasty.

Jenny sipped her brandy in between bites and enjoyed its soothing effects. It relaxed her and she felt her tense muscles, stiff from the day's long journey, unbend. She gobbled three buttered rolls and then sat back in the hard wooden chair, brandy to her lips.

"To a bargain well made," said the Earl, raising his glass to his bride. "I shall be eternally grateful that you accepted my offer."

She leaned forward and allowed her glass to touch his and then downed the libation, feeling it sear her throat and warm her body. She blushed and said in a quiet voice, "I . . . I am not unhappy with the arrangement, my lord. After all, I had some reasons of my own for welcoming it. I only hope you do not regret it . . . in later years."

"I shall not, though I would have, had I been fool enough to get tied up with the Digby chit," said the Earl, remembering his near escape.

His serious expression suddenly made Jenny want to laugh. She covered her mouth but could not stifle the series of giggles that bubbled forth.

"Oh . . . h-ow dread-ful!" she exclaimed, giggling ludicrously.

"What is it?" the Earl grinned, thinking his wife had had enough brandy to drink.

"I ... I could just picture you in constant attendance upon Lavvy ... it would not have done! You are so austere, and Lavvy ... is Lavvy. Do you know my romantic friend thinks you preferred me to her because of love at first sight, and doesn't realize 'twas because she giggles and I do not!" said Lady Waine, giggling uncontrollably.

The Earl found her adorable gurgling irresistible and the sound of their laughter filled the room.

They lay back upon their wooden chairs, and as Jenny wiped the tears of mirth from her eyes, the Earl regarded his bride with affection. She had startled him with her generous offer to help the innkeeper's daughter. It was a step away from the norm, and to be sure, the Beau Monde would have raised an eyebrow.

She had then shocked him with her unseemly behavior of actually entering the innkeeper's kitchen. This was an solecistic move in itself. And then to actually pump water and wash in a public kitchen was totally unfitting and indecorous. Yet ... he admired her for it!

Another female would have complained unendingly after a long and tedious journey. She had not done so. Then, having been finally brought to an inn, another female would most certainly have ordered the keeper to show her to her room and bring up warm clean water! Jenny, having seen the poor man was alone and in an anxious state of mind, could not be so thoughtless. He smiled. His Jenny was a true lady and he had been wise to choose her.

"I think, child, that 'tis time for you to bid me goodnight, for your eyes are beginning to droop," said the Earl gently.

"Thank you, my lord. I am frightfully tired, but please do stay here and have your wine. I shall just go remind the innkeeper to call me if his daughter has need—"

"You shall not do so, child. If there is an emergency, he can advise me, and if I feel you should be awakened, then I will do so," said the Earl in a tone that would brook no argument.

Jenny found nothing to object to in this, as she felt the Earl would naturally call her if she were needed. She rose and found that he refused to stay behind, pleading that he, too, wished to turn in.

The innkeeper led them up the steep narrow flight of stairs, a glass-covered taper raised to show the way.

He stopped before the first door off the landing, which he had prepared while the Earl and his lady were dining. The door was opened and Jenny walked in, surveying the small but cosy room mechanically. There was a small fire lit before the bed, which had been turned down. A cushioned wing chair armed the fireplace, and behind the long dark drapes had been drawn to hide the moon beaming at the window.

On a night stand beside the four-poster bed a large candle burned. A dark oak door was framed between the night stand and a wardrobe closet in the corner of the room. Jenny stared at it, thinking this must be the communicating door. Well, what of that, she thought. There was one between our rooms last night ... and Jason did not try to use it.

She turned to find the Earl standing in the doorway alone, for he had dismissed the owner of the inn.

Jenny gave him her hand. "Good night, my lord, and thank you for your friendship and patience with me."

He smiled at her but only kissed her hand, without speaking. He moved away and she closed the door.

The effects of the brandy were swirling around in her head. She felt the heat from the fireplace and held the chair back for support as she steadied herself.

With a sigh, she reached for her overnight bag and pulled out her nightdress. Then, reaching for the buttons at the back of her dress, she gave an exasperated exclamation. She managed to get two undone, but though she tried desperately with all sorts of manipulations, she could not reach the remainder. Jenny put her hands on her hips and wanted to scream. There wasn't a female in the house to help. She could, of course, sleep in her dress and hope that in the morning the owner's wife would be back ... She'd probably be sound asleep, Jen, she thought miserably. Then, in that moment, she made up her mind. She went to the communicating door and knocked gently.

Jason appeared almost at once, still dressed in the same

clothes. She blushed furiously. "I—I am having a bit of a problem. You see, these plaguey buttons of mine—"

"Ah," said the Earl, smiling sympathetically. "I am sorry, Jen. I assumed all the inns we would be visiting would have serving girls about to assist you with such things. Had I known, I certainly would have brought the maid I hired in London along with us."

"Oh no, Jason, it was not your fault. How could you know?" said Jenny sincerely.

He turned her around and picked up her long tresses and put them over her shoulder. Quickly and with a skill born of experience he had the troublesome things undone.

"There, child! In the future you shall not have to worry your pretty head with such things."

She thanked him and speedily disappeared behind their shared door. Within a thrice she had thrown off her blue muslin, laid it over a corner chair, and wiggled into her nightgown.

The flimsy pink silk was sleeveless. In fact, the only things connecting the front to the back were two ribbons tied at her shoulders. She snuffed out the candle on her night stand and went to warm her hands by the fire. She stood there in her slipperless feet, staring into the hearth, hypnotically held by its satanic beams. The lights of the flames flickered wildly through the thin material, glowing upon the innocent beauty of her nakedness. A knock sounded at the communicating door, which caused her to jump.

Jason opened the door and stood in the archway. He was wearing a dark brocade dressing gown and holding a black velvet box. He stopped short as his eyes beheld her, and he felt as though his breath had been wrenched from him. He could not move, was afraid that the vision before him would somehow change if he took a step. His eyes appraised her as she stood there, transfixed before him. The flames flickered over her, exposing her exquisite form. His eyes traveled over her white shoulders to her young rose-tipped breasts, lingered, and then wandered to her waist and hips so perfectly curved, down to the firmness of her legs, and then quickly back to her lips. Jenny, suddenly aware that he was touching her with his eyes, moved for her shawl and wrapped it tightly about her.

The Earl took two quick strides and put the velvet box between them as an offering. His voice came hoarse and deep in his throat. "Jenny ... I have here the Waine diamonds. They are always presented to the Waine bride upon her wedding. I had planned to place them around your neck when we reached Waine, but find that I can no longer wait. I wanted to see them on you."

She opened her eyes wide at the glistening stones, marveling in a small voice over their size and brilliance. The Earl lifted the collar of diamonds and rubies and went behind her. She picked up her long hair with a scoop of her hand and he fastened the stones about her slender neck. She exclaimed delightedly at the coolness of their touch and would have run then to her mirror had not the Earl's mouth caressed her shoulder blade. She stood there, frozen by his touch, while his lips traveled across her shoulders. He moved her hair away with his hand as he kissed her tenderly. Each of his kisses seemed to burn her flesh. Slowly and firmly he turned her to him, and still his lips forestall to seek out her own, but continued their course, finding the hollow beneath her neck and wandering toward her breasts, which heaved tumultuously against him. His lips caressed her ears, her forehead, her eyes and cheeks. He whispered her name, and then his mouth sought hers, pressing her hungrily to him. He was kissing her wildly now, for he could no longer control himself. He was exalted with the knowledge that she returned his passion willingly!

His hands traveled down and around her slender hips, finding their way deftly and with finesse over her body. Then just as deftly he was fondling and cupping her supple breasts. She gasped and pulled away, putting her hand between them, but he thrust it aside and held her against him.

"Jenny ... I want you!" he said, his voice deep and lusty with desire. Then all at once she remembered ... she remembered Johnny. *"No!"* she shouted. "You gave me your word! You promised ... never to force me!"

"Nor have I! You want me as much as I want you.

125

Why do you deny it?" came his low voice, husky and compelling.

She yanked herself away. "It is a lie! A lie! I don't want you . . . I don't!"

Jenny's heart was overidden with a sudden rush of fright and guilt. Frightened at her own passion and guilt that she had somehow betrayed the memory of her lost Johnny. "I—I kissed you . . . yes, for a moment I imagined that you were John . . . that it was he holding me on our wedding night. Not you! How could you ever believe I would let you touch me?" she said, sobbing. "I told you . . . I could never let anyone love me." She covered her face with her hands and turned her back upon him.

Thus she did not see the look of startled pain in Jason Waine's eyes. He was hurt and angry. His mouth was set and his face was white. He took a step toward her . . . and then stopped. For a moment he could not think, could not speak . . . knew only a deep pain searing through him. He felt a constriction of his heart and knew a need to scream. Without a word, he turned and slammed the door that connected their two separate rooms.

Never before had a woman denied him. Never before had a woman hurt him, and Jason Waine was hurting. He stormed about his room, taking off his dressing gown and flinging it wrathfully to the oak floor.

"Damnation!" he said out loud. He had always known the satisfaction of having his amorous advances welcomed . . . in fact, invited! That he had been perhaps too precipitate with Jenny he was well aware of. He had sensed that she had become suddenly frightened. Oh yes, he was no fool. He was conscious of the passion he had aroused in her, and conscious, too, of the fact that he had scared her off. What stung Jason Waine was not that she had denied him. He did not mind her refusing him her body. No, 'twas her words that lashed. He felt as though he had been gashed across the face, across his eyes, and deep into his throat.

That she could claim she had returned his kisses because she imagined him her lost love returned he found intolerable! That she should repel his kisses, his touch . . .

that would have been her right. It was what she had said that tormented him. He felt as if she had plunged a knife ruthlessly into his heart, twisted it, and that knife thrust had left him breathing, but in excruciating pain.

He threw on his buckskin breeches and his shining hessians. He drew on his linen shirt, tucked it in angrily, and donned his kid waistcoat and buckskin riding jacket. He then reached for his top hat and planted it firmly and rakishly upon his head. He opened the hall door, thought of banging it, but contained this wish, and strode down to the stables, where he saddled his roan and rode out into the darkness.

There was a tavern in the village, and he meant to visit it and shake off the cold that clutched at his insides ... the cold that made his forehead hot and his eyes burn!

"Damnation!" he swore out loud again and his horse's ears pricked attentively. He slowed the roan to a canter, for he was too good a rider to gallop over unfamiliar roads at night. His mind was a whirlwind of bitter thoughts. Jenny had warned him. She had said her heart was with a dead soldier. Oh yes, she had warned him, and he had said it did not matter. He now found that it did, very much! He felt a roaring sense of injustice swell within his breast and knew that he was jealous ... good lord, jealous of a dead man! "Devil take him!" he said to the skies.

It was all-consuming, this jealousy. It caused his heart to beat violently and his head to drum incessantly and mercilessly between his ears. "Confound you, Jenny! You are surely a witch," he said to the night air.

Jason Waine had always been a possessive man. He had never allowed another man to touch the woman who was enjoying his favors. When a woman was under his protection, he had always expected all her attentions. He recalled once having visited one of his light-o'-loves. The dainty ladybird had put her arms around him in a welcoming embrace, just as he had noted another man's walking stick leaning against a corner wall. He had felt a sudden revulsion come over him and had disengaged himself from her arms. He then shrugged himself back into his greatcoat and with a sneer had told her to be sure to

127

remember to return the gentleman's cane when next the stranger visited her. He had left the wench then and had never seen or thought of her again . . . until now!

Yet here . . . here was something different. The child was being faithful . . . but not to him! She was being faithful to a dead man!

You are besotted, he told himself angrily. Besotted by a chit that is pining for someone else. Well, Jason, that is just retribution for you! Since the carefree age of twenty, you have managed to avoid the foolish state of being in love . . . and then you go and do it with your own wife! You! With all the loveliest of the Beau Monde to choose from, you choose a bride who is in love with a dead soldier! More fool you, he told himself bitterly.

"Ha!" exclaimed Jason Waine defiantly. "I will teach the chit!" he said to his attentive but bewildered horse. "I'll find a nice cosy tavern, a bottle of their best, and a warm country wench!"

However, when the lights of the gay tavern loomed up out of the darkness and he heard the raucous mirth invitingly call, he felt no real desire to enter.

He did though. And he drank a bottle of their best . . . and he took a plump country pretty upon his knee . . . and he felt sick at heart!

## Chapter Twelve

*Ay—there it is! it wakes tonight.*
*Deep feelings I thought dead;*
*Strong in the blast—quick gathering light—*
*The Heart's flame kindles Red!*

EMILY BRONTË

Sobbing pitifully, Jenny flung herself upon her bed. She cried long and hard, staining her flushed cheeks and the pillow beneath her. She felt torn by conflicting emotions.

Shame had positioned her on the defensive, propelled itself within her unreasonably until she spit out against herself, though her angry words were at Jason. Shame made her rage on at him uncontrollably.

She had not at first seen his face, as her own was buried in her hands, but just as he had turned to leave, she caught a glimpse of his eyes, and even through her own contention she was able to feel for his. She had seen a hurt, stricken expression take command of his face, and Jenny felt overwhelmed with a new sense of guilt!

"You wicked girl . . . wicked!" she chastised herself between sobs. "You allowed him to kiss you, touch you . . . and oh faith, Jenny, you wanted him! Forgive me, John . . . I wanted him. . . ." Her tears stormed down her stained cheeks and once again her head drooped to the wet pillow. She felt totally shaken.

It was a long while before she had spent herself with crying, but when at length she had, it was with the realization that her promise to herself had been broken! She had proclaimed that she would never love again . . . and yet somehow the unwanted sensation had crept into her soul. Jenny rose from her pillow with the realization that she was in love with Jason Waine; had been in love with him from the first moment she had looked into his deep blue eyes and felt her body tremble!

"In love with Jason Waine!" The words caused a trebulation within her mind. "In love with a rake!" She reminded herself that his kisses meant little to him. " 'Twas no more taken for love than the first time he kissed me," she whispered to her empty room.

She curled up on her bed and pulled the blanket to her chin. He had never uttered one word of attachment . . . only lust . . . and lust was not what she wanted. And now, now he was gone, for she had heard him leave.

Her troubled jumbled thoughts kept her eyes open, and though the hours dragged on, she found sleep impossible. Then suddenly she could think no more, feel only emptiness, and her lids dropped.

Jennifer awoke the next morning and went immediately to Jason's room and knocked. There was no answer. She walked slowly to her vanity and sat down. A knock sounded at her own door and a warm, robust voice called cheerfully, "Would ye be wanting some help, Lady Waine?"

"Yes, do come in," said Jenny, who had rushed and unlocked the hall door.

A round appled-cheeked woman beamed at her and ambled into the room carrying a pitcher of warm wash water.

"Oh, you must be the innkeeper's wife. How . . . how is your daughter?"

"Oh, 'tis that grand she is, m'lady . . . her and her baby boy," said the woman proudly.

Jenny congratulated her, and after asking the expected questions, requested the woman to wait and help her button her gown. She donned a crisp muslin gown of brown, dotted throughout with white velvet. The sleeves were short and puffed, the neck low and scooped, trimmed with white banding. A wide white ribbon hugged her waist and flowed down the back of her skirt. The innkeeper's wife helped Jenny dress her long gleaming hair in a semblance of curls piled at the top of her head and a straw chip hat was set angularly thereon. Jenny made quite a fetching picture, though her eyes lacked the sparkle of a bride's.

"Oh, m'lady, 'tis that pretty you be!" exclaimed the innkeeper's wife.

Jenny thanked her quietly and ventured mildly, "I . . . I suppose his lordship has ordered breakfast belowstairs?"

"Why no, m'lady. The Earl . . . he said coffee and biscuits was to be sent up here to you. He left just about ten or fifteen minutes ago."

"I—I see," said Jenny quietly.

"I'll just go and fetch your—"

"No, that won't be necessary. I'll come down and have my coffee while I . . . speak with my driver."

The woman dropped a curtsy and ambled out of the room with Jenny following slowly.

Jenny walked across the main room toward the front door and spotted the drivers conversing idly by the team, which had been already hitched.

Jenny approached them timidly. "Excuse me, gentlemen. His lordship—I assume he is riding his roan—did he give you any message for me?"

"No, m'lady," said one driver with a deprecatory cough, aware that all was not well with the newly married couple. "Lord Waine . . . he jest say he is riding on ahead and for you to follow in the carriage."

Jenny's head drooped as she turned and reentered the inn. She found hot coffee, muffins, sweetcakes, and biscuits awaiting her, but was barely able to swallow the hot liquid. With a sigh, she thanked the innkeeper and his spouse, whose bill had already been seen to, and sadly returned to the coach.

She sat quietly, one finger tapping her lip, her mind lost to cogitation. Well, Jen, what did you expect? You insulted him . . . and he is a proud man! You have hurt his pride. Did you think he would take that lightly?

For the next few hours, she watched the road, yet never caught a glimpse of her husband. She had berated herself for a fool, a cruel, wicked fool. Then slowly this feeling ebbed and she began to feel irritated.

"What the deuce does he think he is doing?" she asked the empty seat facing her. "After all, it is ridiculous to leave me all alone for so long . . . he is acting like a child!"

The coach slowed to a stop some forty minutes later and Jenny heard the bustle of running stable boys as they came forward to attend to the horses. Jenny's door was opened by her groom and she was met by a pretty serving maid who offered her the message that there were no other inns for quite some time and his Lordship thought she might want refreshment.

"Oh . . . is his lordship inside then?" asked Jenny hopefully.

"Oh no, m'lady . . . m'lord left just a while ago . . . but he did arrange a private parlor for your ladyship."

"I see," said Jenny dangerously.

Lady Waine's meal was hurried and when she required the serving girl to pause a moment and reveal the reason for such rushing, the pretty maid replied, "His lordship . . . he said not to let you linger, m'lady."

Jennifer digested this and by the time her luncheon was at an end and she was hurried back to her waiting coach, m'lady was close to fuming!

The carriage bumped and rumbled along the rutted highway and the jostling built Jenny's irritation to a nicety. "Leave me to travel and . . . and eat alone, will he?" remarked Jenny out loud, once again resuming her conversation with the empty seat before her. As anger began to take hold, her chest heaved beneath the strain and one could almost see the smoke emitting from her dainty little mouth. Then suddenly something within burst! She opened her door and shouted to the grooms, demanding that they stop the carriage at once.

Startled, they proceeded to brake and rein in the team. Jenny hardly waited for the coach to come to a complete stop before she picked up her skirts and jumped nimbly down. Her face was flushed with resolution and anger and her voice came hard between her teeth. "Please saddle my horse."

"But Gawd, m'lady!" objected the driver, aware that his lordship would not approve this deviation from his instructions.

"At once, sir!" said Jenny, for her mood would allow no interference.

The driver and groom eyed each other, but as they had no recourse but to obey their mistress, the groom climbed down from the box and proceeded to saddle Jenny's Whisper. This took a few moments. However, it was soon after that Jenny was mounted and riding over the open fields of tall grass.

She had a strange feeling that although the Earl could not be seen, he was not so very far off and probably keeping the coach under some surveillance. She had no intention of allowing this intolerable situation to continue into the morrow, for she would not be made a fool of—especially upon arriving at Waine Castle.

"The very idea!" she stormed out loud. "He . . . he wants to disgrace me, does he?"

Jenny's eyes snapped and viewed not the passing scenes as Whisper moved onward at a slow trot. She had been right in assuming that the Earl was not so very far ahead. He had, in fact, been backtracking whenever he felt the coach was overdue. He waited at the crossroads, and though the milestone clearly indicated the way, would not continue until the coach arrived so that he could be sure they would not lose the road. When several minutes elapsed and they did not appear, he began slowly walking his horse back down the road to discover what had gone amiss.

He finally came across the coach two miles back, pulled along the roadside with his two postilions standing dejectedly about waiting for their lady.

"What the devil?" ejaculated the Earl, surprised. "Where is Lady Waine?"

"Had a notion to ride, m'lord," answered the groom, screwing up his thin mouth.

"Ride? Well then, why didn't she ride along the road?" asked the Earl impatiently.

The groom shrugged his small shoulders and scratched what was left of his gray hair beneath his cap. "When we suggested that to her ladyship," offered the groom sulkily, "she said she didn't have a notion to do so."

"Didn't she, though?" hissed his lordship ominously. "In which direction *did she* have a *notion* to ride?"

They pointed unhappily toward the north fields, and without another word, the Earl followed the line of their leveled hands.

Jenny had slowed her horse to a walk. She was furious and her anger had helped her to overcome the hurt and anxiety within her. Suddenly she heard a rider at her back and reined in, waiting. He checked his own horse no more than half a foot from her and she could see his face was that of dark, yet surpressed, fury.

"Will you tell me, my lady, where the devil you think you are going?"

She smiled sweetly. "For a ride, my lord."

He was close to spluttering, so acute was his agitation. He sucked in his breath. "You will be kind enough to stop this foolishness and return to the coach at once!"

"Will I?" Her tone was sweeter still.

"Damnation, Jenny, do not try my patience!" he hissed.

She clicked her heels and threw over her receding shoulder, "Go to the devil . . . my lord!"

The Earl was after her in a moment. He was in a wild rage. Only a second passed before he had overtaken her, held her bridle in his gloved hand, jumped off his own horse, and yanked her roughly off hers. He had never allowed himself to strike a woman—few had instilled this desire in him—but he wanted to hit Jenny!

She looked up into his irate face and her heart softened. "Oh Jason, do forgive me. I . . . I did not mean to put you to so much trouble. And Jason, what I said last night . . . 'twas not . . . well, that is, I wanted to speak to you last night, but you . . . you were gone."

"You wanted to speak with me last night?" asked the Earl, frowning.

"Yes. I . . . I did not want to leave things . . . well, where did you go, Jason?"

"I was out . . . seeking consolation!" he answered her bitterly.

Jennifer stiffened and it occurred to her that perhaps the Earl had not really been hurt by her angry lashings last evening. Perhaps . . . perhaps only his pride was affected. Automatically, she thought of Johnny, who had loved her. They had many tiffs, but he had never gone off to seek *consolation*. Their arguments and misunderstandings had always been settled together. She found the knowledge that the Earl had no attachment for her more painful than she had anticipated.

"I—I am so glad you were able to be consoled, my lord. Well, yes, as I was saying, I did wish to explain my . . . my outburst last night. What I told you was untrue. I think I have recovered. I—I mean I was wrong for trying to make you think that I had not! However, my lord, we had made a bargain . . . and I am going to ask you to hold to it!"

Jason Waine regarded his bride as though she were the rope, the only means by which he could escape some dark, barren pit he had fallen into. The darkness had been dispelled. He wanted to lift her off the ground and swing her about in his arms. He had found that the brandy had not consoled him, neither had the fair wench, but these words of Jenny—these soothing, enchanting words—they made his spirits soar! As to the nonsense about keeping his promise not to touch her . . . 'twas pride, he believed. He preserved a grave aspect and as-

sured his bride that her privacy and person would here-
after be respected.

He helped her mount her horse and adjust her skirts
around the sidesaddle. He jumped neatly upon his roan
and escorted her back to their waiting carriage. Their
horses were once again tethered side by side at the rear of
the coach while the Earl and his lady took their places
beside each other within.

The groom and driver eyed each other knowingly and
the coach rumbled forward.

Jenny turned inquiring eyes to her lord and suggested a
game of cards to while away some time. He was anxious
to regain his position with her and readily assented. The
rug was spread out between them and the deck of cards
produced from the side pocket of the coach wall. The
machinations of the game carried them for the next two
hours, as both were good players and enjoyed the tricks
of the game. Jenny was a cautious gambler and thought
out her moves carefully . . . yet skill and luck were both
on her husband's side.

Now and then her eyes went to his face and one could
almost hear the sigh within her. She loved him. She knew
it and it troubled her deeply. She had loved John Dillingham nearly all her life. She had never known any
other male as intimately as she had her John. They had
roamed about at will. She played with him, climbed trees
and hills with him; and she had loved him . . . in the
natural course of things. When she lost Johnny Dillingham, she lost a part of her youth and her past.

This strange new wave of emotion was entirely different. It was sudden, without logic, without her bidding . . .
and yet it was complete in its overthrow!

She loved Jason Waine with all her being and wanted
him to return her love, and this wish was beginning to
seem hopeless. He had showed that he wanted to make
love to her but she knew that this meant little. She had
learned in Brussels that men of this stamp often fancied
women without any deep attachment. She could not give
herself to him *that way*. She just couldn't give herself to
him so totally, knowing he would pledge her nothing in
return . . . that he would continue to visit other women.

This caused her to shudder and the Earl asked if she was cold.

She returned a negative answer and turned her gaze to the window. She had been thrown into confusion when he had so blithely announced his whereabouts last evening. It had hurt to hear him speak of seeking consolation so off-handedly, and Jenny knew the torment only jealousy can evoke. She was both determined to win him and yet shy to venture.

On the other side of her sat Jason. Exhilarated beyond description. She had actually retracted all she had said to him last night. She had wanted to tell him, see him last night, and found him missing! He dearly lamented his absence and envisioned what might have been had he stayed. He regarded her piquant face and was struck with the thought, By God! I love the chit.

They had been so absorbed with the workings of the game and the movements of their thoughts that neither had noticed that the landscape had changed almost drastically.

The rich lush green had become shades of yellow, brown, and gray. The road had become flat above the rise of ground. They had been traveling at a steady pace and had made excellent time.

"Well, well, we are ahead of ourselves, my dear. Here we are at the Lewes Inn. I hadn't expected we'd reach here before nightfall. What say you to watering the horses here and pushing on?"

"That would be fine with me, my lord. I'm most anxious to reach Waine Castle and meet everyone there."

"I can't imagine why—but then, there is no accounting for a woman's whims."

She laughed easily and the Earl and his lady made their path to the inn ... each determined to forget what had occurred between them on the previous evening.

# Chapter Thirteen

Jenny eyed her sleeping husband, wondering how he could manage to keep his eyes closed over the bumpy road. However, his lordship had not slept well on what had been his third night of marriage. They had pushed on past Lewes Inn and had actually reached Hastings by nightfall, where they had spent the night.

They had rooms across the hall from each other, as the inn was nearly fully occupied and they had been lucky to get rooms at all. They had breakfast at eight in the morning and had now been on the road some three hours. This was the fourth day, and Jenny was weary of traveling. She wanted to be there and sighed audibly.

"Tired, my love?" asked his lordship from beneath his top hat.

"Do you know you have a perfectly odious way of asking after one's comfort without even showing the effort of movement?" said Lady Waine.

"Ah . . . but I *do* ask," said his lordship, remaining in his relaxed position.

"Then since you do, yes, I am tired. I want to end this journey and . . . and . . . oh, I just want to be there!"

"Poor child . . . let me see, what does one say to a child when it becomes fretful?"

"Odious, horrid, and . . . and brutal!"

"No, I don't think those words particularly soothing," offered his lordship.

"Oh!" returned his wife, folding her arms and glaring at his top hat. He moved his hat to one side so that one blue eye was able to take in the sight of his wife's indignation.

"Do you know that you are a glorious creature when you are angry?"

"Am I? How fortunate since I am liable to be angry quite often when in your company, sir."

"Even after I tell you that we are about to tread Waine lands."

Jenny's eyes lit. "Oh, Jason, are we here?"

For answer her husband smiled whimsically and spread out his hands, indicating a stretch of land darkened by the numerous pine trees knitted closely together. The road forked and they veered to the right and ascended gradually. All at once Jenny could see the waters beating stoically against the rocks. She pressed her face, childlike, against the window and gazed enthusiastically as though she had never before seen this view.

"It is so wondrous, Jason! I loved the sight of the sea from Dover . . . when we traveled to Brussels."

"Did you? Yes, it has a mesmerizing beauty . . . but not quite to my liking."

"How can you say that . . . 'tis your home, Jason."

"It is my *estate*. It has never been my home, and the sea has always looked unwelcoming."

Jenny did not answer him but returned her eyes to the passing scene. They gradually climbed and she could feel the wind playing mischievously with the coach. It was just past noon but the sun was hidden by a profusion of irregular clouds, and then Jenny saw Waine Castle. It filled her large dark eyes, and seemed to meet the clouds hovering above it.

The road had been molded in a circle, brushing up against the Castle walls, pushing past, and then meeting itself again. This created a wide round circle of badly kept lawn. However, Jenny did not at the moment notice the condition of the grounds. It was the Castle that had caught, held, and dismayed her. The structure was a huge mass of gray, dull, cold stone. Jenny had expected what most romantics expect when the word "Castle" is introduced into their minds—a fairy-tale building with gold pinnacles, silvery turrets, drawbridges, excitingly dangerous moats, and walls covered with proud dark ivy. What Jenny got was a rectangular stone building with a conical turret on its right, another on its left, and a battlement roof stretched across between the two. The walls were not silver but grayed, and instead of ivy they seemed to be troubled by an unattractive moss. The windows were not arched and few were ornamented with terraces. The only embellishment Waine Castle boasted was a large coat of arms over its sizable front doors. These were some ten feet in height, double, and made of hard oak planking with mighty studding.

The sea could be seen on either side of the Castle, whose facade faced the northwest.

The Earl put a finger to her chin and turned her to face him. "Ah, Jenny, you are disappointed in your new home?"

"Well, in truth, Jason, I did not expect anything ... quite like this."

"Rather foreboding, isn't it?"

"Indeed it is, Jason ... and it needn't be!" She had by now scanned the grounds that could be seen from the confines of the coach and found them sadly lacking. "Why is it so stark? Why not put in flower beds and do something about that atrocious lawn ... and ..."

He kissed her finger, but she withdrew it and he frowned. "My mother used to keep a rose garden, and then Gwen took it over ... but she left some time ago, as you know, and it hasn't been attended to. My stepmother was left an independence, and though she continues to live at the Castle it is not her home and therefore she spends very little on its maintenance."

"Well, I shall—I mean, if you do not object," she said, suddenly shy.

"Object? Jenny, you are my wife and entitled to dress up any and all of our homes."

"Will not your stepmother object?" asked Jenny doubtfully.

"It is not for her to object. The dower house is hers ... she may move anytime she wishes," replied the Earl dryly.

She sighed. "I do hope we are not all going to be ... uncomfortable, Jason."

He gave her a quick look and his voice came hard. "I

139

have already told you, Jenny, that if Lillian does not find things suitable, she and Julian may go to the dower house—which is, I assure you, quite lovely."

"But, Jason, they don't want to. That is obvious, for if they did, they would have already made the move."

They had no time to delve into this further, for the coach had already halted before the great double doors and a footman dressed in blue livery was holding the carriage door open for them.

They reached the massive oak doors, which were swung wide open to receive them. A short man with thinning dark hair and a wooden expression above his white starched neckcloth said in tones that hinted of deeper feelings, "Welcome . . . welcome home, my lord, and may I say on behalf of the staff—and, of course, myself—how extremely pleased we are to have you and your bride with us."

He bowed more than was customary and Jenny felt a strong inclination to giggle.

"Thank you, Gravesly," said the Earl, smiling and motioning to his wife. "I am pleased to present Lady Waine."

The butler bowed reverently and reiterated his felicitations before the Earl dismissed him and guided Jenny toward a dark door immediately to the right of the center hall. Jenny had been secretly admiring this hallway with its huge round oak table, its armor suits, and crossed swords. There were a few baronial chairs that caught her eye because of their workmanship and antiquity. However, she made a mental resolve to pick some flowers and brighten the center table.

The room that Jason led her into was surprisingly inviting. The size was large, and yet, it was comfortable and cosy. There was a fire blazing in the grate. Two sofas made right angles to the fireplace and there was a coffee table in the Gothic style. Two worn gold brocade Chippendale chairs flanked the fireplace as well. There was but one central window, with gold faded hangings, and ranged on either side of the window were bookshelves.

Jenny decided that she liked the room, and sat down upon the sofa with a sigh.

The Earl planted himself close beside her on the sofa and was about to remark on her loveliness when an elderly maid bobbed into the room and placed a tea tray with biscuits on the coffee table. She smiled warmly at the Earl and received his cheerful greeting in return. She gave Lady Waine a long, curious glance and received a friendly smile for her efforts.

Satisfied with the results of her investigation, she hurried off to impart her considered opinions of the new mistress to the staff awaiting her news in the kitchen.

Jenny poured the tea in silence, handed a cup to Jason, and turned to see the door being closed. Jason stood up immediately, waiting for the newcomer to approach.

Jenny was at first startled, for surely, she thought, this woman was far too young to be Jason's stepmother. She looked at first glance not much older than herself. Lillian Waine was tall, imposingly so, and built along magnificent lines. Her hair was the most unusual shade of pale yellow Jenny had ever seen. It was, she thought, the color of bleached gold—almost white in its intensity and yet sparklingly alive with gold tints. She wore it drawn back from the sides of her face and wound in wide soft braids at the top of her head. Two waves parted at the center of her forehead and were clipped just above her ears. Her brows were light and finely etched and her eyes were clear but an indistinct blue.

Her nose distracted slightly from her features, for it was a bit too long and straight, giving her a stern look. Her mouth was thin, cherry colored, and parted at the moment in a smile. She went first to Jason, giving him her cheek to kiss, and then turned quickly to Jenny, both her hands extended, the smile still fixed upon her face.

Jenny was conscious of a strange feeling. Something was wrong. Lillian Waine was seemingly beautiful, though her gown of purple silk was dated, and Jenny thought too harsh a shade for her paleness. She seemed friendly, and yet Jenny felt repelled by her.

"Jenny, my child, do say I may call you Jenny ... so informal. How pleased I am for you and Jason! Though you must chastise your husband for keeping it a secret so long. You can't imagine what a surprise it was to receive his letter . . . but never mind all that. *I* have seen to everything."

"Has Lady Waine's maid arrived, Lillian?" asked Jason.

"Yes, dear, she is awaiting Jenny above stairs . . . in the master suite. We prepared it just as you asked," answered Lillian. There is, in fact, a hot bath being prepared for your . . . wife."

Jenny exclaimed appreciatively, for this is just what she wanted. She mumbled some pleasantries and then excused herself, asking the direction of her room.

"La, child, you will never find it on your own. I shall come with you," exclaimed Lillian amicably.

"There is no need to trouble yourself. Perhaps one of the servants? . . ." ventured Jenny timidly.

"Nonsense. I want to spend a little time with you. I am sure we will be great friends." She turned her head to Jason and said in an odd tone, "Jason, I should like a word with you when I return. You will wait here for me?"

He nodded, but his face took on an expression Jenny was beginning to recognize. Jason Waine's countenance told that he would brook no unpleasantness. She wondered as she followed Lillian Waine up the flight of stairs what she wanted to discuss with Jason and why he had become so stern-faced.

The doors of the second room on the second floor were thrown open and Lillian entered, her hands clasped in front of her and the smile fixed upon her face. Jenny followed her and once again felt dismayed. The room was large but austerely dark. There were three glass doors side by side which led off onto a small rectangular balcony with a severe iron railing. Jenny moved to the middle door and gazed out upon the front drive. She turned with half a sigh and grimaced over the faded print of yellows and browns covering most of the walls. There were brown area rugs on both sides of the four-poster bed, which was covered with a brown velvet quilt. The room was barren of other furniture with the exception of a small vanity against the fireplace wall. The hangings over the glass doors spoke of better days, although the low swag valence of rich brown velvet looked as if it had

142

been recently cleaned. The drapes were tied back with gold ropings.

A plump woman of some thirty-odd years peeped through a doorway located in the corner, at the head of the room. She wore a gray linen dress and a neat white lace cap over short brown curls. Her cheeks had a well-polished look and her smile was warm and somehow reassuring.

"How do you do, m'lady. I be your personal maid . . . if you please."

"Well, I am pleased," replied Jenny quickly. "What is your name, dear?"

"Joan, m'lady . . . Joan Deckles. If you like . . . your bath be ready for you."

"I would like . . . very much."

"Well then, Jenny I am so glad to see you are making yourself right at home," put in Lillian Waine suddenly. "If you will excuse me? . . ."

"Yes, by all means . . . and thank you," replied Jenny quickly.

She waited for Lillian to disappear before turning back to her maid. "Joan, I noticed a door when I was coming down the hall—the first room on this side. Is that a closet or a small bedchamber?" asked Jenny curiously.

"Oh no, m'lady. That there," she said, pointing to the doorway she had just crossed, "is your dressing room. And this," she said, moving across the room to another corner door on the opposite side that Jenny had not noticed, "be his lordship's dressing room."

The Earl's communicating door was opened and they walked inside to find a rather thin small man (boasting the title of gentleman's gentleman) unpacking the Earl's overnight portmanteau, as his other baggage had arrived and been unpacked two days before.

It was a small room, with a single day bed huddled in the corner. There was no fireplace, but it housed a large bureau. It was a dark ugly room and Jenny pulled a face. So, thought Jenny, Jason is at my head and my dressing room at my feet. It seems I am well housed.

Her musings were interrupted by the gradual rise of voices. Joan was flinging wild abuses at the little man she

143

referred to as Winfred. It seemed that Winfred had made the error of objecting to their unexpected intrusion. This caused Joan to take strong exception. As Winfred was clearly quite flustered and Joan unrelenting, Jennifer decided to put a stop to the bickering. Putting up her hand, she said, "Enough . . . both of you! Winfred—that is your name, is it not?" She waited long enough for him to admit that it was. "Well then, Winfred, you must agree that as his lordship's wife, I have the perfect right to open his door and enter his room whenever I choose. However, you did not realize whom you were addressing and we will let it go at that, shall we?"

He acknowledged this and gave over quick apologies, to which Joan folded her arms and continued to mumble.

Jenny laughed and admonished. "Enough, Joan. I won't have our two most prized servants indulging in this absurd rivalry."

Winfred, much abashed, continued his apologies as Jenny led Joan out of the room. The communicating door was closed, but not before Joan threw back a superior smile at the Earl's valet.

Jenny was relaxing in her bath and reflecting over her first impressions, and a thought struck her: Why was not Julian present to greet them?

Lillian Waine eyed her stepson with something close to malice. "You are and have been a despicable boy, Jason. Even as a lad you were spoiled and willful. You have married that child simply to do your brother out of his inheritance!" she snapped.

Jason Waine smiled, but without warmth. "Ah, you see how differently two people can look upon the cold facts. I have always understood the contents of the will to mean that *my* inheritance would become *my brother's* only if I did not carry out the contingencies of that will. I have done my father's bidding—which was to marry, settle down, and possibly produce a Waine heir. Are you not pleased? No, I see you are not. Somehow you have looked upon my inheritance as Julian's. I must say, *mother,*" he slurred the title insultingly, "I do not fathom your reasoning."

"How dare you! How dare you speak to me like that! You led Julian to believe that you would never marry! You bragged about going through life without the hampering of a woman's strings. Of course, I have looked on the estate as Julian's ... I have always believed you would not marry. You have given us a shock, Jason. It was an infamous thing to do ... and I'll find a way out of it, I warrant you!"

"So you have already informed me several times over, madam! However, I cannot see what all this raging is going to accomplish. I *have* married ... and that appears to be that!"

He was weary of this woman and her unending tirade. He had known it would come. Expected it as inevitable, had even discussed it with Gwen, and was heartily sick of it.

Lillian Waine picked up her flashy purple skirts and swung around, leaving her stepson without further comment. He stood for a long while and gazed at the door she had slammed behind her and found once again the old feeling of revulsion and disgust. How could his father have loved her ... and having loved her, how could he have actually married her?

## Chapter Fourteen

*Who see'st appall'd th' unreal scene,*
*While Fancy lifts the veil between:*
*Ah Fear! Ah Frantic Fear!*
*I see, I see thee Near.*

WILLIAM COLLINS

Jenny had fallen off to sleep after her soothing bath and awoke to her maid's gentle knock. It was just five o'clock and still quite light out, yet she was rushed, as the Waine Castle kept country dining hours.

She chose a lovely gown of red silk. It was high-waisted, low-cut, and sleeveless, its only embellishment being a white lace spencer. The gown clung to her youthful fig-

145

ure, and she appeared what she was, exquisitely alluring. Her chestnut locks were piled high on her head, a few curls allowed to escape their pins and spring down upon her shoulder. She wore pearl drops in her ears and a clasp of pearls about her neck.

Jason knocked upon their door and she bade him enter. He stood in the doorway, looking himself the embodiment of elegant masculinity in a cutaway dinner coat of superfine blue, a white silk waistcoat, and dark blue pantaloons. His black gleaming hair fell about his head in interlocking waves and Jenny had a strange desire to reach out and touch him.

Husband and wife gazed at each other admiringly, and then Jason broke the spell by coming curtly forward. His elbow was extended and she placed her hand gracefully upon it.

"You look bewitching, Jenny." His eyes wandered over her figure and he felt a slight twinge of annoyance at discovering that the lace spencer hid little of her low-cut gown. "No doubt my brother and cousin will find you ravishing," he said, sounding even to himself a bit stiff.

He led her down the stairs into the central hall, and across to the double doors she had noticed earlier that day. Inside was the dining room. They entered to find it, or so it seemed to Jenny, filled with people. It was an unusual room, as it housed, in addition to a tremendous dining table and long sideboard, a sofa and many chairs fringing the enormous fireplace. Servants were coming and going through a rear door, which apparently led to the kitchens.

Jason called her attention to a young man who had stepped forward, and as Jenny raised her eyes, she felt her breath leave her. Here was the most beautiful young man she had ever seen. He had the same silky fair hair as his mother, and his fell in velvety layers to his neckline. The top of his hair hung over his forehead, making an entrancing gold fringe. His brows were sandy-colored and thick. His eyes were pale blue in a face that was lean and angular. He was as tall as Jason, though leaner (Jenny thought him perhaps too thin.) His clothes were worn with care and Jenny was sure that they came from one of the finest tailors in London. He was grinning broadly at her and Jenny felt a sudden surge of liking for him.

"So . . . this is my sister?" beamed Julian Waine. "Welcome . . . Jennifer, is it?"

"It is . . . but do call me Jenny."

"Jenny it is! By jove, Jason has caught himself an angel. Are there any more in that outlandish place you come from?"

"No, I have no brothers or sisters, and Devon, my friend, is *not* outlandish!"

"Of course, it isn't love . . . not if that is where Jason discovered you. But no sisters, you say?"

"No, but now I have Gwen . . . and you may fill the post of brother," said Jenny, feeling strangely at ease with him.

"By gad, I will and gladly," he pronounced with enthusiasm.

She then turned to find another young man, one closer to Jason in age, waiting to be presented. He was also quite tall and inwardly she referred to this as a "Waine trait!" His hair was a sandy brown, worn in soft short waves of indistinct styling. His face was pleasant, if one disregarded the severity of his mouth and the solemnity in his light brown eyes. His clothes were carelessly worn on a frame that was angular but well built. Jenny eyed him carefully and was idly reminded of a minister.

Howard Waine admired Jennifer gravely, his eyes resting on the transparency of her lace spencer jacket, and he remarked that if she was cold, he would be pleased to fetch her a wrap.

Immediately, Julian barked cheerfully at him. "You fool, Howard! Do you want to deprive us of such a lovely sight. Wrap her, indeed! Hush up, man."

Jenny joined in their laughter and found herself completely comfortable with these men. Jason took up her hand and gently pulled her toward a woman standing quietly talking with Lady Lillian. Helen Browne was just past twenty. She was of average height and her figure was good, though her drab clothes did her little credit. She wore her light brown hair knotted at the nape of her neck, though short whisps curled at her forehead. Her eyes were fine and dark in a countenance that was clear and held a hidden prettiness.

"This is Miss Helen Browne, Jennifer. She is governess to the Wendall boys," said Jason, smiling kindly.

Jennifer had just enough time to acknowledge the woman's proud curtsy before two young boys came flying at her.

"Hallo. We saw you this afternoon when you arrived," said the older boy, grinning. "I'm Jamie. And this," he said, pulling his brother forward, "is my brother Peter. He is only nine! But I'm eleven, you know."

"Are you going to stay?" asked the smaller boy, gazing hopefully at Jenny. "I hope you're going to stay . . . you're so lovely."

Jason and Jenny laughed in unison while Miss Helen chided the boys.

"Well now, my buckos, don't I get a welcome?" teased the Earl, grinning.

The Earl was immediately pounced upon, for even in the few times he had visited Waine Castle, he had managed to endear himself to the boys.

Jamie, the elder Wendall, had a tendency to gravity. His main loyalties were toward his brother. He protected, steered, and ruled his younger brother, who, in turn, worshipped him. They were inseparable. Neither had ever really experienced motherly love, and while Miss Helen was the first governess they had allowed to remain on, for any length of time, they merely tolerated her more than they had the others. Both boys had unruly ginger colored hair and bluish eyes. Their faces were covered with freckles and their noses turned up at the tips. Jenny studied them with a warm smile, thinking they looked like veritable elves.

A lackey announced dinner and they filed toward the dining table. Jenny and Jason faced each other, each occupying the far end of the rectangular table. Howard sat on Jenny's right, while Julian armed her left. Lady Lillian and Miss Helen faced each other at the Earl's end of the table, and the Wendall boys sat across from each other at the center of the table. Jamie announced to Jenny quite proudly that this was a special treat, for normally they took dinner in the schoolroom.

Jenny found conversation with the stern Howard trying and at times dull, but she noticed something she had picked up earlier in the evening. Lillian Waine had been silent during the introductions, but Jenny had glanced her way once and was surprised to find the woman eyeing Howard Waine in a curious fashion. During the dinner she noted it again and was sure that Howard seemed to avert his gaze intentionally.

However, this was soon forgotten, for if Jenny found Howard's dinner wit wanting, she could not think so of Julian's. Julian, she found, could keep up a steady flow of conversation that was hilarious. He amused her with a stream of anecdotes and she felt as though she had known him a long, long time.

"Dash it, Julian, you must own that Hyde Park is nothing when compared to our riding paths through the downs and pine forests," said Howard.

"Ay, that I own, Howard, but I'd rather expatiate in the hub of London than in all your downs, forests, and deserts, and at any rate, I know all the paths and roads here and around," countered Julian, defending his position.

"Well, and what is wrong with that, lad?" asked Howard raising his brow.

"Deuce take it, man. There's no excitement in knowing! I detest knowing the road one is to go, and being interrupted by the damned finger posts, or a blackguard roaring for tuppence at a turnpike," said Julian amicably.

"But Julian," said Jenny, smiling brightly, "what a sophist fellow you are. What has that to do with anything?"

"Nothing at all, my pretty . . . but 'tis true nonetheless and serves to show that even my equestrian nature could not keep me from London's call!"

"You are, my boy, a sad rattle," said Howard Waine, shaking his head but allowing his mouth to form one of his rare smiles.

"Ay that I am. But I can remember a time, Howard, when we rattled together over this old place in search of excitement. You were not so prune-faced then, my friend." He turned to Jenny. "Don't let him fool you, Jen. He really has all the proper spirits at bottom!"

"Pray, what do you mean?" inquired Jenny, her eyes lighting up at all this raillery.

"I can remember his face when we discovered the Priest's hole," said Julian portentously.

"Priest's hole?" ejaculated Jennifer excitedly. "Oh, never say there is one! Julian, of all the most glorious things to own. You must show it to me at once."

Julian cast her a mischievous look. "I say, Jen, should love to . . . but what would Jase say about it? Might want to show it to you himself."

"Well then, I shall ask him, and if he does not, then you shall . . . promise?"

He laughed merrily and said she was a naughty puss, for it would surely muss her gown. In the end he gave his promise and a curious look crept into his eyes. When they had left the table, Jenny felt that she had found a friend at Waine Castle.

Miss Browne took her leave of them and Jenny frowned. The girl had cast her dark eyes upon Jason, who had barely noticed her departing form. Then with a warm good night to Howard, she had turned and bade Julian the same . . . but the look she gave Julian sent a chill through Jenny.

The boys followed Miss Browne after Jenny detained them long enough to place a kiss on each one's cheek. The remaining members of the family turned and eyed one another, and Jenny was aware of a wary sensation among them.

It was Julian who suggested a game of whist and Jenny agreed readily, urging Howard and Jason to consent to it. Lillian excused herself, exclaiming that she was exhausted and wished to retire. Jenny watched her go with what could only be called a sense of deliverance. Without knowing why, she had formed a dislike for the woman, and much as she chided herself, she could not dispel the feeling.

150

Jenny relaxed and found an easy comradeship among her male attendants. Even Howard had lost his prosey countenance and joined their jesting good-naturedly. Some two hours later Julian threw down his cards with disgust. "What a mean hand that was!" He stretched out long arms above his head and rose from the table, making his leisurely way toward the decanter of brandy adorning a marble-topped server. He poured three glasses and asked Jenny over his shoulder if she wished for anything. She declined and he handed first one glass to his brother and then the other to his cousin before taking up his own and planting himself in his seat again.

"Jason, I wonder if we might discuss something . . . before you retire tonight," asked Julian hesitatingly.

The Earl regarded his half-brother thoughtfully. "Of course, Julian." He was rewarded with a broad grin and the game continued. It was another hour before Jenny, who was beginning to feel the effects of a long day, glanced at the clock and exclaimed, "Faith, 'tis past twelve already! My goodness, gentlemen, it has been very enjoyable indeed, but I beg you will excuse me."

Three men immediately rose to their feet as Jenny pushed her chair back and stood up. Julian expressed his desire for her to remain, but Jenny firmly bade them all good night, avoiding her husband's eyes as she did so.

Julian watched the newly-weds and his brows rose. The thought occurred to him that if Jenny were his bride, she would not be retiring alone.

Some time passed and Jenny found she could not drift off to sleep. She lay awake with her tumble of thoughts when she heard a stirring in the room at her head. The Earl's day bed creaked, and with a sigh, she turned over and clung to her pillow. A tear dropped quietly to its linen resting place.


"Good morning, m'lady!" said Joan, pulling open the velvet hangings and tying them back with the gold ropes.

Jenny sat up in bed and rubbed her eyes. When next she opened them, she found a tray of sweet-smelling coffee being placed on her unsteady lap.

"Oh, Joan, do be a dear and place this on the tea table

by the glass doors. I'll wash first and then have my coffee on the terrace."

Jenny washed as Joan moved about the room with a good deal of exuberance. A wrapper was fetched, and clicking her tongue, the maid insisted m'lady don it before sitting outside . . . sun or no sun!

Jenny opened the terrace door and the crisp morning air stroked her face. The sun shown warmly and she felt the exhilaration of a new day.

Joan bustled about in the room preparing Jenny's day dress while Jenny sipped her morning coffee and dreamt of roaming the grounds with Jason by her side. More than anything, she wanted to be with Jason. Then all at once she saw him.

She started to call out his name when it stuck in her throat. He had walked out from the house, starting down the drive. Her eyes had been filled with him and had overlooked the oncoming rider until his hand had gone up in greeting. It was then that Jenny saw her. A lovely woman wearing a sky blue riding habit was riding down the drive toward Jason. She was astride a magnificent bay, and Jenny was all too acutely aware that the horse's rider was just as magnificent. The woman brought her steed to a halt almost directly beneath Jenny's window and Jenny drew back, not wanting to be seen. She heard a light musical voice. "Jason, darling Jason, how marvelous to find you up and about already . . . and *alone*. I rode here on precisely *that* hope."

Jenny watched the Earl reach up and help the golden-haired woman dismount. Watched her plant a lingering kiss upon his lips and then link her arm through his. She did not hear Jason's response, but she heard the woman's low intimate laugh . . . and then heard them laugh together.

Jenny felt her world begin to rock and put a hand up to her eyes. She heard Jason say in a voice deeply underlined with something—she was not sure what— "I have heard about Sir Giles . . . Hester, I am truly sorry!"

Hester's eyes glittered. "*You* should be Jason, but we cannot go into that now."

"No, but do accept my condolences. I would have offered them sooner, but I did not hear until last night. Howard told me of your loss."

Suddenly Jenny wanted to get away. She sensed an intimacy between Jason and this woman and only knew she couldn't bear to hear any more. She ran back into her room and donned the pretty muslin dress her maid had laid out. It was white, embroidered throughout with blue bows. The sleeves were puffed and etched with blue banding. The neck was scooped and banded with the same blue. The dress was tight-waisted, with clinging lines, and there were rows upon rows of ruffled skirting that started below the knee. Jenny's hair was brushed out and tied at the top with a blue ribbon, and she looked enchanting. Picking up a shawl of the same material, she rushed out of the room and nearly collided with Julian, whose room was across the hall from hers.

"I say there, Jen, you look fetching in that gown," came his merry voice.

Jenny wanted to run to him and sob her heartache onto his broad lean shoulders, but instead said, "Julian, I am so very glad to see you, for you are just the man to take care of my needs."

"Could have told you that, m'dear. Thing is dashed unlucky, you know. Didn't get to that *not very* outlandish place first."

"Seriously though, Julian, would you be kind enough to show me about the grounds? His ... his lordship has company, and I do so want to go out."

"Eh ... company, you say?"

"Yes, and ... and do you think we could sneak out the back without anyone seeing us? I would dearly love to explore."

Julian's eyes narrowed curiously. "Jason has company and you want to sneak out the back door. Sounds too smokey by half, my pretty. Who is this company he is entertaining?"

"I ... I have not been introduced to her," said Jenny in a small voice.

"By God, the devil take the female. Is Lady Hester here already. All right then, child, put your best smile on.

153

I'll take you anywhere your sweet heart desires." He bowed grandly. "At your command, madam."

Jenny found it easy to laugh with Julian, who was, it seemed, rarely serious. He took up her hand in a brotherly fashion and led her down the hall in the opposite direction of the grand staircase. At the end of the hall they came to a door, opened it, and found a landing that led down to the back of the house. After passing through a narrow hall, they found themselves in the rear courtyard. This was entirely closed in by a stone wall with only one exit gate. They passed through to find the sea calmly splattering its wails against Dover's chalk.

Jenny moved to the edge of the cliff hanging and felt awed by the vastness of white irregular heights stretching defiantly against the sea. The blue tide was full and the sun blinked on the white spray. Jenny listened to the sounds of sea gulls sqawking incessantly and grimaced at the hovering birds.

"Even with their screeching, this is a gloriously beautiful scene," she said in a whisper. Her words were drowned by the roar of the waves brushing against the pebbled shingles. They flung the pebbles aimlessly on each return, making a slow, steady, tremulous cadence.

"What did you say, love?" asked Julian, smiling at her.

"I said," replied Jenny, raising her voice considerably, "that the sea and heights of Dover are glorious!" Then suddenly she skipped away, making a rush for a path she thought led to the beach below.

Julian called out sharply and caught her arm. "Jen! I say, love . . . not another step."

"But why, Julian. I should so like to walk along the beach."

"And so you shall . . . but not by taking that path. 'Tis a decidedly dangerous one to take and ends abruptly at a stone wall. Come on. If it's the beach you intend to walk along, then 'tis to the right we must go."

They walked along the path in silence, with Julian admonishing Jenny to have a care and helping her along over particularly rough spots. They reached the sandy beach and Jenny sucked in some air.

"Oh, this is just marvelous, Julian. You must have loved it here as a child."

Julian's face darkened a moment. "Yes ... I did for quite a long time. Ah, but then came Eton, and Cambridge, and the inevitable lure of London. Find it dull sport at Waine now."

"Your mother would miss you, I imagine, if you were to leave."

"Precisely why I don't leave."

"I see," said Jenny slowly. Then after a moment: "She is a beautiful woman ... I'm surprised she hasn't remarried."

"Mama?" Julian laughed. "Mama is a beauty ... but she is nearly forty, you know. Where is she going to meet anyone, stuck here at Waine and never going out? Have tried to convince her to come to London with me and set up an establishment, but ... well, never mind that," said Julian his tone going hard suddenly.

He took up her hand and his eyes danced. "Come on, let's have a good run."

They ran across a stretch of beach and nearly fell with fatigue. Laughing and swaying with mirth, they leaned against a boulder for support.

After a time, Julian eyed her and asked curiously, "Now tell me, Jen, how did you ... well, how came about this marriage to my brother?"

She surveyed his face for a moment and said quietly, "Do you mind, Julian?"

He looked at her and chuckled. "You mean because of the inheritance thing? No, nonsensical girl. If I mind, it's because Jason snapped you up before I had the good sense to find you."

"Not even a twinge ... I mean about the inheritance?" pursued Jenny.

"Well, I suppose I'd be a liar if I said I had never thought about the money. There is too much of it *not* to think about it. One does, you know. However, I am not ... well, let us say that I do not have the same grand notions my mother has. My father left me quite a comfortable sum and my needs have been in the past quite modest. Now, *Jason needs* the inheritance—his needs are great.

155

He lives high ... but that is neither here nor there. Things are what they are. You are Jason's wife, and Jason *has* inherited. I was merely curious how Jason came to marry you."

She smiled saucily. "We met in that outlandish place, Devon. And though he came to propose to my best friend, he decided her giggles would never do, and instead dropped his handkerchief my way. Apparently, I picked it up."

She succeeded in causing Julian's jaw to drop. She giggled over this and then sighed. "Oh, Julian, it is beautiful here. I do wish my room overlooked this view."

"So do I!" agreed Julian Waine, gazing at Jenny intently.

She turned to eye him and blushed, for his meaning was clear. "Do you know," he said, quickly changing the subject, "on a clear night you can actually see the lights from Calais?"

"No! All the way from France? It doesn't seem possible," she said, wide-eyed.

"It is. 'Twas between Dover and the Calais area that so much smuggling went on, you know, and it's said they used lanterns for signals. One night, if you will permit, I'll bring you here and we'll watch for the lights." Then his tone went suddenly abrupt. "Come on, Jen, I had better get you back to the house before they send out the Bow Street runners to hunt us down. This is quite unorthodox—stealing away my brother's bride on his honeymoon."

She blushed and allowed him to take up her hand and pull her gently up the slope to the unkept lawns of the Waine grounds. They circled the house, passing a long rectangular low building, made up for the most part of glass. The glass was black with dirt and it was apparent that no one had taken any care of this building in quite some time. It was some fifteen feet in height and appeared to be level with the ground.

"Julian, is this the hothouse?" asked Jenny with dismayed shock, for she felt it a crime that such a thing could have happened to a building that had probably house, at one time, rare tropical plants.

"Yes, love, though it's fallen into sad disrepair these

last six years. However, I daresay there are still some fine peach trees growing in there." He frowned and then continued. "Funny thing about this place—there was a story that some tunnel or other connects the castle and this building. Never found it, though. Had a notion Jason knew where it was ... but then, he never let on, not even to Gwen."

"Oh, Julian how thrilling—a real tunnel?"

"Hmmm, yes ... makes a rare tale. Rumor had it that one of our illustrious ancestors was a Jacobite, or perhaps a Jacobite sympathizer. At any rate, he was the devil who supposedly had the thing constructed ... as a means of escape. Led to an old shed originally, until the hothouse was constructed in its stead."

"Pray, Julian, you must help me find it," said Jenny.

"Told you, love, looked for the maddening thing. Never could find a trace of it."

"Well, then, you did not look thoroughly enough," retorted Jen, not to be put off.

"I did too, my girl, and what's more, you are not to go searching for the thing by yourself. Likely break your pretty neck." He then stopped and gave a low whistle. "Oh, oh, love ... well, nothing for it, must plod steadily on," he said as the sight of Jason and Lady Hester met their eyes.

Jason and his female companion made their unhurried way across the center lawn toward them and Jenny felt an ache in her heart as she saw the woman's arm was still linked in Jason's.

Jenny's own hand was still in Julian's firm grasp when she caught the angry look in her husband's eye and stiffened. She tried gently to withdraw her hand from Julian but her brother-in-law retained a firm grip, and his voice came low. "Buck up, Jen. We'll brush through this creditably ... see if we don't." Secretly he was concerned, too, for he had not missed the hard look in his brother's jealous eyes.

"Where have you two been?" Jason asked, his voice hinting at deeper shades of annoyance, his eyes flickering objectionably to their hands.

Under such scrutiny, Julian allowed Jenny to pull her

hand quietly away, and they both stood there, Jenny glaring defiantly and Julian amicably.

It was Jenny who found her voice in time to answer her husband. "Julian was kind enough to take me for a walk along the beach and show me some of the grounds."

Jason's eyes narrowed, but he turned to Lady Hester and made the necessary introductions. Jenny received a frosty smile and gave one in return. Julian coughed. "Er ... Jase, ol' fellow, if you and Lady Hester don't mind, we'll excuse ourselves. Haven't breakfasted, you know, and your bride is famished."

Jenny's eyes thanked him, for there was nothing for it, Jason was forced to excuse them and the two almost ran toward the house.

Lady Hester and Jason watched them go, each with feelings held in check.

"Really, Jason, she is but a child. A pretty one, of course ... but not exactly in your style, is she?"

Jason would not allow his wife to be spoken of in such terms and cut her short. "Ah, but then, my *interests* are so diversified, Hester. I shall call for your horse. As you can see, I have been neglecting my duties as a husband ... and it would not do for Julian to carry the brunt of my obligations."

A few minutes later he strode into the dining parlor to find his wife and brother doubled over with laughter. Jenny dried her eyes and smiled indifferently at the Earl. She was wild with jealousy and still quite furious with him for having stayed in Lady Hester's company for so long. She had laughed loud and naughtily, hoping that Jason would hear her and think she was quite capable of enjoying herself without him.

He regarded her calculatingly and said without smiling, "What do you two find so amusing?"

"Oh, Jason, I hope you won't mind. I was poking a little fun at Lady Hester," said Julian.

"Oh?"

"Yes ... remember last summer? I was telling Jen what an awful seat she has. Don't you remember? We went for a ride and she couldn't guide her horse. There she bounced with her horse chasing after mine—tried to nip my leg off—and Lady Hester screaming in a high hat and her sky blue riding habit, making an absurd figure of herself. The grooms had the devil's own work to keep her from tumbling or having her clothes torn off by the trees and thickets of the pine forest."

The Earl recalled this former scene and grinned good-naturedly. "Yes, brat, I remember . . . but it is not at all the gentlemanly thing to do, you know."

"Hang it, the lady is a perfidious creature and don't deserve the gentlemanly thing!" Julian grinned.

The Earl raised an eyebrow but thought it better to ignore the remark. The Wendall boys exploded suddenly into the room, with Miss Helen just behind them. The two men stood up until she was seated. The conversation took on a lively vein, which they all seemed to enjoy, until Jenny mentioned the hothouse.

"Jason, I should like to have a few men set on the job of washing it down," said Jenny quietly.

The Earl's brow went up. "Oh? Have you been there already?"

Jenny blushed. "Yes. Julian and I came across it this morning on our return to the house. And do you think we could hire a few gardeners to dig out some flower beds?"

The Earl answered that he would set Howard to the task of hiring men to do her bidding. Then, just as suddenly as they had arrived, the boys rushed out, with their governess in hot pursuit. The Earl rose from the table and offered his arm to his wife, saying that he would be pleased to show her some of the Castle.

Jenny almost jumped to her feet, so great was her pleasure at the proffered treat. They passed Lillian Waine on their way out of the room and Jason was quick to note Jenny's relieved expression.

"Ah, I see you have not developed any great liking for my stepmother."

"No. Perhaps it is wrong . . . but I hold her in ineffable aversion. There is something else, Jason, for which I have no explanation and yet there it is," she said, frowning.

"Ah, feminine intuition. Gwen was forever throwing that at my head. Well then, out with it—what is this thing you have no logical reason for?"

"It was what you said . . . about thinking she was capable of many things, but not . . . not murder. I don't agree. I think her quite able to dispose of anything or anyone that stood in her way."

He patted her arm patronizingly but forebore to answer this. They had reached a long wide gallery. The aisle boasted a wall of rectangular-shaped windows of exceedingly large proportions overlooking the enclosed rear courtyard. On the wall facing these windows were hung countless portraits of various sizes and frames. Jason took her on a tour of these. He paused before a large portrait of a seemingly gentle blue-eyed man and said with the hint of admiration in his voice, "This is Alfred Waine—"

"Oh, he is the one who dug that tunnel!" exclaimed Jenny interrupting.

"Why, yes . . . however did you know?" queried her husband, surprised.

"Julian told me about it this morning. I think it so exciting."

He smiled indulgently. "Howard and I had a marvelous time with his personal papers. We discovered them in the tunnel, you see . . . very incriminating letters about his activities during those turbulent times."

"Then he was a Jacobite?" asked Jenny, wide-eyed.

"Most decidedly."

"However did you find the tunnel?" asked Jenny.

"Ah, you don't think me so unwise as to tell you that. I don't want you looking for the thing, Jenny. It is a singularly dangerous route, for 'twas built some hundred and fifty years ago."

"Do you mean you will not show it to me? That is most . . . most disagreeable of you, my lord," stormed his wife.

"I can see that, once again, I have dropped below reproach. However, I must insist that you forget this wild notion you have of locating the tunnel."

He took up her hand and led her to the next portrait, rattling off an amusing legend connected with the vision before her. She found the Waines an interesting bunch, and then all at once she was standing before a portrait of Jason. She removed her hand from his and went up close to gaze at him when he was twenty.

"Jason . . . this is you! How beautiful a boy you were."

He bowed. "Thank you, Lady Waine. My father had that painted of me by Lawrence. There is Gwen's . . . beside mine."

She glanced at Gwen's hurriedly but returned to his. "How . . . innocent your eyes were."

"And how sinister they are now?" he asked, amused.

She turned pink. "No . . . no, that was not what I meant. But you are much worldlier now, you know."

"Ah, undoubtedly . . . it comes with age. We shall have to have Lawrence paint a portrait of you, Jenny."

She looked away from him. "Not yet, my lord."

"I agree. We should wait until we can have one painted with a child upon your knee . . . our child!" he said quietly.

"My lord!" snapped Jenny, shocked. Really, the gall of him. One minute he is dallying with Lady Hester, the next speaking to her of . . . of things that could not be . . . not now, when she believed him in love with every pretty woman he was acquainted with.

Suddenly his voice became clipped. "I am afraid, Jenny, that I am going to have to leave you now and do not expect to return before dinner. Howard wants me to visit one of our better tenants and take a look at his problems. I hope that you will be able to amuse yourself."

Her face fell for a moment, but she smiled again hastily. "Oh, as to that . . . perhaps Julian will be able to keep me company."

To this all she received was a quiet "Perhaps."

The Earl had gone, and after a few moments' indecision, Jenny made for the main house in search of her brother-in-law. She stopped short in front of the parlor doors where she heard the crescendo of angry voices.

"So, Julian . . . that is it! You are far too interested in your pretty Lady Waine . . . but it will not do," came a hard feminine voice.

"Let it go, Helen! Lord, girl, this has gone too far! First of all, I won't allow you to speak of Lady Waine in that tone. She is my sister and certainly I like her. It would be a difficult thing, indeed, not to like her."

"You more than *like* her Julian. I saw the way you looked at her when you thought no one was watching."

"Leave it be, Helen, I am warning you. Listen to me, girl . . . even if I were to chase after my brother's wife—which I ain't about to do—but if I were—for that matter, if I were to sleep with every girl between here and Folkstone—'tis nothing for *you* to remark upon. What happened between us was a mistake. 'Twasn't me came to your room, you know. *You* came to *mine* . . . and kept coming. I can't abide your jealous tantrums . . . nor will I! I am not yours for the bidding, Helen. God knows I didn't want to hurt you and tried to break it off gently, but you won't let go! You hound a fellow into the ground, you do, and it's driving me to distraction! Now I'm telling you to your head, Helen, leave be . . . you'll get nothing more out of me!"

"But, Julian, I . . . I love you."

"Then you'll have to stop. God knows I've given you cause enough to hate me. Now I have to go, Helen. You heard Jason ask me to ride out to the west field."

Jenny's eyes had opened wide and she thought that the sweet-tempered youth she had come to like so quickly could be ruthless when it suited him. Quietly she backed away from the door and made her way down the long hallway again. She had passed a door earlier but had not bothered to look in. She now peeped inside to discover the library. She went across the room and scanned the dusty shelves, pleased to find some of her favorites. There were Jane Austen's recent works, and the much criticized *Queen Mab* by Shelly, there were the collections of Pope and Donne and all of Byron's published works. She picked up a copy of *Lara* by Lord Byron and sat down to read. Her head was brought up by the sound of swishing silk. She looked up to find Lillian Waine standing in the doorway.

Her stepmama-in-law stood there in a dress of yellow silk embellished by numerous green ribbons, and the vision made Jenny's eyes blink. Lillian Waine's pale eyes held an angry sparkle. "Jenny, am I to understand that you have changed my menu for tonight's dinner?"

Jenny regarded the woman's wintry expression and

kept her temper in check. "Oh, I do hope you don't mind. Cook presented the menu to me while I was at breakfast ... I had no idea you had already arranged for something you particularly wished."

It was at this point that Lillian Waine made a strategical error. Mistaking Jenny's gentle grace for weakness, she pounced haughtily. "Well then, in the future, Jenny, you will leave all such matters to me! You need not concern yourself with the running of this house."

Jenny had been raised and bred a lady. She knew her station in life, and while she had no wish to inflict hurt or exert power, she was not made of the stuff that stands aside at the first show of opposition. Jason Waine was her husband and she was Lady Waine. This was her home and she would run it as she had been trained to do. She was the mistress of Waine, and Lillian Waine was, in fact, a guest in her home. Jenny would not allow herself to be so boldly put down and could not refrain from putting up her chin. "My dear Lillian, I am certainly not going to have *you bothered* with the management of *my* household. No, indeed, what a shabby thing to do! I would never dream of taking such advantage," said Jenny with cold sweetness, freezing Lillian in position.

Jenny had said what had to be said, as politely as she knew how, and yet she knew it had been a declaration of war. Lillian Waine glared for a moment and then silently turned on her studded heel and left the room.

Jenny sighed. Here was her first enemy. What an odd thing. She had the son for friend and the mother for foe! She thought of her aunt and papa ... and how very far away they seemed.

It was some thirty or forty minutes later when *Lara* had been read and cried over that Jenny put the volume away and got to her feet. She passed the butler in the central hall and made her way outside.

She picked her way through the tall grass toward the west side of the Castle, passing the hothouse and then heading south a bit, when she noticed a rose garden in full bloom. "Well, in sad condition, but lovely all the same," she said out loud. She was about to return to the house for a pair of cutting sheers when she noted a small toolshed not far off. She walked gingerly through the tall grass and made her way to the shed door. Leaving the door open, she picked up her skirts and began rummaging through the shelves in search of a pair of gardening sheers, when suddenly she was standing in the dark. She turned startled eyes toward the door, thinking that the breeze had not been strong enough to slam it closed ... yet evidently it had. She shrugged her shoulders and gave the door a push. It would not budge. Jenny pushed harder and banged against its handle. Aghast, she kicked at the door when all at once she realized it was locked. The shed door was locked!

## Chapter Fifteen

She was locked in! For an entire minute, Jenny stood there in the blackness, staring at the door unbelievingly. This could not actually have happened. She had to be mistaken. Perhaps it was merely jammed. She smiled to herself. That was it. She was being silly. She found an iron bar and hammered at the door. She tried wedging the bar, but to no avail. The door was most certainly locked from the outside. She could feel the strain against the handle when she pushed.

"All right, Jen," she said out loud. "Let us not panic. A breeze ... whoosh ... slams it closed, possibly jams it, but locks it? Oh no, I know of no breeze so well educated. Well then, how does a toolshed door get locked from the outside? Obviously, a creature of some sort of intellect—enough to operate a lock—sees an open door, shuts it, and then locks it. Ah, this creature, then, has enough intelligence to perceive an open door ... but does not see that directly in front of that open doors stands a lady in white? Well, white no longer." She shook her head. "All right, then, let us carry this further. What sort of creature would carry on such a prank? A child creature, of course. Great sport, to be sure, capture a lady in the toodshed. The Wendall boys, of course! Then the thing to do is to wait for them to decide the lady has had enough of a scare."

She then found a dusty wooden crate and plopped down, resigned to her fate and patiently awaiting her release. After ten minutes had elapsed, she wondered, "I do hope they don't intend to frighten me any longer. I mean ... boys do put frogs in one's soup, and in one's bed, and now and then lock damsels in toolsheds—at least, I suppose that boys do all those horrid things, all of which must have happy endings ... I hope."

The crude but serviceable chair she had made for herself was beginning to pain. After half an hour had passed, Jenny stood and pounded on the door. An apprehension began to take hold of her and her calmness started to ebb. After another fifteen minutes dragged by, she became exasperated. "After all," she said out loud, "a joke is a joke, and I don't mind one at my expense now and then ... but this is really doing it a bit too brown!"

Jenny began pacing to and fro, finally gave that up, and returned to the door and began knocking wildly. This availed not and Jenny began to panic. She stumbled in the dark and fell, tearing her gown and bruising her knee. She was beginning to find the darkness and the boredom unbearable. She made a resonant solemn oath to wring the necks of the Wendall boys when she was released; changed her mind and promised not to touch them if only they would free her.

However, two more hours passed and Jenny began to cry. She knew instinctively that this was no mere prank and felt certain now that the Wendall boys had *not* locked her in the shed. She beat at the door until her arm ached. She tired of shouting and dropped back onto the wooden crate. She was hungry, cold, and frightened. Silly girl, she told herself, why should you be frightened? Surely you will be missed and the grounds will be searched. Surely Jason will return and find you. Jason ... who wanted no wife. ... She brushed this awful thought away, but yet, it was Jason who had sent Julian off today so that she

165

would be alone! Jenny began shouting again. Her mouth felt dry and her throat sore, yet she could not give up. She was filled with fear, fear of the spiders she sensed crawling around her, of the squeaks and squeals of the field mice she heard scurrying about the shed. She tried over and over again to get the door to open by using various tools she found. Then all at once a large rat was at her feet and Jenny screamed. She screamed with all her heart, she was still screaming when the door was nearly flung off its hinges and a male voice called her name.

She was crying and shivering as she fell into his arms and was carried out into the late afternoon light.

Jenny clung to her savior's neck, too upset, too grateful for his presence to question how he came to be there. "Mac . . . oh, Mac . . . I couldn't bear it anymore." She was sobbing from the long tediousness of being caged for hours.

He held her tightly before setting her on her feet and then tried to bolster her spirits by saying laughingly that he would have carried her to the house, had he not been afraid of incurring Gravesly's ill opinion.

She released a little hysterical gurgle and leaned against his strong arm. Lieutenant McMillan frowned over her appearance. "My God, Jen . . . you have been hurt!"

"Oh, no, not really. I was stumbling about in the dark for hours and hours, Mac . . . and then a rat bared his teeth at me. I . . . I could see his eyes glow in the dark, Mac . . . it was horrid!"

"Shh, child, 'tis over . . . though I mean to discover how it came about," said Mac gravely, his dark eyes taking on a hard expression.

Jenny was now able to turn her gaze full upon his cherubic countenance. "But, Mac dearest, how came *you* to be here?"

"Do you mean to scold me, Jen? I could not keep away. Indeed, I think if I had, you would have been a good deal put out with me!" he said, looking sheepish.

"Scold you? Why, Mac, how could you think such a thing? Especially after your dramatic rescue. Why, if it had not been for you, I might have been eaten alive by those horrid things—or worse, I might have spent the night imagining that I was about to be." She hugged his neck and allowed him to help her to the house.

"Now, my handsome lieutenant, you will tell me what has brought you to Dover."

"Well, for one thing, not a lieutenant any longer, Jen. Sold out! M'father needs me. He is . . . he is not well and wants me to run the estate for him. Which brings me to the second thing. Had some loose ends that needed tying up here in Dover, and then in London. When I received your letter, there wasn't enough time to get to the wedding, so I came straight here, as you mentioned you'd be coming to Waine Castle."

They had by now reached the front doors, which were opened hurriedly by Gravesly, as everyone had been alerted of her ladyship's disappearance. The butler expressed his concern and sincere hope that her ladyship had sustained no injury and advised her that he would have tea brought to her immediately.

She led Mac to the parlor, where he situated her before the fire and knelt beside her, rubbing her hands and remarking with a frown that they were frozen.

Lillian Waine entered the scene at this point, exclaiming thankfully that the lieutenant had found Jennifer. "Those dreadful boys . . . to have locked you in the toolshed all day!" she remarked after hearing where Jenny had been.

"Well, it isn't really fair to blame them . . . we are not sure it was them, are we?" said Jenny, eyeing Lillian strangely.

"As to that . . . I'm going to go and ferret them out immediately!" said Lillian, turning on her heel and leaving the room.

"Jenny?" said Mac gravely. "If the boys did not lock you in, then who did?"

"I . . . I don't know, Mac. If it was the boys, it can be chalked up to a nasty prank that somehow grew out of proportion. I daren't think who else might have done it . . . or why. How did you happen to find out I was missing?"

"Well, as I said, I decided to pop in and see how you were managing here at Waine . . . with the Earl. . . ."

"You neglected to say the *evil* Earl." Jenny grinned.

"Well, Jen, if you must know, I was a bit worried. His lordship does have quite a reputation, and I thought you might need . . . a friend."

"It surely looks as though I do!" replied Jenny dryly.

"I arrived here about half an hour ago to find that your husband was away from home, his brother off somewhere, and the women in an uproar over your disappearance. So, my child, I took matters into my own hands and began searching . . . your scream gave it away."

"I should thank that rat then, for you must know I had given up shouting and may have missed you."

The door opened again and the Wendall boys were pushed into the room by the irate Lillian. "I want you to apologize to Lady Waine at once."

"But why? We haven't done anything," said Jamie darkly.

"At once!" snapped Lillian.

"Please, Lillian, if Jamie says they have done nothing to apologize for, I believe them. Please let them go."

Jamie and Peter shot her a grateful look and flew out of the room before Lillian could detain them.

"Really, Jenny, you were far too lenient,"said Lillian.

"Was I? I don't think so . . . I believe them, you see."

The boys had been intercepted in the hallway by the Earl, who had heard some of the story from Gravesly. He eyed them grimly and asked them if they had locked Lady Waine in the shed.

"Dash it, Uncle Jason, why would we do that? We like her," said Jamie.

"Ay, we like her," reiterated his brother Peter. "She is real pretty."

The Earl frowned, but accepted this and allowed them to escape to their rooms. He entered the parlor to find Lillian pouring tea and the lieutenant still rubbing Lady Waine's cold hands. His wife's disheveled appearance brought it forcibly to mind that she had suffered a great deal more than he had been led to believe, and he strode quickly to her side.

Mac released Jenny's hand and stood up, moving

toward Lillian and engaging her in idle conversation while the Earl questioned his wife.

"Jenny, my poor dear, are you all right?" His eyes held concern and she reached out instinctively and touched his hand wanting to reassure him and amazingly comforted by the sound of his voice.

"Quite all right, my lord ... thank you," she said softly.

He kissed her hand and turned to Mac. "It seems I have you to thank for coming to my wife's aid. I do indeed thank you ... Lieutenant McMillan, is it?" He had been advised of the gentleman's presence by his butler.

"Mr. McMillan, my lord. I have sold out. It was an honor to be able to serve Jenny again. We are old friends," said Mac quietly, eyeing the Earl speculatively.

"Mac, you will stay with us here. I could not let you stay in town, so I won't hear any objections," said Jenny.

"Oh. I am in full agreement with Lady Waine," interjected Lillian, glancing provocatively at Mac. "I will go arrange for your room to be prepared."

She hurried out and the Earl excused himself, saying he would be back momentarily. Mac and Jenny were left to themselves.

Jenny had not missed the look Lillian Waine had given Mac, or the look her friend had returned Jason Waine's stepmother, and she teased him now.

"It seems my stepmama-in-law is taken with you, Mac."

"She is a fancy piece, that one!" remarked Mac thoughtfully.

"Mac!" exclaimed Jenny, just a bit shocked.

He laughed. "Always had a fancy for older women, Jen. You know that ... they know how to play the game."

"You are disgusting, you odious thing," said Jenny, with the hint of a chuckle.

"A perfidious fellow!" agreed her friend.

"No, if you don't mind, I will excuse myself and go upstairs, for I am sure that my face is in far worse condition than my gown."

"Now that you mention it, Jenny, you do look a sorry sight," teased Mac.

"Horrid! I don't remember you ever being so horrid."

"Ah . . . but you have never before given me reason, you naughty thing."

"Oh, Mac," she exclaimed, dismayed. "Are you really put out with me . . . for marrying with such haste?"

"Put out with you? Now how could I be? I want you to be happy. If I am put out . . . well, 'tis only with your choice. I would have preferred that the man of your choice were one who could love you as you deserve."

She blushed and averted her eyes. "I won't be too long, Mac." With which she hurried from the room.

As she made her way toward the grand staircase, Julian's voice halted her.

"Jen . . . I say, Jen, then it's true . . . for your gown is torn, and there . . . your arm is bruised." he said touching the wide scratch on her forearm with a deep frown.

"How . . . how did you hear of it?"

"Just came from the stables, love, and they told me you have been lost all day . . . locked up in the toolshed."

"Yes, I was locked in all day," she said quietly.

"Upon my word, was it the Wendall boys? Must have been those brats! I'll thrash them for this," he exclaimed angrily.

"No, Julian, I don't think it was them."

"Gammon . . . must have been. Who else would do such a stupid thing? But here, never mind that now. What you need is a hot bath and a good rest . . . then I'll take you for a walk, Jen."

"We'll see, Julian."

He frowned as he watched her climb the stairs and turned toward the parlor, where he met Mac.

# Chapter Sixteen

*Hence, viper thoughts, that coil around my mind.*

SAMUEL TAYLOR COLERIDGE

Jenny walked up the staircase slowly and pensively. So, Jason had sent Julian out of her reach—that she already knew, and yet it nagged at her. Why? Why had she been locked in the toolshed? Was there something sinister behind it? Who would do such a thing?

Jenny was aware of a chill tingling her heart and knew a fear she had never been acquainted with before.

The Wendall boys, Miss Helen, and Howard Waine were not present at the dinner table that evening. The boys took their meal, as was their custom, above stairs. Miss Browne declined to join the family, as she complained of a headache and remained in her quarters, and Howard Waine was engaged with friends in the neighborhood.

Mac was seated on Lillian Waine's right, Julian faced them, and the Earl and his Lady made up both ends of the table whose leaves had been dropped to accommodate conversation.

Julian was much in awe of Mac. His questions were all for Waterloo. "You cannot imagine, sir, how very much I had wanted to enter your very regiment. But m'mother held the purse strings at the time and would hear none of it! She was set on my finishing up at Cambridge. Now, 'tis too late . . . I mean with Boney beaten! No one else could possibly stand up to Wellington," he said dejectedly, reflecting upon his ill luck.

Jenny smiled inwardly, thinking him very boyish . . . very much like her John had been. She turned to glance at her husband and found his eyes gravely surveying her and she lowered her eyes to her pheasant.

William McMillan smiled indulgently, but Waterloo had cost him too many friends and he could not regard it

171

romantically. "Be thankful you were not there, lad. I have often wondered whether it was worth it all. So very many of our best . . . our best men were lost—Howard, and Brunswick . . . lord, so many—and for what? To put the *Bourbons* on the *throne!* Egad, Julian, think on it a bit."

Julian regarded Mac disbelievingly, for this was sacrilege and his estimation of McMillan's character took a severe plunge. "Surely, sir, you cannot mean that?"

"Not mean it? Blister it, boy, haven't you been attending to what I've said? No, no, of course you have not. Waterloo was a bloodbath. Picture it . . . suddenly we were there facing the French, and then just as suddenly the land oozed red—"

"Oh, Mac, please stop," objected Jenny, putting a hand to her eyes.

"Oh, do forgive me, Jenny. Of course, this is not the topic for dinner."

"However, the lieutenant has introduced an excellent point," added Jason.

"I don't see it!" retorted Julian.

"All right then, think how many of our greats fell to put down that tiger of a man, Napoleon. Now Wellington sits back and collects his pension and the Bourbons once again display their stupidity to the world, just as their ostentatious predecesors did! When Napoleon's wild name was spoken, men trembled . . . and now he is nothing. And France is nothing!" said Mac.

Julian had heard the unpardonable . . . all the more so because some of what Mac was saying seemed to make sense. However, he protested loudly.

"I must agree with you to some extent," put in Jason grimly. "I, too, have often regretted the installation of the Bourbons, and one must indeed grimace at the Duke of Wellington's . . . er, rather stupendous pension."

"But . . . but, Jason, surely you cannot mean that!" said Julian, aghast. For he had always looked up to his older brother and considered him a "top sawyer." "Wellington deserves every penny! He fought and won against Boney!"

Jenny thought it was time the conversation took an-

other direction, "That is all very interesting, Julian ...
but I have something to say to you."

He gave her his light blue eyes immediately. "Anything, love ... so as it comes from *your* lips."

"Julian!" objected his mama. "Your brother may not
like you to speak to his lady in such a manner."

Julian ignored his mother and continued to give Jenny
his full attention.

"Well, you may not like to hear this, my friend, for I
am quite put out with you. As I remember, you promised
to show me the priest's hole. You promised faithfully,
Julian ... and have not done so yet!"

"Well, listen to the love!" retorted Julian, grinning
broadly. "Goes and gets herself locked up for the better
part of the day ... *your* husband had me running all over
the county ... and then you accuse me of shirking my
duties. It isn't fair, madam, I protest!"

This caused a chuckle to go round and the tension that
had arisen seemed to be dispelled.

"Well, you must take care of the matter directly after
dinner," demanded Jenny.

"Well, and I won't either, puss! It's not the sort of ac-
tivity one indulges in after dinner," he said, laughing.

"Julian Waine, of all the poor-spirited things to say,"
retorted Jenny challengingly.

"But, Jenny, just think ... your pretty yellow gown
will get all wrinkled and blackened. And besides, m'girl,
I'm engaged with friends tonight. Off to the village, you
know."

"Oh. Still ... it shouldn't take you so long, after all."

"No. And that is final, my pretty. If Jason won't do the
thing, then I'll take you to it first thing in the morning ...
so don't be put out with me, puss."

Jenny turned to her husband, who had been strangely
quiet during this exchange. She was also quick to note
that Mac and Lillian were already conversing on what
seemed to her very intimate terms.

"Jason, would you mind ..." she began.

"No!" said Jason.

"Oh, but Jason, I should so like to explore it," she
pleaded.

"No, Jenny. It is nothing but a small hole, and a dirty one at that. If Julian is willing, he can show you the confounded thing tomorrow."

She pouted prettily. "Can I not do anything to change your mind?"

He hesitated, stood up, and came around to her chair. He held out his hand for hers and helped her up, walking her away from the dinner table as the meal was at end and coffee would be served by the fire.

"You want me to change my mind," he said, pulling her down on the sofa beside him. "Well, then, what are you willing to do to *get* me to change my mind?"

"Oh! You are horrid, Jason Waine! All you can think of is getting me into your . . . your . . ."

"Schhh, naughty little thing. Yes, it is all I can think of. You *are* my wife, you know."

"Yes, I carry your name. Need I remind you how that came to be?"

"Devil take the terms . . . I know them well! However, I don't seem to remember anything in our . . . bargain that said I would be expected to initiate you into the joys and sorrows of exploring a priest's hole!" he said sarcastically and at once disliked himself for it. Her face fell and she blushed bright pink. He threw up his hands with exasperation. "All right then, brat, so be it!"

He stood up and took her hand, turning his head as Julian waved himself away. He also noticed that Mac and his stepmama had come to an interesting friendship.

The Earl and his lady made their way across the central hall, toward the picture gallery, where Jason stopped abruptly. He went to a large portrait, which turned out to be the notorious Alfred Waine, and took it down from the wall. There inserted deep into the wall was a thick metal ring. Jenny watched wide-eyed as the Earl pulled, and heard the sound of grating wood against stone from the recesses of the hall. Jason took her elbow and motioned her down the corridor to the small wooden steps leading to an overhead storage room. The pulling of the metal ring had released a lock that held the steps in place against their stone wall. The Earl now pulled these away by using a great deal of strength and was obliged to heave

174

heavily in the process. Directly behind the hollow stair-well reposed a lantern, which the Earl lit and took up.

He led the way with Jenny clinging to his arm, and pulled open an undersized wooden door.

Jenny gazed about her with a tremendous surge of disappointment. The priest's hole was nothing more than a barren room of small proportions. There were no windows, no furniture—discounting the table and chair situated in its center—and definitely nowhere to hide treasures and other imaginable goodies. Jenny's face fell ludicrously and Jason could not refrain from exploding into laughter. "My dearest Jenny, I don't know what you expected to find. It was used to hide individuals the Waines did not wish found."

She stamped her foot at him good-naturedly. "Stop it, Jacon Waine! You are abominable to laugh at me. It is just that it sounded so enticing . . . so much more interesting than it has turned out to be. I would think that you Waines would have hid at least one small treasure in here."

"We haven't had a treasure for centuries . . . that is, until my father accumulated one." He pinched her chin fondly. "Come on, sweetheart . . ."

She blushed rosily, for he was gazing tenderly down at her. The Earl took her shoulders in his large hands. . . .

"I say, you two, have you seen the thing already? Mind if I have a look?" came Mac's voice from behind them.

Jenny pulled away immediately and the Earl's emotions curdled with a very natural sense of annoyance at McMillan's bad timing.

"Hello, Mac," called Jenny. "You will never credit it . . . but 'tis nothing more than a . . . a dirty barren closet!"

He chuckled. "Eh, rather thought it would be. But let's have a look," he said amiably, passing her and peering inside. "A bit untidy, isn't it? I say, my lord, you should have your sanctuary swept up a bit . . . never know when it might be needed."

The Earl's sense of humor was not at all tickled. His countenance remained stolid and he offered his lady his arm. "Shall we withdraw to the parlor? I fear it is getting a bit chilly here for *my* wife."

They entered the parlor silently and found that the hearth was cackling with a fire that had been started recently. Jason moved to the stainwood cabinet and poured out two glasses of port, while Mac made himself comfortable beside Jenny on the couch. The port was served with a dark look, and Jenny, feeling it incumbant upon her to break the silence, requested her husband to fetch her a galss of madeira.

As his lordship picked up the bottle of clear mild wine, Lillian entered the room. She had removed her velvet spencer, exposing her gown of black clinging silk. It was audaciously cut and beaded along the bodice and again around the hem of the skirt. A single black feather adorned her fair silken hair and she looked inviting. She glanced toward her stepson. "Ah, madeira ... do pour me a glass as well, Jason." Then she turned toward Mac. "My, how cosy ... have you seen the horrid little room? Yes, I can see that you have. I could have told you it would prove disenchanting ... but you would see for yourselves!"

She placed herself on the sofa facing the hearth at Mac's elbow and smiled rapturously at him. Jenny watched them and was surprised to note that Mac seemed to be encouraging Lillian's lustful whispers.

Conversation became stilted and twenty minutes later Jenny decided to excuse herself. She gave the Earl her hand, which he held a moment, bringing his blue eyes to hers. He said nothing and yet she felt her breath take to the air!

Long after she had washed, undressed, donned her nightgown, and dismissed her maid, Jenny lay awake in her bed. She was wondering with a tingling sensation whether or not he would walk through their communicating door and visit her. She wanted private conversation with him and hoped that he, too, would want to speak with her before he retired. However, deep in her heart she knew he would not visit her room this night. Her pride kept her aloof, but her growing love for him haunted her thoughts ... reminded her of his turbulent kisses. She wanted to surrender herself and her pride into his keeping . . . and then she remembered Lady Hester.

Jenny bit her lower lip, turned her face into her pillow, and felt a twinge of pity for herself.

Armed with sharp cutting sheers and an empty flower basket hanging over her bare arm, Jenny made her way across the front lawns toward the rose garden. She had risen that morning to find the sun grinning at her. She donned a pretty blue muslin gown, swallowed her coffee, planted a straw bonnet upon her head, called for a flower basket and cutting sheers, and finding no one to detain her, off she went. She wiggled her way among the overgrown bushes, selecting the pinkest of the pink buds, clipping them and dropping them into the basket.

Jenny shook her head over the red roses, for they had been allowed to grow wild and had lost their original fullness and richness of color. Aphids covered many of the blooms and Jenny made a mental note to have things set to rights . . . when a hearty voice called her attention.

"I say, Jen . . . revisiting the scene of the crime?" said Mac merrily.

"Good morning, sir. Actually it took quite a bit of determination just to venture this close to the flowers. There is no chance, I assure you, of getting me anywhere near the shed," she said, moving away from the rose bushes and fingering the bouquet she had collected. "These should dress up the hall nicely. The house is so barren of flowers . . . have you noticed, Mac?"

"No. The house has you, Jen. That is more than any house—or man—could ask for," said Mac, his voice strangely distant.

"Why Mac, 'tis not like you to sound so glum!"

"If I sound . . . glum, it is because you are another man's bride." But this time his tone was light and teasing.

She laughed and quizzed him with tilted head. "Ah, but that leaves you free to pursue *that man's* stepmama!"

He gave one of her long chestnut curls a playful yank. "That, Jen, is very naughty of you."

She eyed him and thought him looking his best. He walked beside her, his hands clasped behind his back. His dark hair curled carelessly about his cherubic face. He wore a dark brown riding jacket and buckskin breeches. His cravat was neatly tied and his boots shone. He looked every bit the fashionable gentleman. Jenny remarked upon this and he grinned.

"And so I should. I'm off to visit with m'father's solicitors. Must make a good impression if I'm to handle the thing creditably."

"I do hope your father will recover, Mac," said Jenny, frowning.

"As to that, Jen . . . there is little hope. That is why he wanted to see me established."

"Death—'tis inevitable, and yet I will never get used to the idea of losing someone . . . completely."

"Never say you still pine for John?" asked Mac, one eyebrow up.

"No, not for John. Just for . . . for that kind of love."

"Upon my word, what do you mean. You are married, Jen. Never say you ain't in love with the Earl?" asked Mac, frowning.

Jennifer blushed. "Well, as to that . . . yes, I suppose I am . . . but, you know, Mac . . . well, I couldn't go into details when I wrote to you. Oh lord, I have to be honest with you Mac . . . I always have been. Jason Waine married me in order to inherit—"

"Yes, Jen, that I knew," interrupted Mac quietly. "That is why I came so quickly . . . just in case *you* did not know and were perhaps . . . hurting."

"Oh, Mac, you sweet darling. But the Earl did not deceive me. We made a bargain. He would go his way and I mine. We are married in name only . . . but I think that I have fallen in love with him," she said quietly.

"Oh God, Jen, my Jen," said Mac, suddenly grim. He looked penetratingly at her. "Jen, you say in name only . . . I had heard talk from the servants about the two of you . . . they said he does not visit your room—"

"Mac!"

"Servants do talk, Jen."

"I know that, but I didn't expect you to listen."

"I listen to everything that concerns you."

"What shall I do, Mac?"

178

"Damn the man's eyes," said Mac between grit teeth. "If he takes advantage of you—"

"But Mac, I want you to help me, not damn him! I want him to fall in love with me."

"Jen, would that I could spare you the hurt. God knows you have had enough, but the Earl is a well-known rakehell—"

"Stop it! I won't hear one word of disparagement about him."

"This must be said, Jen. He is used to the wildest of orgies . . . and women. He is not capable of settling down. If he were, he would have done so long since."

She heaved a deep sigh. "All that you say, I know to be true, and yet . . . well, never mind. I see Jason, so hush now!"

They looked up to find Jason with his arm linked through his brother's, both apparently in good spirits and walking toward them.

Julian was the first to wave. "Hallo, you two. What have you been up to. You've missed a grand breakfast . . . for I daresay 'tis all cold by now!"

Jenny patted her nonexistent tummy. "That is what I had intended. Since I've come to Waine, I have been eating too much."

Jason suggested they call for their horses and give them some exercise. Jenny agreed happily and bade them wait for her. She put down the basket of roses, picked up the cutting sheers that had clattered down the steps and deposited them carefully in the basket beside the flowers, and then ran into the house to don her riding clothes.

Jason called for a stable boy to saddle their horses and bring them to the front steps. He then turned to Mac, inquiring politely whether he wished to join them. Mac declined and said that he was off to Dover.

Mac made his way toward the stables, but Julian detained him, saying that his horse could be brought along with theirs.

Jason then excused himself and went back into the house, where he was intercepted by Lillian.

She was looking magnificent in a gown of bright yellow, though she was ornamented with too many jewels and they spoiled the effect. Her rather vague blue eyes were glittering with anger. "Jason, I wish to speak with you."

"Not now, Lillian. I wanted to have a word with my wife, and as we are about to go riding, there just isn't time."

She opened the parlor door. "I must insist, Jason."

He sighed heavily, entered the room, and turned with folded arms to face her. "Well, Lillian?"

"Don't you dare take that attitude with me. Puffed up in your own consequence ... always have been!" she snapped. "I want to know what this is all about—this nonsense you have been putting into my son's head."

"I have not put anything into your son's head, madam," retorted the Earl, irritated.

"He hasn't mentioned his wanting to leave for India for months. Then you come along, and suddenly he begins talking of nothing else. I won't have it ... do you hear me?"

Suddenly Jason relaxed, believing he had been hard on this woman. She had but her one son. The neighbors shunned her, she had virtually no friends, and now her son wished to leave for a foreign land. He found it possible to pity her.

"Listen to me, Lillian. I have not encouraged Julian to take off for India. *He wants* to go. Has an idea of following in our father's footsteps and making himself a fortune. Wants to be rich as a nabob. But it's not the money he is pining for, it's the excitement. He wants to travel, wants to set a goal and attain it. The boy has backbone ... you wouldn't wish it otherwise."

"What do you know ... or care? You have robbed him of his home, his money, and then you encourage him in these foolish schemes. India ... of all the filthy disease-ridden lands—"

"Lillian, this will get us nowhere. I have not encouraged him. He is my brother and I have offered him a sizable sum if he wished to stay on. He does not. He has asked me to put up the blunt for his travels, and I said that I would gladly put up anything he needs. I am also giving him a few recommendations, which he might find useful."

"Oh, Jason, I have never really asked you for anything. Please do not foster this plan of his . . . I could not bear it if he were to leave me."

"Lillian, he is a man. He must make a life for himself . . . and so should you."

Her eyes lit with hatred. She could not understand. "I loathe you, Jason!" She turned on her heel and ran from the room.

Jason Waine watched her go and felt a sadness flicker within. He turned and stared into the empty fireplace, unlit today because they had been hit with sultriness.

Jenny came downstairs hurriedly. She had donned a light green linen riding habit. Her hair had been brushed and pinned in curls all over her head and a small straw hat was tilted prettily upon these. She tripped happily out to the front steps to find the horses standing with only the one groom in attendance. "Where is everyone?" she asked, surprised.

He replied that Master Julian had gone off to the stables after another riding crop, Mr. McMillán had left, and his lordship had not come out yet.

Jenny sighed and looked around, noticing that the flowers were still lying in the basket upon the stone steps. She reached down for the basket handle and was surprised to note that the sheers were on the ground beside the basket. She distinctly remembered placing them inside the basket. She shrugged and took the bundle inside and handed it to Gravesly with instructions to leave the flowers in water until her return.

The front door was still open when the Earl left the parlor and crossed the hall and he was able to catch sight of his wife turning her back to the house. He called hastily, "Jenny!"

She waited for him to come up alongside and smiled at him.

"You look charming . . . I am sorry I have kept you waiting."

"Everyone has kept me waiting! Mac is gone. Julian is off in search of a new riding crop, though I daresay he—ah, here he is now."

"Hallo!" said Julian, mounting his mare. "Bit fidgety,

are you?" he asked his horse, as she was pawing the ground and beginning to champ at her bit.

"Come on, you two," said Julian as his horse circled them.

"Listen to the man!" exclaimed Jenny as her husband hoisted her into her sidesaddle.

They walked their horses down the drive where the roundabout met itself and singled off. Here they posted to the main pike, falling in step alongside one another. A narrow wooded path no more than five feet in width was reached and Julian led them onto it. Jason and Jenny rode alongside each other for a stretch. Jenny allowed her horse to break into a gallop and caught up to Julian. Jason overtook them and walked his horse on ahead.

Julian turned to Jenny and she was startled by the strange glint in his eyes. "We will have a moon tonight. If you like, I'll take you down to the beach and show you those French lights . . . as I promised."

"I think that would be lovely. Perhaps Jason would like to join us?"

Julian's brows rose and then drew together. However, Jason had overheard and held back his horse so that they were standing three abreast.

"Join you . . . join you where?" asked Jason.

"At the beach tonight to see the lights from Calais," replied Jenny.

Jason regarded his brother with a combination of amusement and concealed annoyance. "Why, that sounds delightful. Yes, certainly if you two decide on it, I most *definitely* will join," he said meeting the eyes of his brother.

Julian flushed darkly but made a quick recovery by drawing attention to the upcoming scenery. "All this—" he gestured with his hands—"is Waine land!"

They walked their horses to the clearing where the path forked off, and Julian continued. "If you take this to the right you will reach a creek with a small bridge that gives us access to Bridgewater Farm. Papa had the bridge constructed, as it saves some two hours getting there. The other path leads us onto some of the finest riding territory in this county."

"Well, then, to the left we go. Though I should like to cross the bridge sometime ... it looks lovely," replied Jenny.

"It is. We used to picnic there quite often when we were younger," remembered Julian.

The path did indeed spread out and become a fine riding area. It was a smooth, untroubled stretch. There were few rabbit holes and fewer ruts to disturb their run. Julian, who was in the lead, cursed and they reined in, for they could see the field gate had been locked. "Damnation! I forgot to have the gate left open yesterday. I always jump it, you see. But I don't think you should, Jen."

"Not jump it!" said Jenny defiantly. "Ha!"

Julian turned and went back enough paces to give his horse momentum. He was up and over the obstacle lightly and with an expertise that Jenny admired. She laughed and followed suit, landing a bit more roughly, for the gate was of an unusual height. Jenny and Julian turned and chanted for Jason to follow. He grinned at them and began his run.

Then it happened! So quickly that it left them breathless and stunned. Neither Julian nor Jenny was able to speak, for Jason lay unconscious upon the ground.

Without realizing how she got there, Jenny was at her husband's side. She held his bleeding head in her lap and began sobbing. Julian was right beside her. Somehow the impossible had happened and Jason's saddle strap had given way ... but there was no time to speculate upon how and why. She cradled the Earl's head and noted that the cut was not deep, but the blood was making his black locks sticky and he had a pale look about him. She tore off a piece of her petticoat and patted the blood gently, calling his name. It was no more than a moment, though it seemed an eternity to Jenny, before the Earl opened his eyes and blinked at them. "What ... the ..." he said feebly, making an attempt to move.

"Be still, Jason, don't get up yet," pleaded Jenny agitatedly.

The Earl held his aching head but managed a smile. "Don't be a zany, love. I am quite able to stand up," he said proceeding to prove his statement by getting to his feet and reeling.

Julian had half expected this and managed to catch him with both arms. Jason fell heavily upon his young brother's form and he smiled wryly. "More fool I."

"Quite!" agreed Julian with an admirable effort at a laugh.

They stood thus, Julian and Jenny eyeing the Earl with misgivings, until the Earl's eyes found his saddle. "How the devil did that happen?"

He took a few unsteady strides and went down upon his knees, fingering the saddle straps with a frown. Jenny followed him to the woeful heap of leather humped upon the warm earth. Her eyes followed his hands to the strap he held.

"By God!" came Jason's voice, low and harsh.

Julian bent down to feel and see what Jason had discovered. The strap he was holding had been severed—not with age, or wear, but cleanly and deliberately.

Jenny looked from one to the other. "What . . . tell me, what is it? Why do you two look like that?"

Julian spoke before Jason could stop him. "It's the strap, Jen! Someone . . . some demon has cut the strap!" His face was deathly white.

Immediately Jenny's thoughts went to the shears. She had been sure she had left them in the basket, but when she had returned, they were on the ground! "Oh no . . . oh pray, Julian, what are you saying?" she asked, her voice rising to a hysterical note.

Jason stood up and put an arm about his wife. "Nothing, my sweet life . . . please do not mind Julian's fancies. He is mistaken."

Julian looked at first bewildered and then contrite. "Lord, Jen, I'm . . . well, I'm an addlebrained blackguard for pitching such gammon at you."

"No, you are not at all a rattleprate, Julian, and that strap *was* cut! Oh faith, Jason!" She turned desperate eyes to her husband. "You . . . you might have been killed!"

184

They stood in the clearing and eyed one another. The meaning was too dreadful to voice. And yet it was there . . . not to be denied!

## Chapter Seventeen

A solemn graveness held the returning party silent. The saddle had been left behind and Jason rode slowly beside his wife and brother, seated on his roan's bare back.

When they reached the front steps, Jason slipped off his horse, observed Julian aid Jenny off hers, and excused himself, refusing to have a doctor called in to see to his bruises. Jenny pleaded with her sad dark eyes but he flicked her nose, saying he wanted nothing more than a hot bath and a change of raiment.

Julian and Jenny stood transfixed, watching his retreating form.

"I . . . I am so frightened Julian . . . and daren't think," faltered Jenny still shaken.

"Well, I ain't! Someone is going to pay for all these tricks!"

"Never say you think that the same person who locked me in the shed slit the strap of Jason's saddle?" asked Jenny, surprised.

"Well, what else must I think? I tell you what, Jen. Those two young scalawags are getting out of hand. They don't know the difference between a prank and dangerous tampering."

"I can't believe that they are behind this," said Jenny, shaking her head.

"Depend upon it. Thought Jase would tumble off onto the lawn. They were probably hidden in the thicket, waiting to see and have a laugh over it."

"They . . . must be aware that such a nasty trick could

get the rider hurt. And they are very attached to Jason ... why would they want to laugh at his expense?" argued Jenny.

"I don't know, Jen ... but I mean to find out. Are you coming?"

She shook her head. "No, you go ahead. I want to sort things out alone for a while." He left her abruptly and went into the house in search of the boys.

She turned and found the stable boy leading the horses to their stalls. Impulsively, Jenny dashed after him and found that he was the same young lad she had conversed with earlier.

He looked up at her, startled, and hastened to assure her that he had already sent his brother with the cart to fetch his lordship's saddle.

"That is all very well, but 'tis not what I wished to speak with you about," replied Jenny gently. "I would like you to think about this morning and tell me honestly—you needn't fear reprisal—were you with the horses the entire time after they were brought from the stables?"

"If you are thinking that I put a saddle on without checking his lordship's strap m'lady, you be wrong!" said the boy defensively. "Couldn't have done such a thing—"

"Yet the strap is broken, lad," interrupted Jenny quickly. "However, if you say that you would have noticed a worn strap, I believe you. What I asked was not intended to put any blame on you. I merely want to know if you were with the horses after they were saddled, and whether or not you remained with those horses until we took charge of them?"

The boy eyed her suspiciously, for this still sounded to him as though it might lead to bringing down blame on his head. However, his instinct told him Jenny would not cause him any hurt and so he answered. "Well, m'lady," he said, scratching his dust-covered burnished hair, "I saddled the horses, brought 'em up front, and then Master Julian—he told me to go fetch his riding crop."

"I—I see. Then Master Julian was alone with the horses?" she asked, feeling as though her heart were being pumped beyond its natural size.

"No, m'lady. There was Mr. Howard with him ... and

186

the new gentleman, Mr. McMillan. They were with him a bit."

"What? You say Mr. Howard was there? I did not see him. No one advised me that he was here this morning."

The boy gazed at her and rubbed his nose with one of the leather leading strings he held in his worn, grimy hands. "Don't know 'bout that, m'lady. Just know he was here."

"Yes, of course. But then, what happened? For you said that you went to fetch a riding crop for Master Julian, yet when I came out, I found you with the horses . . . not Julian."

" 'Twasn't my fault, m'lady. Master Julian . . . he swore at me, said 'tweren't the right crop I brought. Off he goes in a huff. Then ol' Griddles—that's the head groom—he calls me, so I hurries off, leaving the horses with Mr. Howard and t'other fellow. When I gets back, they both were gone. Weren't my fault. How's I to know they'd up and leave the horses standing like that? Though, in truth, that gent McMillan did have his 'orse awaiting. But I thought Mr. Howard would be there a spell. How was I to know they'd all go off and leave the 'orses like that?" the boy wailed.

Jenny stood there, frowning, but bade the boy continue, for she assured him she put no blame on his shoulders.

"Nothing more to tell, m'lady. Then you came out, spoke to me, and then off you went back into the house. Then up comes Master Julian and sends me off to Griddles again . . . and that's all I can tell you."

Jenny studied the boy for a moment and then spoke to him authoritively. "Now listen, lad, you are not to speak to anyone of our little discussion—anyone other than his lordship, that is. If the Earl should question you, then, of course, you will answer him. However, I want your word of honor that our little talk will go no further. Somehow, a . . . a practical joke was inaugurated, and it got a little out of hand and I want no unnecessary gossip."

"No one ever asked for my word of honor before, m'lady," said the boy, puffing out his chest. " 'Tis that you have and anything else *you* want!"

Jenny unbuttoned her riding jacket and took out a sixpence from the inner pocket and placed it in the boy's hand. He stared disbelievingly at the fortune and began a series of bows that did not end until Jenny had left the stables.

Jenny returned to the house, her countenance grim and her thoughts in a turmoil. She made her way toward the stairs, when she was attracted by the sound of voices in the dining room. She knew it was wrong . . . but then, so was that severed strap, so she bolstered herself and stepped toward the door, putting her head against the wood.

"How dare you, Howard . . . and how could you? Just yesterday you held me in your arms . . . and now . . ."

Howard Waine sounded incredulous. "Only yesterday? Lillina, how can you? It is over . . . has been over these three months and more. Now don't make us any more wretched then we already are!"

"Over! Who was it, then, only two weeks ago that rested his head on my pillow? Why, Howard, have you forgotten that night?"

Howard Waine had the good grace to stutter. "Y-you take unfair advantage, m-madam! I . . . I do not like to say things to you that may hurt, but you leave me no choice. 'Twas *my* pillow . . . for you came to *my* cottage. And as for the rest . . . well, there is no denying that you are a beautiful woman and that I am only human. I make no excuse for myself in this cursed situation, but pray, Lillian, we . . . we were never in love with each other—you cannot possibly claim that, especially after last night!"

"What do you mean 'after last night'?" asked Lillian.

"You were seen, Lillian," said Howard Waine quietly.

"Seen? Damn you, what do you mean?"

"You were seen leaving Mr. McMillan's room in the early hours of the morning!"

Jenny sucked in her breath on the other side of the door and had a moment in which to be shocked, as Lillian did not immediately answer this accusation.

"By God, 'tis that little witch—Helen! I thought I heard a sound from the stairs leading to her quarters. How dare she? Well, let me tell you something, Howard Waine, you

188

haven't wanted anyone but that little creature since the first time you saw her. I felt it at the time. But you won't get her ... do you know why? No, I can see you don't. Because my son has had her ... had her from the first week she was here ... had her these three months and more!"

Jenny could almost see Howard Waine shaking Lillian and heard his cold brutal voice come between clenched teeth. "Be quiet! I won't hear any more of your filthy lies! I came in here to question you with regards to my cousin Jason."

"Question me?" said Lillian with a hysterical note.

"Damnation, yes, Lillian. The Wendall boys gave me the news just moments ago that someone cut the strap on Jason's saddle. Apparently your son tried to blame Jamie and Peter, but that won't fadge."

" 'Tis their doing, depend on it. And at any rate, 'tis none of your affair."

"Oh, you think it is none of my affair when my cousin has apparently had an attempt made on his life—especially when the only person who stands to gain by Jason's death is his brother Julian!"

There, the unspeakable was out in the open, thought Jenny on the other side of the door.

"You ... you repulsive parasite!" screeched Lillian Waine. "I should like to remind you that *if* an attempt has been made on Jason's life, it was an extremely poor one since he has survived it with but a mere scratch! *Secondly,* my son is not the only one who stands to gain by Jason's death. What of yourself? What of all the extra little bonuses you have been hiding away from the Waine estate all these years? Perhaps Jason was coming too close to the truth? What of that last purchase—that new grinding mill—did Jason discover that you made a nice percentage on that? Well, did he?"

Presumably Howard Waine found this practically unanswerable, for it was a long while before Jenny heard his response. His voice came unsteadily. "You are mistaken, Lillian. And, indeed, you are a fool ... among other things!"

Jenny heard him cross the floor and she rushed to the

stairs just as he slammed out of the dining room and to the front doors, which Gravesly held open for him.

Jenny looked at Gravesly, whom it seemed came out of the woodwork. Where had he been standing? Had he seen her eavesdropping? Gravesly retired to the kitchen without looking up at Jenny and she sped up the stairs and hurriedly ran into her room. She plopped herself upon her bed and put her hands to her head.

This had become a nightmare of stupendous proportions. She had learned much, almost too much. Ugh, she shuddered. Faith, Howard Waine—who had reminded her of a minister on their first meeting—had been having an affair with a woman ten years older than himself. Her own dear Mac, who was even younger than Howard, had actually . . . . My Goodness, she thought, shaking her head, Lillian Waine seems to prefer younger men . . . or perhaps that is all that is available to her here at Waine!

But worse than these sordid revelations was the fact that she knew in her heart that the cutting shears had been used to sever Jason's saddle strap! Both Julian and Howard Waine had had the opportunity—for that matter, even Lillian had had the chance to do the thing. Was it really possible that Howard had been stealing from the estate? Had Jason discovered him . . . or was he about to?

She stood up and ran to Jason's communicating door and knocked frantically.

Jason opened the door himself, saw the expression on his wife's countenance, and dismissed his valet. He was wearing his buff-colored breeches, and his black shining hessians with the gold tassels, and nothing else. Ordinarily this would have brought the blush to Jenny's cheeks, but at the moment her mind was too busy to take notice.

"My dearest child, what is it? Why do you look so frantic?" said the Earl soothingly.

For answer, Jenny rushed headlong into his arms. He held her a while, stroking her hair silently, waiting to hear what was troubling her.

Without thinking, for she was beyond that now, she had thrown herself against him. Her hands pressed against his bare broad chest and she was conscious suddenly of a safe, secure feeling. At that moment she only knew that she loved this great, handsome man and wanted him away from these clouds of doubts.

"Jason, oh, Jason. I'm so afraid."

He wedged his hand between her chin and his chest, forcing her face upward. "Look at me, Jen." He waited for her eyes to meet his. "There . . . now let me first tell you that there is nothing to be frightened about. You have been jumping to conclusions, I can see that. It is quite possible that the strap was not deliberately cut . . . a nail may have torn through it when it was hanging in the stables—"

"No, the stable boy says that he would have noticed if the strap was worn in any way!"

"Ah, you have already spoken with the stable boy. That should have been left to me, Jen. We don't want any unnecessary gossip running rife here—"

Again she interrupted. "He . . . doesn't know why I questioned him . . . and has already promised not to discuss it . . . with anyone."

"All right then, let us just say that the lad is mistaken and did not notice that the strap was damaged and is afraid to own up to it."

"No, Jason, I do not believe that."

"Then the only other answer is that the Wendall boys were out for a lark and misjudged the sort of prank they were playing."

"*You* do not believe that."

"No, I believe that the stable boy did not notice the strap was about to give way."

"But, Jason, both Howard and . . . and Julian were alone with the horses and"—

"Stop it, Jen! That is beneath you. You cannot possibly think that either of them would stoop to such a thing? For what—money? Howard has no reason, Jen. He stands to lose a great deal more with me dead, for he does not really get along with Julian and might lose his post if Julian were head of the household."

Jenny looked away from him and said quietly, "Is it possible that Howard has not been totally honest with regards to the management of the estate?"

He took her face in both his hands. "Jenny, Jenny, all

this is the most absurd nonsense. It is, of course, immensely gratifying to see you so concerned over my welfare ... but you need not be!"

Suddenly she realized that she was being held most intimately by the Earl and that he was half naked! She jumped back with a hand to her mouth and blushed an adorable shade of pink. "Oh, my lord!"

However, it was too late, for the Earl had chuckled and quickly swept her up in his arms. His voice was low and full with tender amusement.

"Now, my little sleuth...." His lips touched hers gently, yet possessively, but she stiffened and he quickly put her away from him, only the flicker of his eyes betraying the control he was exerting upon himself.

Jenny looked doubtfully up at him. Her lips felt as though they were on fire and her body was trembling from his touch. She could not deny to herself what she felt for him ... and at this moment there was a look on his face that hinted of his heart. Yet he spoke not of love and Jenny's eyes fell.

"Jenny, I have to go into town and won't be back for a while. I don't want you playing the sleuth and speaking to anyone of my little incident. Forget about it all. Do you understand, Jen?"

She nodded gravely but said nothing and turned to go, but his voice halted her. "Jen ... be careful, my pretty. And when I return, we'll go off alone, you and I ... we have much to discuss."

Her eyes met his fleetingly, but as he said nothing more, she moved away and entered her room, leaving him to finish dressing.

# Chapter Eighteen

Helen Browne strolled past the hothouse and shouted for the boys impatiently. She was out of temper these days and found her job as governess trying and unbearably dull. She wanted and yearned for excitement and she still wanted Julian.

She had accepted the post as governess in the Waine household a little more than three months before because she had no other choice. She was the daughter of a local shopkeeper who had died penniless. She had thanked Providence and her father's foresight for having spent every extra penny he had on her education. At least she had that. It had enabled her to apply at the Waine estate ... an estate rich with bachelors. She had hoped the Earl would come to stay, but when he seemed out of reach, she turned her eyes toward Julian. After all, she told herself, Julian's mother was naught but an innkeeper's offspring, and so she set her cap at the handsome boy's feet.

Even in her drab gowns, Helen Browne's figure was attractive and she could on occasion create an aura of prettiness about herself that Julian had been quick to notice. He was himself bored in the country and not adverse to the idea of having a mistress at hand. However, as time progressed, Helen began to hint of marriage and he realized he had best put a stop to her fanciful notions.

Helen had hoped for a child with which to trap him, but this had not come about. She had tried everything to force his hand, but had only succeeded in turning him away. Yet until Jenny had come to Waine Castle, he had still come to her room at night. But suddenly he stopped altogether, and Helen Browne blamed this on Jenny.

The Wendall boys had been dodging the adults after

Julian's thundering accusation earlier that morning. However, Helen Browne had spotted them, so they saw there was nothing for it but to come forward out of the thicket.

"Go to the schoolroom . . . it is time for your lessons. And goodness, do wash up first. You are both a ghastly mess!"

"No!" said Jamie, looking straight at her.

Helen Browne had always had a difficult time with the Wendall boys, yet they had never before openly defied her. She was surprised by it and stared hard at Jamie. "Whatever do you mean?"

"Don't mean to be rude, Miss Helen, but we don't want to and we don't think we have to listen to you anymore. You are no better than the other governesses we've had. In fact, Miss Helen, Peter and I think you are not altogether respectable!"

Miss Browne was too stunned to speak. She recouped herself enough to hiss, "How dare you? What do you know of such things? Now, do not defy me any longer! Go to the schoolroom at once!"

The younger Wendall pulled at his brother's white sleeve. "Perhaps we better, Jamie. Don't want to stir up a fuss."

Jamie eyed his brother severely. "Hush up, Peter! We are not going in yet, Miss Helen, and that is final!"

Miss Helen's face drained of color and the two young boys suddenly appeared before her eyes as two sly devils. She gritted her teeth, for she was not sure what had brought on their attack. "We will discuss this later. For the time being I shall let it pass because I am not feeling at all well today. You may go now. But be sure this will not be passed over!" She then watched them disappear again into the thicket and turned and quickly managed a sunny expression for the man who bore grimly down upon her.

Howard Waine's grave aspect was more severe than usual. There were tight lines about his mouth and he greeted Miss Browne solemnly.

"Why, Howard, whatever is the matter?"

He gazed at Helen Browne longingly. He had been in love with her almost from their first meeting. She was everything he had ever wanted. She was demure, and to him, infinitely alluring. He liked her quiet reserve and the hidden sparkle in her eyes. He had been all too aware that she was infatuated with his younger cousin, Julian. He knew that Julian did not love Helen and thought that with time her infatuation would lose itself. He had courted her gently, wooed her tenderly, and she had returned only friendship. Yet this had been enough to sustain him. It carried him and reaffirmed his belief that he would be able to win her over with time.

Lillian Waine had thrust a blow to his heart, for he had never even suspected that Julian had really noticed Helen. He had thought it had gone no further than a one-sided platonic inclination on her part. The idea that she had been Julian's mistress—might be still—hurt him as nothing before ever had. He knew not what he would do and hoped against hope that Lillian had lied.

"Are you free for a while, Helen. I . . . I need to talk to you," he said, as though his body were bursting from within.

"Of course, Howard," she responded at once. She liked Howard Waine, had, in fact, a very deep regard for him. She had been interested in her own welfare for so long that it often surprised her when she found herself caring for this big grave man. She had often wished to reach out and reassure him, for she was aware of his attachment for her; but there was her future to think of . . . there was Julian, who would one day be rich! Helen Browne saw the distress in his eyes and frowned, waiting for him to speak.

"I have just come from a . . . a discussion with Lillian. She has made some very ugly remarks. I am sorry, Helen, I'm afraid *I* brought these on by allowing it to slip that I knew of her liaison with the new guest."

"Oh no, Howard, how could you?"

"It . . . it was unavoidable at the time. At any rate, she has made some nasty accusations with regards to my honesty as acting agent of the Waine estates. However, that is not what troubles me. What has me worried on that score is that there *is something* I did not wish Jason to discover for a few months yet to come. An experiment I took up with the Bridgewater Farm tenants. It entailed an additional expense, which will not prove itself worthwhile for some months to come. I was really hoping to . . . to astound Jason with my cleverness by waiting for the September harvest. I now see that it will look very strange, indeed."

"Oh, Howard, why did you want it kept a secret?"

"You see, though I am agent for the Waine estates, Jason was only able to entrust the eastern lands to my management. He has other properties near Nottingham and Bath that are managed by his lawyers. I hoped that this particular experiment would prove my ability . . . and that I would then be given the *entire* estate. It would mean a very comfortable income and a larger house."

"I—I see," she said quietly.

"I wanted that attractive income, and the larger home, for . . . for *you*, Helen."

She stopped and turned to look into his face and saw deep in his eyes a pain. Her hand reached out and touched his cheek. He held her hand over his face and lowered it to his mouth, kissing it desperately, and she felt his tears wet against her fingers.

"Oh my God . . . oh my God. What else did Lillian say to you? What else, Howard?"

For it dawned on her that Lillian might have told him about herself and Julian.

"It doesn't matter. I know her for the contemptible prevaricator that she is. I . . . I knew that you were interested in Julian. There is nothing in that. . . ."

"Oh, Howard, Howard, you deserve better. I cannot accept your very sweet offer."

"Helen? . . ."

"No. Now, there is something else we must discuss—you are going to have problems with Jason Waine, and we cannot allow that."

"No, I know, I don't have the receipts for the cash expenditures . . . I merely recorded the cost without view to being questioned."

"No receipts? Howard, if Lillian were to make a scene over this, she might convince Jason of almost anything."

"Yes, I know. I shall have to think of something to retrieve my position. But . . . Helen!"

She cut him short quickly. "Howard!" came her scream. "Did you see that creature?"

"Good Lord, yes. We can't have a wild boar so close to the Castle. It could be dreadfully dangerous."

"Yes, it could," said Helen quietly. "We should arrange to have it disposed of as soon as possible ... don't you think?"

In spite of Jason's desire for secrecy with regards to what he insisted on referring to as an accident, the house buzzed with the news. By that afternoon there was no one who had not heard about his fall and discussed the various aspects of the mystery.

Jenny had gone to her room, washed, and changed her riding habit for a day gown of yellow organza sashed with a wide brown velvet ribbon at her waist. Her bonnet was made of straw and ornamented with the same shade of brown that encompassed her small waist. She made her way unnoticed to the back courtyard, where she found Julian gazing out across the gate to the sea. He turned when he heard her footstep and came up to her quickly, taking both her hands in his and raising them to his lips. "You look a beauty, Jen. Not still upset, are you?"

She shook her head, for she felt there was no sense in saying she was, for he would then try and convince her she should not be. He drew her hand through his arm and gently guided her through the open gate to the precipice overlooking the dark waters.

She was aware of a tender glint about his eyes as he said softly, "I'll pass on that walk of ours tonight, for I have just remembered that I am engaged with friends ... and would probably be sad company for you and the Earl."

"Why, Julian, how so?"

"I could not with any degree of equanimity watch you walk beneath the stars with my brother," he said quietly.

"Julian!" said Jenny, truly shocked.

Suddenly he laughed and pinched her cheek. "I know, I'm an artful thing and should be horsewhipped for flirting with you so ... but you are an irresistible creature, and my blood is all meridian!"

They walked about a bit and then he led her into the house for lunch. This was a gruesome experience because Lillian was in a terrible temper. Finally Jenny escaped, though Julian did not join her. She walked toward the hothouse and hoped something would soon be done about its appearance. She then turned her back upon it and faced the sea. After a few moments she sighed and retraced her steps toward the castle. She hugged the sidewall of the gray stone and was surprised when she noticed two huge evergreen trees standing staunchly alone. They had grown ungainly with time. Odd, she thought, gazing at the two trees. They were clumped together without rhyme or reason ... and yet had been planted there. They were the only attempt at landscaping around the Castle, and caused her to remember something Johnny had once taught her. Look for a landmark, he had said when they were out in the piney woods. A landmark—Jenny's eyes lit up! He had taught her to pick out something that stood out differently from the rest of her surroundings. That way, he had explained, "you won't get yourself lost, girl." Jenny came closer and touched the dark bushy yew. Poor things, you have been sadly neglected and need a good pruning. She bent down and picked a clump of the weathered small needles, thinking they would make good mulch for her roses ... and there it was.

She could not believe what she was seeing, but there, beneath one low green branch, was something round and rusted. She brushed the needles that partially covered it and found it hard to contain her excitement.

A rusted heavy metal ring about the size of a grapefruit caused her heart to throb. She pulled at it, but it came off in her hands. She threw it down impatiently and went down upon her knees, unmindful of her dress. She brushed at the dirt and weeds and found a metal hoop, weathered and cracked with age. Beneath that she spied traces of a solid metal plank. She would have to dig away some of the dirt, she thought, and got to her feet, remembering the storage shed in the rear courtyard. She hurried there and pulled open its wide weathered wooden door. There she found several shelves that held many assorted tools. A shovel emerged, and then she gave a squeal of delight as a crowbar came forth. Thus heavily armed, Jenny returned to her discovery. Heedless of her dainty hands, she attacked the shallow layer of earth and uncovered the metal shield. Some twenty minutes later, with a gown now torn and muddied from exertion, Jenny felt the shield move. She heaved a thankful sigh, rested a moment, and then managed to tilt the plate upward. Lord, but this is heavy, she thought ruefully. However did those Jacobites get in and out before they were seen?

The metal plate was up and Jenny was able to slide it to one side. She almost leaped with unbridled joy. Priest's hole, indeed. She had discovered the secret tunnel! For there before her were the stone steps. She ran back to the storage shed and grabbed the lantern she had seen earlier. She lit it and returned to the opening. Slowly and gingerly she descended the steps. It was a steep decline and she pressed her hands against the cold stone wall for support. She reached the bottom and put her lantern up before her, peering around in the blackness of the narrow walk. Whoever had built this had done a good job, she thought. There were oak beams siding the walls and the ceiling, and although the floor was made of dirt, it was as hard as stone. The walls seemed to be made of rock and minerals. She treaded carefully, remembering something Jason had said about rats, bats, and other odious creatures she had no wish to meet. It did not take her long, even at that slow pace, to attain the end of the passageway and another set of steps. She mounted these and was obliged to bend her head when she came to the top step. The exit was totally different than the entrance. This panel was made of wood and Jenny wondered how it had stood up against nature's forces. Even the heavy metal had corroded from the salt air. She felt along its edges and found what she had been looking for—a hinge! "A hinge!" she said out loud. "That means with a little push, you should swing open," she said hopefully.

She gave it a little push, and then another. It took, in fact, several hard shoves to get the trap door to creak. Finally she managed, by putting her shoulder to work, to get the thing open. She found it much harder to scramble out of the opening than she had to scramble in. The stairs had not been constructed so that a lady could gracefully emerge, and she found that she had to exert some effort in the process. However, when she finally emerged, it was with no little elation! She had come out to find herself in the hothouse! She had never been inside before, and scanned her surroundings. There were many garden chairs and tables strewn about and the trapdoor was secluded in the corner. She marveled that Julian had never found it. Really, it was so easy. One could leave by way of the courtyard—drop literally out of sight and lay low in the tunnel—or make one's way to the greenhouse. Jenny closed the trapdoor and surveyed it. One could not see the hinges from this side . . . and with the entire floor to examine, she supposed it could be overlooked. She wiped her hands against each other, but as both hands were quite black, this did nothing more than spread the dirt a bit more evenly. Dismayed, she looked down at what *had* been an exquisite gown. Oh, good gracious, I must run back and change before Jason comes in! She made her way back to the evergreens and replaced the metal lid, spread out the needles, and shoved some of the dirt back over the plate in an effort to hide the telltale evidence. She picked up her tools and ran back to the courtyard shed and replaced them and the lantern. Hurriedly, she turned the corner and started for the stairs and ran directly into Mac.

"Hallo there, just the lady I wished—by jove, what has happened, Jenny? Are you all right? You look as though you have been attacked by the lord knows what. Dash it, Jen, speak up! You've got me reeling!" said Mac, really concerned.

Jenny had to think quickly and the only thing she could come up with was, "Oh, I have been gardening, and I'm afraid I slipped and fell. 'Tis nothing," she said, for the first time telling Mac a lie.

"Gardening, is it?" he looked past her and then swept her a sunny smile. "You are bamming me—afraid I'll tell the Earl? Now, Jenny, you know better!"

"Honestly, Mac, you know what I am about flowers."

"Yes, I remember. Look, m'girl, if you go and change, I'll take you for a walk."

She beamed. "Oh, good. We have had so little time together. Will you wait for me here . . . or in the front?"

He played with the fobs at his waist. "Here, Jen. Now, don't be long!"

She scurried into the house and up the back staircase, which put her at the far end of the second-floor hallway. Her she made a wild dash for her room. She found the wash water had cooled considerably, but did not dare ask Joan to bring up hot water, lest it attract attention. She suffered through the ordeal, stuffed her gown beneath the bed, donned her white and blue, brushed her hair, hid her muddied slippers, and grimaced over her feet. She took another minute to pour water into her foot basin, raised her skirts and dipped her feet. When the remaining signs of tunnel exploration had been washed away, she scurried back the way she had come. The entire procedure had taken her less than thirty minutes, leaving her quite proud, though somewhat exhausted.

Mac stood in the courtyard, patiently awaiting her reappearance. She went toward him, giving him her hand. "I hope I haven't kept you too long."

"You are amazing, Jen. I have never known a woman who could change in less than an hour . . . and yet, here you stand!"

She giggled. "Here I stand . . . and here I might fall. I'm very close to needing hartshorn."

"Where would you like to stroll, Jen?" he asked, bowing gallantly.

Suddenly she remembered that he had spent the night with Lillian Waine, and because this was still fresh in her mind, she reacted a bit stiffly. "I have never taken the east path."

"What is it? What is wrong, Jen?" asked Mac, sensing her reserve and unused to it.

"Nothing, oh, nothing at all, Mac. I suppose I am just a bit tired."

"Then let us go inside and relax, child."

"No, I want to have this time with you." She sighed. "Mac, something awful has happened this morning!"

"I know. It was all over Dover before I took my leave," he said, his aspect grave.

"My goodness, Jason won't like that. What are they saying?"

"Simply that the Earl met with an accident. Can't keep people from jabbering about a thing like that. Bound to be all sorts of speculation regarding it. However, I daresay there is nothing to it! *I* don't think for a moment that it could have been deliberate, so don't worry your pretty head over it."

"But what if it was . . . deliberate?"

"Couldn't be! It is not possible to think that Julian attempted such a dastardly trick. And who else has enough cause? You can be sure the strap was cut by careless handling, and overlooked—nothing more!"

Jenny did not think it right to spread gossip, and as what she had overheard Lillian accuse Howard of was unproved suspicion, she could not bring herself to speak her doubts about Howard. They rambled on the worn path, which ran parallel to the sea until the path forked, leading to a wooded path.

"Shall we continue along the sea, Jen, or will you trust me beside you in the thick of the woods?"

She laughed. "It won't be the first time I have trusted you, sir, in the thick of the woods."

They made their way slowly into the rich green forest, but had not gone more than twenty feet when Jenny stopped short and clutched at Mac's arm.

Jason Waine was leaning back against a white birch tree. Jenny could just make out his profile . . . and that of the golden-haired Lady Hester! Jenny blinked, for he had said he was going into town, and she could not believe he had lied . . . and yet, here he was. She was seeing it with her own eyes. Hearing all with her own ears.

"Oh, my darling Jason, if only you had waited, we would not now have to be separated . . . meeting like this," said Lady Hester, pressing herself against the Earl, putting her hands to his shoulders. "Don't you see, Jason, Sir Giles died in time for you to marry me and fulfill the terms of your father's will. Whatever are we to do with that child now in our way?"

Jenny could not see the Earl's expression, but she did see Lady Hester's and what she saw there caused her heart to explode. She didn't wait to hear any more. She couldn't wait to see the Earl take the woman into his arms. All she could think was, Jason is here . . . with her . . . listening to her.

She picked up her skirts, and without waiting for Mac, ran desperately back toward the house. Mac chased after her, calling her name when he was a safe enough distance from Jason Waine's hearing. "Jen!" he shouted as he caught her by the arm. She shrugged him off furiously.

"Leave me, Mac. I have been a stupid, stupid fool! He is everything you said he was—everything! He lies with his eyes. Oh, Mac, I feel as though I am breaking!" she cried and took off again wildly. She ran past the trees, down the winding path, thinking, "How, how did you ever think you could hold him. Why, why did his eyes speak of love? Why, why did his kiss speak of tenderness, of depths? . . . She sobbed and the tears slid down her cheek. Could a man be so cruel? He talked of having a child . . . he said he wanted to hurry back to be with me . . . while all the time he was planning to meet her!

She brushed the tears away from her cheek and somehow found her way back to the house. She ran past a startled Gravesly to the parlor door, flung it open, and thankful that it was empty, rushed inside. She threw herself on the couch, and determined that she would not cry, gripped her fingers until the knuckles were white and the fingers purple. She tried to school her thoughts and regain her composure.

Mac entered and came to her side at once. "Jenny, listen to me, girl. It may not be what you think. It was probably an accidental meeting. Perhaps the Earl was out looking for you, and Lady Hester came along . . . anyone can see that she is a forward piece. 'Twas not *he* that did the talking. Dash it, Jen! You are, after all, jumping to conclusions."

"How can you say that to me?" said Jenny, swinging around on the sofa to stare at him. "I have seen and heard them. She was and is his mistress! He told me he was going to town . . . and instead he was with *her*!"

203

"Deuce take it, girl, stop your prating! He *was* in town—saw him there myself! I tell you, girl, that he has just returned. He was probably looking about for you and came across Lady Hester instead."

Jenny sniffed. "Then why go into the woods with her?"

"Silly chit, what's in that? You were in the woods with me."

"That is different. I was not in your arms," she said, putting up her chin.

"That, m'girl was no fault of yours," said Mac teasingly.

She giggled tearfully at this and he put his arm around her shoulders, drawing her head against his chest and patting her fondly. "My sweet Jen, you are naught but a child. The Earl can't help but love you. I would myself if you didn't have this lamentable habit of always ruining my best coats by crying into them."

A trembling giggle again escaped her, for it did seem as though it was Mac she always sobbed her troubles to. She gave him a warm embrace. "Oh Mac, dearest and best of friends, what would I do without your support?"

Neither of them had heard the door open silently and close. The Earl's voice sounded across the room like a whiplash and they jumped apart.

"Do I intrude?" said the Earl, his voice harsh. "If so, I do most humbly beg pardon. But I wish to have a talk with *my wife* . . . in private. I am sure you understand, sir." He looked darkly across at Mac.

Mac nodded stiffly, stood up, and took Jenny's hand, dropping a kiss upon it and giving her a quick wink. "If you need me, all you have to do is call. I shall be within easy reach!"

He then made his way to the door, and with a final smile at Jenny, left the room.

The Earl and Jennifer faced each other, each waiting for the sound of Mac's retreating footsteps.

It was Jenny who broke the awful silence. She said, her eyes blazing, "Well—my lord?"

"I should like to know, Lady Waine, why you were in McMillan's arms when I so inconveniently and thoughtlessly interrupted you?" said the Earl, feeling as though he were being ignited from the deep recesses of his mind.

Jenny gasped, *"My lord!"* she gave a short, hard laugh and said with cold disgust, "If you will excuse me, I think I will retire to my room." She rose and started to move. However, he stepped in front of her, blocking her path, and ruthlessly grabbed hold of her arm, pulling her to him. His voice came stingingly hard. "You have not answered me, Jenny!"

"I do not think your question deserves an answer!" She was wild now and stood defiantly glaring at him, her face a storm of emotions.

"Oh ... don't you? I find that singularly interesting! You were in here alone, and in the arms of another man, and yet brazenly advise me that it needs no explanation!" He delivered this in the way of a slap.

She pulled away from him, bruising her bare arm in the process. She felt her face burn as she lost all self-control. Her words came spilling out. *"You—you disgust me!* You stand there and coolly interrogate me about my apparently questionable activities ... when you have just this moment returned from the arms of Lady Hester!"

There it was out. She had not meant to tell him that she knew, and a sob escaped her. She put her hand to her mouth and turned her tormented eyes away, racing out of the room before he could prevent her. Indeed, he was too stunned to do so!


# Chapter Nineteen

*Much ado there Was, God Wot,*
*He would love and she would not.*
NICHOLAS BRETON, 1591


The Earl sank down upon the sofa. Here now, he thought, here now was something unexpected. He had thought he had heard the rustle of skirts when Hester had delivered her moving heart renderings. He had dallied only long enough to tell the lovely lady that it was ended between them. He had agreed to meet her for that sole purpose. Theirs was a finished affair. He had left her abruptly, for he disliked scenes and the lady had given every indication that she was about to enact one. He had come rushing back to the Castle, for he was anxious to be with Jenny. Then he had opened the door and found his wife in McMillan's arms. He was quite certain that Jenny's affection for the fellow was sisterly. He had no doubt that there was an explanation ... and yet his jealousy had won over.

He could not bear with complacency the sight of her, for any reason, in that particular position with anyone other than himself. He found even the sight of her in conversation with his brother Julian shot hot fluid through his veins. He had never felt that way over a woman before, and it was beginning to wear on him. Her attitude had galled him to unfathomable rage. Then all at once she had stunned him with her spitfire announcement. Jenny had obviously seen Lady Hester at the moment the confounded woman had flung herself into his arms. Apparently Jenny had waited for no more ... and it had been the rustle of Jenny's skirts that he had heard. The Earl rubbed his chin and cursed the fates for having put Jenny on that particular path at that precise moment!

Here now was his problem. He had made his farewells to Lady Hester, not because of any strong desire to be faithful to the woman he loved, but simply because he no longer wanted the fair Hester. Jason Waine wanted only one woman, she was his wife. However, he had never thought very deeply on the question of constancy. He knew himself to be in love with Jenny. He wanted only Jenny ... at the moment. He heaved a sigh and stretched out his long legs and crossed them at the ankles.

He placed his hands over each other, covering his temple, and closed his blue eyes. Now Jason Waine, what do you intend to do? he asked himself ruefully. You lust after no other woman *now* ... but who is to say when you might again? Jenny will have you on her terms only— and those terms call for faithfulness. Can you promise such a thing?

The Earl had always prided himself on his honest behavior with the females he had enraptured. He had never before promised what he would not or could not do. Loving Jenny, and he was beginning to realize that his love had depths hitherto unexplored, he would not hurt her.

'Tis faithfulness she expects, Jason. Without it, you'll never have her. So, man, are you willing to give her up?

The thought of giving Jenny up brought the Earl to his feet. No damnation, no!

"All right, then, Jason," he pursued out loud. "Promise her constancy and hope for the best." Then suddenly her large dark sad eyes loomed up in his mind. He remembered his earliest feeling, that of wishing to dispel the sadness. "No, by God. I can't hurt her . . . nor will I! If it's my soul she wants, 'twill be my soul she gets!" he said, going to the door and flinging it open with a flourish. He took the stairs angrily, two at a time, and reached Jenny's bedroom door quickly. He took hold of her door latch and found it locked. "Open this door, Jenny!" he commanded.

"No—go away!" shouted Jenny. "I . . . I never want to see you again." He had no patience left to quibble words with her. He merely took a step backward and then with a swift force lunged his foot forward with a hard heave-ho. Having dramatically and successfully broken the lock, he then proceeded to push the door open so forcefully that it banged convulsively against the wall.

Jenny stood, looking like a magnificent goddess. Her dark eyes flashed at him defiantly. Both were unaware that the servants had gathered at the bottom of the stairs, and it was more than one female heart among them that wished she were viewing this scene. The male servants exchanged glances, nodding approval of his lordship's masterful methods of . . . er, obtaining wifely obedience.

Jason loomed above her in the entrance, and for a moment he wondered what the devil he should *now do!* This, however, was answered for him as Jenny fired up his temper once again by exclaiming in a cold, contemptuous voice. "If you will kindly take your leave and send some one up to repair my door, we may consider this matter closed."

Her cool attitude infuriated him. He had come up to offer her his unending love, to promise her fidelity . . .

lord, what more could she want of him, he thought. Had she cried, or looked frightened, he would have sank down upon his knees—well, perhaps not that, but certainly he would have taken her in his arms most tenderly. But no, here she was, this chit of a girl, trying to make him appear foolish.

He laid claim upon the broken lash and slammed the door like a shot. He then turned wrath-filled orbs upon her and she could see the fever in his deep blue eyes. "Devil take the door . . . the lock . . . and—" He stalked across the room like an animal gone crazed, while she watched in amazement. Never before had she witnessed such violence . . . or passion. She watched as he flung the communicating door open, strode over to what had been the poor piece of furniture he had been occupying each night, and said, "and Devil take this, for it's not another night that I will spend in it! Do you hear me, Lady Waine?" said he, flinging the bed on its side.

Lady Waine regarded her husband. She herself was furious and needed to suck in air before she could answer. Satisfied that she had steadied herself, she opened her mouth to speak in tones she hoped would be cool and low-pitched, as she was certain that by now everyone in the household had heard what should have been for her ears alone. However, this very admirable intention somehow went awry, for when she did at last open her mouth, it was to shout in a volume that was as loud as his own, *"I hear you, and so does everyone else, my lord!"* She then managed to lower her voice and say, "I don't care how many beds you heave your vile temper upon. There is one bed you will not have access to . . . and *that,* my lord, is *mine!"*

He went to her then with the full intention of silencing her with his kiss, but she managed to deliver what she hoped was a solid kick to his shin. However, having been made the recipient of such a blow early in their acquaintanceship, he was foresighted enough to dodge this attempt. She pulled free and ran, but he was on her in a thrice and had her pinned to him. She screamed, and while the servants waited breathlessly for more, Jason Waine ruthlessly kissed his wife!

"No, Lady Waine, you will be still and listen to me!"

"You needn't shout in my face! As to being still and listening to you, I don't suppose I have any choice since there is no doubt as to who is the stronger here," said Lady Waine sarcastically. "I take leave to tell you, my lord, that you are *no* gentleman!"

"I believe you have once before made that observation to me. However, for the moment, we shall let that pass. What I am *not* is a liar ... and madam, I take leave to tell *you* that I have not made love to Lady Hester or anyone else since we have been married. What is more— though I never thought to hear myself say these words, I say them *now* to *you*, and with all my heart—Jenny, I love you and don't intend to make love to anyone other than yourself."

This announcement made Jenny turn purple with rage and the Earl regarded her with no little surprise. After all, he thought, I just made a concession that should have sent my sweet love into transports.

"You say you do not lie ... you say you have not made love to any woman since we were wed? Get out! I will hear no more!"

"But Jenny—"

"What of the night you sought *consolation?* What of Lady Hester and what I have seen with my own eyes? Get out! Get out! Oh, please go and leave me alone."

The Earl released his struggling wife and his eyes clouded over. He was hurt. He had told her he loved her, and she did not return either affection ... or interest. He looked at her a moment and then quietly left the room.

The servants scattered, as they realized the Earl had lost the battle and was descending among them.

Jason Waine walked out of the Castle and aimlessly toward the west woods. He ran his hand through his hair. The chit was driving him mad. She didn't believe him! How could he make her believe him? He walked past the hothouse. He heard the pheasant's call and the scampering of a squirrel through the brush, and he heard Jenny's voice telling him to get out!

Jenny watched him go and suddenly knew she wanted him to stay, but she was frozen with indecision. Then all at once she made up her mind and ran down the stairs, past some of the lingering servants, who exchanged wide-eyed expressions at such "goings-on." She saw Jason's retreating form and called his name, but he did not hear her. Something inside her made her run faster. She had to stop him—she didn't know why, she only knew that he had to be stopped. She could see him enter the southwest woods and screeched his name as loud as she could.

Just then a shot rang out and she saw Jason fall to the ground!

"Jason!" she screamed. "Oh ... Oh God!" and ran toward him. He raised his head, got to his feet, ran toward her, and pulled her down to the ground. Her breath came in short spurts as he held her head in his strong grasp.

"You ... you aren't hurt?" she asked wonderingly.

"No, the bullet hit the tree and instinctively I hit the ground. All right, I don't suppose the devil will try again." He got to his feet and pulled her up beside him.

"What ... what is happening? Oh, Jason, what does it mean?"

"I don't know, love." He turned and glanced toward the hothouse at his back. "But the shot came from that direction."

"The hothouse! Oh, Jason, I ... I didn't tell you I discovered the tunnel."

"You what?"

"I found it quite by accident and went through via the yew tree opening to the hothouse—the hothouse. Oh God, Jason, do you think someone from the house went through the tunnel and came up here to shoot you?"

For answer, his lordship took her by the hand and walked purposefully toward the greenhouse. They opened the door and he moved directly to the trapdoor. It was wide open.

"Did you leave it open, Jenny?"

"No, no, I distinctly remember shutting it," she said, frowning. "Jason, you told me that Howard knows about the tunnel—"

"That does not signify. Come on, let us go back to the house."

They walked slowly, and when they entered the central hall, it was to find Miss Browne waiting. "Good afternoon, my lord, my lady. I heard the shot. Did the gardener get the wild boar, then?"

"Boar?" asked his lordship.

"Why, yes. We were almost in his path this morning . . . and Howard asked the gardener to attend to it. I assumed that—"

"I did not see either the gardener or the boar, but I will go and find out what is being done about the matter," said the Earl.

"No, Jason," said Lady Waine, desperately clinging to his arm.

He patted his wife's hand and gazed at her long. "Don't fret, love. I'm only going to the stables to leave word for the man to come in and see me when he returns from his hunting expedition."

Jenny watched him go and turned to find Helen regarding her strangely.

"If you will excuse me, my lady."

"Yes, of course," said Jenny, pretending not to observe Miss Helen make her way toward the picture gallery. Without reason, Jenny made up her mind to follow her.

She saw Miss Browne make her way to a rear door and went to a small round window and peeped out. She was surprised to see Miss Browne put both her hands conspiratorily into Mr. Howard Waine's and watched them walk off together.

So, Howard Waine is here . . . in fact, he was in the rear courtyard. If he had come back via the tunnel, that is exactly where he would be!

She walked back toward the main hall and entered the parlor, where she rang for a servant.

A lackey appeared and awaited her instructions. "Is Master Julian at home?"

"No, m'lady, he has not returned yet."

"What of Mr. McMillan . . . is he here?"

"No m'lady, he went out sometime ago."

She felt in her heart that it could not be Julian—must

not be Julian—yet Julian could have sneaked back to take that shot. She would have to ask Mac if he had seen Julian in passing.

The lackey moved as if to leave but Jenny came out of her reverie and called him to a halt. "Just ... just a moment. Can you tell me where I can find Lady Lillian?"

"No, m'lady. She called for her curricle more than two hours ago."

"Do you mean she has gone into town?" asked Jenny, surprised.

"I couldn't say, m'lady ... excepting that she didn't take her groom along, so I don't think she went into town. Never does so without her groom."

"Oh." Jenny then dismissed him and stood in the hall, leaning against the center table. She bit her lower lip, her mind aching with frightened logic.

The front doors opened and Jason loomed on the threshold. His face was grave and his deep blue eyes were a mask of hidden thoughts.

"Jason," whispered Lady Waine, going toward him, her hands outstretched.

"Hush, love," he said softly, taking both her hands and giving them a squeeze. "Come, let us go into the parlor."

He situated her on the sofa but remained standing, moving restlessly to and fro, saying nothing.

"Jason, did you speak with the gardener? Was he there?"

"No, Jennifer ... but it is as Miss Helen says. She was right about the wild boar. Some of the stable boys substantiated her story, for they had seen the thing just yesterday evening. The gardener is, in fact, somewhere in the west woods hunting him down. I have left word for him to report to me here as soon as he returns."

"You think it was he? But, Jason, why. Why would he shoot at *you*?"

"Silly chit! Shoot at me? All this business has gone to our heads—"

"Stop it! I am not a fool, Jason. Someone shot at you ... and you know it. You said yourself the shot came from the hothouse. And then, the trapdoor was open—"

"Now you stop it and listen to reason," said the Earl

firmly. "I don't like to admit it, but there it is—nothing for it. You see, Jen, I was somewhat shaken, what with my accident this morning, and then suddenly a bullet whizzes past my ear. Well, I must have been wrong about it coming from the hothouse!"

Jenny had never seen the Earl shaken and knew he was trying to calm her with falsehoods. "But, Jason, if it was the gardener, why did he shoot so high? Wild boars are monstrous things ... but I have yet to see one six foot high!"

"Eh? Well, as to that ... perhaps the fellow slipped upon a rock and threw up his arm. Happens to the best of us. At any rate, when he reports to me, we will know."

"'Tis gammon you are pitching at me, Jason Waine! What about the trapdoor? I told you that I remember closing it ... yet we found it open."

"You must be mistaken. Perhaps you just thought you closed it. You see, my pretty, if someone were indeed trying to kill me, he would need a motive. Julian is the only one with a real motive, and even if I could be brought to believe such a ridiculous thing, *he* does *not* know where the tunnel is!" said Jason convincingly.

"Perhaps he does and has never let on ... though, in truth, I cannot myself be brought to think so. However, Howard knows about the tunnel, and I heard Lillian accuse Howard of mishandling estate funds without your knowledge, so he has motive, hasn't he? And Lillian ... she could have cut the strap when the horses were left unattended. And she may know about the tunnel ... your father may have showed her!" said Jenny.

"So then, my wife, you are determined to dramatize this? Ah well, at least it shows that you care," he said, coming to sit beside her.

"Care? Of course, I care," said Jenny. Then, retrieving her pride, "I . . . don't like to think of *anyone* as a target!"

"I see," said Jason Waine quietly.

The doors of the parlor flew open and on the threshold stood Julian Waine. His flaxen locks were windswept and his blue eyes glittered strangely. His smooth boyish face looked death white. His buckskin coat was smudged with

213

grime and Jenny's eyes noted that his breeches were soiled. Her eyes automatically traveled to his boots ... and she sucked in her breath at the sight. There were evergreen needles wedged into the rims of his boots!

Her dark eyes flew to her husband's and she felt as though her mind and heart were at war!

"Jason! Thank God you are not hurt. Why were you not told to stay away from the west wood this afternoon?" said Julian, coming to sit beside his brother on the sofa.

Jenny leaned over her husband, "Julian, what has happened to you?"

Julian looked down at his clothes and laughed sheepishly. "Oh, this. It is nothing really. Took a bit of a spill coming through the ... er, woods. My horse must have hit a rabbit hole." His eyes went back to his brother. "But *you*, Jason, what is this about the gardener shooting at you."

"Oh good lord, is that what was said?" exclaimed Jason with exasperation.

"Not exactly. I was told the gardener was out hunting the boar ... but I knew that already. Mother told me to stay out of the west woods——"

"You were told?" asked Jenny, frowning.

"All the stable lads at once jabbered that Jase here almost got hit and that Styles was in for it, sure," replied Julian.

"Styles?" asked Jenny.

"He is our gardener, Jenny," said the Earl. "I do hope they don't put a scare into the fellow, for then we won't be able to get a word out of him. Damnation, I told those lads to keep their mouths shut. Look here, Julian, take care of Jenny. I'm going to have another look around and see if I can spot the fellow."

"Oh please, Jason, do not," said Jenny pleadingly.

"Better not, Jase," agreed Julian. "No sense in taking any chances——"

"Now don't you start, Julian," said the Earl glaring meaningfully at him.

"I don't want you adding to Jenny's already wild imagination."

"Eh? Oh, oh, to be sure. But, Jase, have a care."

The two brothers' eyes met for a moment and then Jason was gone again.

Jenny's lip quivered, but she controlled herself and turned to find Julian had stood up and was now pouring out a glass of madeira. He handed it to her, poured himself some port, and sank down beside her on the sofa.

"Are you staying for dinner?" asked Jenny in way of making conversation."

He chuckled. "I wasn't going to . . . but think I will. Seems all the action is at Waine."

"How horrid of you, Julian. All this "action" has been aimed at *your* brother!"

"Not all," he said lightly. "I seem to remember a certain young woman—or should I say *maid?*—getting shut up in a toolshed by some mysterious agency."

She locked in on the one word he had said so strangely. *"Maid*—what did you mean by that? You called me a *woman* and then changed it to *maid*. Why?" she said, frowning.

"I should think it obvious, my innocent. Here you are a bride—nearly a week a bride—and yet you ain't really, are you?"

"Julian!" Her eyes snapped and her cheeks blazed.

"Oh, now don't take a pet. I suspicioned it from the start . . . but I wanted to be sure. Now I am."

"You are odious, that is what you are."

"Jenny, don't think that of me. Not really. It shouldn't matter to me—I mean about your . . . your relationship with your husband. Yet it does. I have told myself that you are *his* wife—"

"Stop it, Julian. Don't speak like this to me," she interrupted.

"Why not? Does not Jason speak in terms he should not to the fair Hester?"

"How . . . how did you know about Lady Hester?" asked Jenny, suddenly shivering.

"Know? What is there to know? I saw her on the road a while back and assumed she had been here. Was I right?"

Jenny's heart began to ache. Was Julian lying? Had he

215

been here earlier—hiding, waiting for a chance to kill his brother?

"It matters not whether you were right about her being here. That has naught to do with . . . me."

"Ah, but it does . . . or do you intend to be the dutiful wife, forever home, forever waiting, with no earth of your own?"

"And you—you would betray your brother? Julian, would you attempt to take his wife in his own home?" asked Jenny uncompromisingly.

"Oh, Jen, why must you see it so? Why speak so blatantly? How can I say the things I need to say to you when you throw ideals and principles at my head and make me shirk at the sound!" said Julian, taking her hand, his light blue eyes ablaze with intensity.

"But, Julian, I can't clothe such things with finery. *I* am aware of the cant of the day. Ah yes, Lady Such is married to Lord So . . . but prances with her cicisbeo! Quite conventional . . . if 'tis quite discreet! *It is* hypocrisy. We go about saying that we eat *meat* because we do not like the sensation that shoots through us when we say we eat *flesh*. Yet 'tis the same! If your intentions toward me are amorous—and I am your brother's wife—either give it up or stand before the blow! *I am your brother's wife,* this is his home, and you have made your first attempt to seduce me!" said Jenny sadly.

Julian looked away from her eyes and said nothing. When his voice came, he turned his eyes to hers again. "Do you want me to tell you I am sorry? Well, then, I am . . . I'm sorry for it all. I'm sorry for feeling as I do. It happened, Jen. It was out of my control! *I am sorry,* for you have made it clear that you will not be mine . . . although you are not really his! *Sorry*—what a word that is! I wish that I had never seen your face or heard your voice . . . and still I am glad that I have. Yes, blister it, you are my brother's wife! Yet you are not . . . are you? You are not really his, but neither are you free to be mine. Lord, I am sorry! Your integrity does you no good in my eyes! Your virtue has set itself an enemy against me. I would almost that you were a lady of the streets . . . so that I might possess you! What, then, do I have left—time? Yes, there is always time, time enough to disenchant and deaden even the purest of ideals and set you free!" He stood up and left her abruptly and she watched him go, unable to stop him, for she had no words to cool his heat.

What did all this mean? Was Julian jealous of his brother's belongings? Had Julian soiled himself from a fall in the woods—or scrambling through a tunnel? And what of Lillian? She had the opportunity to cut the straps ... and so had Julian, for he could have returned from the stables undetected and done the thing! There, too, was Howard. He knew about the tunnel and had been in the courtyard without anyone's knowledge ... and had been with the horses this morning!

## Chapter Twenty

*Oh! dreadful is the check—intense the agony—*
*When the ear begins to hear, and the eye begins to see;*
*When the pulse begins to throb, the brain to think again,*
*The Soul to feel the flesh, and the flesh to feel the chain!*
                                        EMILY BRONTË

Jenny received a message from a lackey that the Earl had taken his horse and would be in Dean that evening, visiting with the Squire Talbot. Jenny repeated the words disbelievingly. The gardener, Styles, had not yet returned, which meant that Jason had not even waited to speak with him.

Mechanically she went to her room and lay across the bed, waiting for dinner to be announced. A knock sounded and Jenny ran to her door. Joan stood there, looking shy and apologetic.

"Why yes, Joan, what is it?"

"I be real sorry, m'lady, but Lady Lillian ... it seems she will be taking dinner in her room and says, as her son has gone out, maybe you would prefer to take your dinner here instead of alone in the dining room."

"Alone? Has not Mr. McMillan returned?"

"No, m' lady."

"Very well, Joan . . . thank you."

"I'll bring it straight up to you."

"Don't rush." Jenny sighed. Suddenly she thought of Aunt Beth and Papa. For the last few days, her life had been so jumbled that she had barely had enough time to think of them, let alone write. . . . Good lord, Aunt Beth will send out every runner in the country if they don't receive a letter soon.

She sat down at her vanity and pulled out her writing paper, setting herself to the task of giving them a full account of her new home and carefully weeding out any details that might worry them.

She was absorbed in her task and did not notice the passing of time or the fact that the one candle affording her light was really not adequate until Joan returned with her dinner tray.

"Oh dear," said Joan clucking her tongue. "You'll be hurting your eyes, you will, m' lady." She bustled about, lighting the wall sconces and making the room cosy for her mistress, while Jenny signed her letter.

She thanked her maid, watched her leave, and without much appetite sat down to eat. She was meandering through a large portion of mutton stew when a sound in the hallway brought her head up. Thinking it was a servant, she rose quickly and sped to the door, as she wished the dinner things to be taken away and replaced with coffee. As soon as she got the door open and peeped out she shut it again hastily. She leaned against it, and for a reason she could not explain to herself, locked the makeshift latch that had been installed. The thought occurred to her that such a minor setback would do nothing to deter Jason Waine had he a mind to enter.

She shook her head, for she had just witnessed Mac entering Lillian's room down the hall. "So, it is really true. Odd . . . I only half believed it," she said out loud to herself. "But then, Mac, you always did go for experienced women . . . it's just that I don't particularly like this one."

The hours ticked by and it was nearly ten when Jenny finally put down Sir Walter Scott. She liked his new narrative poem *Marmion*, about an honorable gallant who comes home to find his bride being given to another. Off he swoops her and they live happily ever after. "I wish life were so gay," said Jenny, snuffing out her candles and slipping into her bed. She lay there an interminable time before sleep commanded her lids to drop.

Suddenly she was awake. It felt as though she had only slept a short while, but she sensed that it was late ... very late. She knew what it was that had awakened her. It was the Earl—she could hear him moving about in his room. She waited, almost hoping he would come to her.

On the other side of the communicating door, the Earl had undressed himself, turned, and grimaced at the small day bed he had been using. Evidently Winfred had set things to rights. He grinned at the thought, imagining what must have flickered through his valet's mind.

The Earl started for the communicating door and stopped, staring at it. He was powerless, he felt. It isn't possible, Jason Waine. You have won over the hardest of females with the prettiest of words, but can find naught to convince your wife that you love her. The long ride to Dean and back had wearied him, and with a sigh, he decided to leave it go. The Earl quietly pulled the covers about him and lay there exhausted and wide awake.

The next hour needled by as each tossed and turned but slept not. With their eyes tightly shut and their minds wildly imagining, two individuals lay awake and apart, wishing they were together and asleep.

Helen Browne entered the dining parlor on the next morning, remarking idly that the day appeared to be quite lovely. Lillian continued to sip her tea. However, the two men, Mac and Julian, rose to their feet until Miss Browne was seated.

Pleasantries were exchanged, but each seemed to be absorbed in their own thoughts.

"I'm off for a cock fight near Folkstone," said Julian amiably. "Care to join me, Mac?"

"Afraid not, lad. I have some last-minute things to take care of in town, and then I'm off."

"No, Mac ... you did not tell me," objected Lillian, turning around, a deep furrow lining her face.

He patted her hand and Julian's brows drew together, though in truth he was quite tolerant of his mother's activities. It was more the fact that he did not really like Mac that caused his present disapproval. He had nothing really tangible to claim any disapprobation for the fellow, it was more a feeling that came over him now and then. He knew the basis of it was probably Mac's closeness to Jenny.

Both Mac and Miss Browne excused themselves a few minutes later and mother and son sat across the breakfast table, lingering over their tea.

"Did you have a look at the dower house, Mama?" said Julian, his eyes grave.

"Yes, dear. I went yesterday afternoon and set about drawing sketches of the rooms."

"Good. We will want to furnish it when we return."

"You are determined in this preposterous scheme of yours?"

"Call it what you will, I am determined . . . more now than ever before."

"Why? Because of that little chit who calls herself Lady Waine?" said his mama scathingly.

Her son frowned. "Tread carefully, mama. I'll not hear anything against her."

"No, no *you* wouldn't. Such a fine boy . . . your father would have been proud."

"You will accompany me, then, as I planned?" said her son.

"No, I don't think so. I would be in your way."

"That is nonsense, ma'am. You will be the toast of Bombay—or any other outlandish place we hit upon. Why, so many men will be at your feet, you'll hardly notice me about."

She smiled fondly at him. "You are ridiculous."

"Mama, there is naught for you here. The people of Dover have always treated you unfairly. I have never understood why you chose to remain after you lost Papa—"

"I loved your papa. This had been our home together."

"But he is dead and we have to alter our plans. You would not be happy alone at the dower house. I promise

220

you, Mama, you will begin to live again if you come with me."

Lillian's eyes went past him and her mind darted, giving her eyes a strange look. "We'll see. After today . . . then we will see."

Julian did not like the look in his mother's eyes, but he would get no further with her this morning. He rose, patted her shoulder, and left the room.

Jason Waine descended the steps just as Gravesly opened the front door to emit Howard Waine. For a moment their eyes met gravely. Jason's own suspicions flickered through his mind and were speedily dismissed. He greeted Howard amicably.

"Jason, could we retire to the library? I wish to speak with you on an urgent matter."

"Yes, of course."

Miss Browne watched them from the recesses of the stairwell and she smiled. She had been up early that morning walking through the grounds with Howard. He had proposed to her again late yesterday afternoon, and then again this morning. She had been finding life intolerable at Waine. The Wendall boys were never around for their lessons, and when she did manage to catch up to them, it was to hear their threats of exposing her.

However, it was not this that decided her. It was the fact that while she was not in love with Howard Waine, she knew she could be, so great was her attachment to him. She told him about her affair with Julian and he had understood . . . had swept it aside. It was then that she put her hand in his and told him she would be his wife. And now, she thought, he was doing precisely what she had demanded. He was arranging to go to Bridgewater with the Earl!

Jenny lingered over her morning coffee. She had no wish to go downstairs. Her insides felt tight and her mind was in agony. Had Jason gone to yet another woman last night? Why didn't he stay to speak with the gardener? What was she going to do about Julian? Things would now be so awkward. These troubled cogitations kept her

221

in her room quite some time. However, she finally put her thoughts aside and made her way downstairs. She started for the parlor when the front knocker sounded and she waited to see who was at the door. Gravesly opened it and standing in the entrance was a small old man in work clothes. His hat was being nervously wrung in his hands and his grizzled chin was pressed against his chest. This must be Styles, thought Jenny, going forward.

"Oh, m' lady," said Gravesly. "His lordship wanted to see Styles—"

"Yes, that is quite true. Please advise the Earl that he is in the parlor with me."

"But, m' lady, his lordship has gone out," said Gravesly hurriedly.

"Oh, when?" said Jenny, frowning.

"About ten minutes ago."

"I see. Very well, then, come along Styles. *I* will see you anyway."

"Yes, m' lady," said Styles, still not looking up.

He followed her into the parlor, where she sat down and invited him to be seated. He declined the offer and stood before her, fidgeting with his worn cap.

"You needn't be frightened ... I shan't bite, you know," said Jenny, trying to put the poor fellow at his ease.

He did not reply and so Jenny decided to plunge into the matter and put him out of his misery. "I should like to know if you managed to kill that wild boar yesterday."

"Yes, m' lady, though it took some doing."

"Oh? You had to shoot several times at him, you mean?"

"No, that weren't the gist of it really. Was ferreting him that took a bit of time. Got him before dark though."

"Then why did you not come here last night as we asked."

"The truth of it is ... I bolted, m' lady. When I came into the stables and sent them after the boar—for he was a big fellow, needed the cart—well, they told me someone near hit his lordship and that I was wanted. Didn't know what to do, so I took off ... for m' daughter's. She lives in town. She sent me back, she did!"

"I see. Then will you be able to answer me honestly if I promise you it will go no further and that there will be no reprisals? Mistakes can happen ... it is not that which has brought you here, but the fact that I want to get at the truth. Could you have shot over the boar's head ... in the region of the hothouse area?"

"No, m' lady. I heard that was where it happened. Didn't do my shooting there at all. Was more'n a mile deeper into the woods. I shot and missed—that is true enough—but not there and not six feet in the air."

She thanked and dismissed him, remaining alone with her fears.

## Chapter Twenty-one

*What Private griefs they have, alas, I know not!*
SHAKESPEARE

A pair of bright eyes, set with a purpose, watched Jason Waine riding off the grounds beside his cousin Howard. The eyes, watched, knowing one of the two riders was on his way to Bridgewater Pass.

A few moments later, carrying a small horsehair blanket, a lone rider made the same trip. There was a strange glint about the eyes, a satanic smile about the mouth. The rider stopped at the bridge ramp and appraised the narrow bridge. It was made of wood, but stood on stone pillars some twenty-five feet in the air above the fast-moving waters. The bridge was some seven feet in width and stretched nearly forty feet across to the other side. There was a short wooden railing that bordered both sides of the bridge. The eyes scanned the waters, glinting as they sighted the large pointed rocks glaring among the foam. Horsehair blanket in hand, the ramp was spanned. The hands laid the blanket down upon the wooden flooring, and one crowbar, one saw, and several wooden chips were uncovered. The same hands removed, after some exertion, two laths of wood by using the crowbar and carefully prying them loose. The wood laths ran horizontally, and after the two slats were removed, the crude but serviceable saw made its incision. The saw cuts were carefully made in the wood in a vertical line, and the two laths were replaced so that they would not appear to have been tampered with. Certainly no one would note it sitting upon the back of a horse! Then continuing the incision vertically toward the ramp, and inserting the wooden chips between the severed laths, so they would not fall away from each other, the hands made an incision of some eight feet down the center. The flooring was cut so that if anyone were to step upon it the wood chips would give way and the laths would fold under, sending their victim and his horse plunging to the rocks below! The eyes glittered and the mouth smiled, well satisfied with the work.

The sawdust was meticulously brushed away. The obsessed eyes seemed brighter, the mouth twisted, giving the visage a devilish aspect. The tools were returned to their blanket and packed tightly to the saddle. The rider was once again returning to Waine Castle, aware that Howard Waine had parted with Jason. The rider knew that Howard Waine was off for Dover, but Jason Waine had already crossed the bridge to the farm and would be returning home alone. The deed was done and this time there could be no escape.

Lillian had watched her son go and sighed. At any rate, he would need suitcases, for he was determined on this trip. She climbed the stairs to the third floor, where she had some baggage stored. However, she stopped short outside the Wendall boys' room.

"Jamie, I think we had better tell Uncle Jason what we know," said Peter.

"I don't know. Might make things worse . . . for then, we'd be bound to tell him we've been holding it over Miss Browne's head."

"It isn't honorable to keep it from him. I like Lady Waine. She is pretty and soft and smells so nice when she kisses me."

"Well, she hasn't come to any harm. We'll watch her and make sure."

"But what about everything that has been going on? What about Uncle Jason? Someone cut his strap, Jamie, plain as pikestaff, you know. And someone took a shot at him."

"Lord, Peter, you ain't suggesting Miss Browne did those things, too!"

"Well, we saw her lock up Lady Waine."

"We better think on it a bit."

Lillian Waine had heard enough. She made her way down the stairs and rushed up to Gravesly. "Where is Miss Browne?"

"I'll have someone send for her, madam."

"Ah, never mind, there she is," said Lillian, spying Helen Browne moving down the long gallery.

"Oh, did you wish to speak with me? I was just on my way to the library to choose some reading for the boys," said Helen.

"Let us go there together, shall we," said Lillian sweetly, nearly bursting with what she had learned.

Helen regarded her strangely but followed her into the library and watched her close the doors.

Jenny flung up her hands. The gardener said he couldn't have shot in the area Jason had been walking. If he was to be believed, she was back where she had started—nowhere. It was too much. She rose and decided to get a book from the library, and came to an abrupt halt outside its doors.

"I have just left the Wendall boys, Helen, and I know everything. Did you think you could get away with such a stupid trick? Whyever did you do such a thing?" Lillian's voice was harsh and nasty. "They will end by telling Jason."

"Let them ... it doesn't matter. I locked her in the shed—yes, I did it—she deserved it. She came here and blinked her eyes in Julian's direction, didn't she? 'Oh, Julian, walk with me here ... oh, Julian.' I couldn't stand it. I was in a rage, and when I saw her go into the toolshed, I just thought I'd keep her there a while. Then it was too late to do anything about it without being discovered."

"You are a fool! 'Tis no wonder you couldn't hold my son," said Lillian.

"I don't want your son. He is heartless, conceited, and puffed up in his own consequence!"

Jenny felt as if the entire world were swerving before her. Even she was beginning to do things she had never done before . . . for eavesdropping was beginning to become a habit of hers, she thought ruefully.

"You realize, of course, that this means your dismissal," sneered Lillian.

Helen Browne laughed bitterly. "It doesn't matter. Howard Waine has asked me to marry him and I have accepted."

Lillian felt stunned and piqued that this plain girl had won Howard away from her.

"Marry Howard?" The words came out seethingly. "Why it is all becoming clear now. I know now what the two of you have been planning—all these accidents. How stupid of me not to have realized sooner. It has been the two of you all along. You think Julian will be accused . . . and then Howard will get it all! You will never see it happen, I tell you, it will never come to pass!" screamed Lillian, incensed.

On the other side of the door Jenny stood frozen. Here now was what she felt was positive proof. Howard had been tampering with Waine money. He was going to marry Helen, and they were scheming to kill Jason and put the blame on Julian. Oh my God!

She rushed from the passageway to the main hall and found Gravesly. "Gravesly, tell me at once where has his lordship gone?"

"I am sorry, m' lady. His lordship did not precisely tell me where he was going. However, I did overhear him speaking with Mr. Waine when they were on their way out."

"Well?" she cried impatiently.

"I believe his lordship is going to look at the Bridgewater Farm."

"With Mr. Howard?" ejaculated Jenny.

"Mr. Waine *did* leave with his lordship, though I am not certain their destination was the same."

Jenny turned on her heel and rushed back upstairs to don her riding clothes.

The Wendall boys had slipped out down the backstairs and hurried away from the Castle. They skirted the road and took the path to the fields, passing the fork that led to Bridgewater, when they noted someone riding away from the bridge. However, as the individual overlooked them, they shrugged their shoulders and continued their hike.

It didn't take Jenny long to change her clothes and run out to the stables, where she impatiently waited for her horse to be saddled.

She heard her name called cheerfully from the stable doors and turned to find Mac standing before her, his leading strings in his gloved hands.

"Mac, how glad I am that you are here!" she exclaimed. "It's Jason—he has gone off with Howard."

"Yes, I know. They mentioned it to me earlier when I met them out here."

"Don't you know what that means? No-no, of course, how could you. . . ."

"Jen, do calm yourself."

"Jason is in danger, I tell you."

"All right, then. I will ride out and meet him—this is not for you."

"No—"

"Jen, you must trust to my better judgment," Mac scolded.

"I cannot, Mac, not this time. I must go . . . I must see him . . . you don't understand." She was wild with fear.

Her horse was brought to her and she took the strings but Mac put out his hand, detaining her.

"Mac, I know you are trying to be kind, but I must go. Please do not try and stop me."

His eyes glinted irritably at her and he shook his head. Suddenly Jenny felt a shiver run through her, but knew it was because she had never before seen him angry with her and he was now!

"All right, then, if you must ride out to meet him, I'll

come along ... just to make sure no accidents befall *you*."

They sped down the drive together, continued down the road, and took the wooded path until they reached the fork, where Mac called her to a halt. "Jen, let us wait here."

"No, we must continue to the farm. We can't let him return with Howard alone."

"He is not with Howard," said Mac strangely.

"How . . . how do you know that?"

"I told you. I spoke with them before they left. Howard went into Dover.

"Perhaps Howard told you that ... simply to create an alibi for himself."

"Jen, please let us wait here. Jason will be safe enough at the farm."

"No, I have to go to him."

"And I say no!" commanded Mac, grabbing hold of her reins.

She exclaimed over his rough usage. Her face was flushed and her eyes kindled. Suddenly he had dismounted and pulled her off her horse!

Jamie exchanged a look with his brother, who sat beside him in a tree they had come to think of as their own. "Know what, Peter?"

"Yes, I think so."

Without another word they scrambled down the tree and dived through the thick of the woods, making for the road.

"Mac. How ... how dare you," said Jenny, in shock over Mac's attitude.

His bright dark eyes glinted luminously at her and she knew an inner fear. There was something ... odd about Mac, something that made her back away in the direction of the bridge.

"It is your fault, Jenny. All of *this* has been your fault! If you had not married him, he would not have to die. But you did ... you betrayed *Johnny* ... you betrayed me ... just as Johnny betrayed me," he said sadly.

228

Jenny gazed at him and felt all at sea. "What? What do you mean, Mac, what are you trying to tell me?"

"You don't know . . . no, you don't know. You weren't there that night—that terrible night of blood and death and and terror, Jenny! Such terror. You didn't see . . . but *I* did. *I saw them*—all of them, my friends, I saw them with their arms shot off and their heads blown to pieces. We saw a soldier's head blown clean off his shoulders . . . watched it roll down the hill and fell on our bellies laughing. Jenny, do you hear? We *laughed!* You still don't understand. John, he didn't understand either . . . he had fought in the Peninsular . . . he was so strange and ready for it all. You have no idea. There was Fenhurst, riding off with a message for Wellington, and we saw him shot off his horse—in a split second. Do you know how old James Fenhurst was? He was nineteen, Jen. Right before my eyes a sniper killed him. I couldn't move, but I heard Johnny curse and take chase. Even then, I hadn't thought of escaping. I rode back into that hell with Johnny beside me. Then John's third horse was shot out from under him. Think on it, Jenny—his third horse. Oh God, I watched him as he knelt before his mare. I heard him say, 'Confound the Frogs! Dash it, Mac, do you see what those devils have done? They have killed my Cherry. Devil take them . . . for I loved that horse. Now what's to do?'

"I helped him onto my horse and we rode back to our lines. He jumped off and cried out to me, as gay as though we were at Vauxhall, 'Now. I'm off, Mac! I'll just get another steed!' He was grinning at me . . . you know the way he had, Jen? I just shook my head. I loved him . . . there was no one like John! I still had my horse and was thanking the fates when suddenly she was down, down by one of our *own rockets!* Those devilish things have a way of taking off—why one chased poor old Rodney Hawkins for twenty minutes while we spit blood laughing! That blasted thing didn't give up until it hit a tree and exploded. And now *one* had downed *my horse!* It happened just as John was leaving and he was back in a thrice, pulling me to my feet and laughing as though we were having a grand old time.

" 'Zounds, Mac,' said John, 'how I am to find two horses is beyond me. All right, don't you fret none, I'll be back with a steed for each of us. Then we'll send those Frogs to perdition!'

"I couldn't bear it any longer, Jen. I had to get out of it . . . any way I could. We were behind the lines, but so had Fenhurst been when he was felled. It was then that I saw the wagonload of wounded being taken back to Brussels. I pulled away, nearer to the thickets and aimed my gun at my left arm, and . . . shot." He turned his face away from Jenny and closed his eyes with the memory. "It was then, then that life ended for me . . . for I looked up and I saw Johnny's eyes—those eyes, staring at me with disbelief, with . . . with horror. I had never seen that look on his face before . . . I had never felt so very contemptible! You see, I loved John, really loved him, as I have never before loved anyone. I tried to explain. I told him how it was . . . what I was going through . . . I told him my mind was reeling. But he was so hard, Jen. Our gay, dashing Johnny was so hard—so unmovable. He turned on me! He said I disgusted him, that I should have put the bullet through my heart, not my arm! I begged him, but he said there was nothing for it . . . he was going to report me! He said this was something he could not let go. He said I was an officer . . . that men depended on me. He turned his back and began walking away. I only knew I *couldn't* let him. He was betraying me, betraying the friendship, the love I had given him. I had never done so to him . . . would never do so. Hadn't I wanted you, Jen?—ah, you did not know, I didn't let you know, all that time in Brussels I wanted you but put you out of my mind for Johnny's sake—and here he was ready to turn on me. At that moment, I hated him. It was so easy . . . one shot, just one shot, and he was dead . . . and *so was I!* Just that one shot and John's glory was gone! He felt no pain, Jen. He died immediately. Never said a word. I know because I held him . . . I held him and waited, waited for him to cock his mouth and grin at me. Then Hawkins found us. He took John away and put me in the wagon headed for Brussels. You see now, don't you, Jen? I had only one chance for redemption. I knew it the moment I told you

230

John was dead. I had to make it up by taking care of *you*. I had to see to it that you were never again hurt. But you betrayed *us*. You married Waine. Why, Jenny?" His eyes were wildly bright and his face was flushed.

Jenny had been listening with growing horror. Mac had killed John. Mac, her friend, John's friend, was sick ... terribly, terribly sick. Slowly she backed away from him onto the bridge ramp and felt an ineffable constriction of the mind. She only knew that he was ill, so very, very ill!

"Don't you see?" he asked pleadingly, following her up the ramp. "I ... I have to make you see! I came here to Waine to set things to rights. Don't you realize yet? It was I who severed Jason's saddle strap. It was so easy ... as though *you* were helping me. Remember, you left the cutting sheers for me! Howard went off after Helen Browne and I was alone with the horses. All it took was the flick of my wrist and the strap was nicked. One good run, one jump should have done it. A big man like Jason, he should have been killed, but he was lucky. Then you came around—do you remember, Jenny?—the next day you came around the courtyard with your dress all sullied. You lied to me—I saw it in your eyes, you were lying— and I didn't like that, Jenny ... you have never lied to me before. It was *his* influence. I forgave you and was determined to finish the job quickly. I investigated and uncovered the tunnel entrance! You didn't hide your tracks very well, Jen. Then ... then, all I had to do was wait for the right moment!

"When I saw Jason walk off alone toward the hothouse, I grabbed my pistol and hurried on ahead through the tunnel passage. I had such a clear shot at him, but suddenly you called out his name and my arm moved—'twas only a fraction, but enough to miss. You saved him that time, but not this time, Jenny, not this time!"

"Mac ... oh please, Mac, you don't know what you are saying!" she cried, the tears spilling over her white cheeks.

"Know?" he queried in a trembling voice. "Know? ... Of course, I know. It is you ... you who does not know. You don't know what it is like to sleep with fiends taking over your rest, to wake up screaming with the sweat staining your face, your mouth bleeding from gnashing your teeth. Oh God, *I know!*"

"Mac ..." she stumbled over his name not knowing what to say to him, trying to forget that he had just admitted to killing John.

"No!" he screamed at her. "No! Not pity. I want your forgiveness ... not pity."

"I give it to you then. Only stop all of this!" begged Jenny desperately.

"Do you mean to offer me a venality, a bauble, Jenny? Your forgiveness for Jason's life?" He laughed harshly and his eyes reflected his mind.

"If that is what it will take ... I offer you *myself*, but let Jason live."

"No. He must die! He must be *erased*. I planned it so carefully, so carefully ... even my liaison with the willing Lillian." He stopped his wild tone and suddenly turned tender. "You mustn't mind that, you know, love. She is nothing to me ... no other woman has ever been anything to me. I needed an excuse to stay if the thing took longer. It was you—always it was you, just as it was only you for John! I will make it up to him—to you—I will make you happy."

"Stop it! Stop it! You cannot make it up to me. You will make me hate you if you hurt Jason!" screamed Jenny, beside herself.

"No, you will not hate me ... not when you know how well I planned it. No one will suspect me. They will look toward Howard ... toward Julian ... but never toward me. Jason Waine will take his plunge today, and then ... it will be just as it should be."

Jenny's body trembled as she spoke. "Listen to me, Mac. I will never be able to ... to think of you as anything but what you are. You are ill ... you need care—"

"I need your care—yours!" shouted Mac, reaching out for her.

She stepped back with revulsion. "You shall never have it. Oh please, isn't it enough that you have killed Johnny, destroyed what might have been? Must you wreck my chance for happiness now? Will that make your nightmares end?"

232

"Stop!" he screamed putting his hands to his head. "This is for *you!* I will make you happy . . . I have always made you happy. Come, come now, away from this bridge."

Jason and Howard Waine had finished their talk in the library, much to each's relief. Jason had been disturbed by the hint that his cousin had been tampering with Waine funds. He, in fact, had not believed it possible, yet he wondered how it came to be insinuated.

Howard's forthright explanation had alleviated both their fears and set them on the chimes of easy friendship once again. They rode away from Waine Castle in the best of good humor. Pausing at the fingerposts, Jason screwed up his mouth. "Do you know, Howard, it is absolutely nonsensical that I should ride over to Bridgewater Farm without you."

"I want you to have a look at that machinery," said Howard, blushing slightly. "It would make me feel a bit better, you know."

Jason laughed. "My good man, you had not intended to put the new grinding mill on display until harvest time, and I don't see why we should let Lillian's ridiculous notions come between our harmonious relationship."

Howard grinned thankfully. "Well then, what are your plans?"

"I think I will ride into Dover with you."

"Good. There is a young addition to the firm of Brougham and Sterlwell, a nice young chap. Has been handling your investment funds rather well, I think."

"Think I'll skip it this time, Howard. Have in mind dropping by one of the shops and buying a bit of a whimsy for my wife. She has had a rather rough time of it at Waine, what with me falling off my saddle and walking about looking like that wild boar."

Howard's face became grim. "I don't like it, Jason. It's all very well for you to put a light face on, but it won't do. You know as well as I do that *someone* cut that strap . . . and someone took a shot at *your* head, not a boar's head. You must do something to protect yourself."

They walked their horses, taking the east road to Dover a few minutes in silence, for the Earl had, in fact, done something to protect himself and was deliberating whether or not to communicate his schemes to his cousin. In the end he remained silent, not because he did not trust Howard, but because when he had gone to his friend's at Dean last evening and explained the whole, Squire Talbot and he had agreed that complete secrecy must be maintained to ensure the success of their delicate trap. For a trap is what they had planned for the Earl's sniper!

Jason and Howard continued to ride toward Dover and another ten minutes passed before Howard cleared his throat, indicating that there was something he wished to say. Jason cocked his brow and silently awaited his cousin's prosey.

"Another thing," began Howard soberly. "If it were my honeymoon, I wouldn't be running off to Dover to buy trinkets for my bride! No, Jason, I'd be attending to that bride personally . . . rather than leaving her to the care of a . . . profligate brother!"

Jason's eyes swept Howard's face penetratingly. "I would not actually call Julian a libertine, Howard. The boy is certainly a scamp, but really, man, you do go too far!"

"I don't think so, Jason. I have reason to believe that Julian is more than just a bit infatuated with your wife, and when Julian is interested in a woman, he usually attempts to get her into his bed! Don't pucker at me, Jase. I know you don't like hemming and hawing, and I thought plain speaking was needed here! Julian has been roving about the country these past few months, sleeping with every wench that catches his eye. 'Tis a fact! Gained quite a reputation for himself with the local gentry. If he is seen with your lady . . . well, might tend to start the gossip mongers!"

Jason's face set in a hard line. "You were ever a bit too prune-faced, Howard. I don't like your insinuations. There is nothing in it if Julian shows Jenny about the place!"

"Never said there was anything to it . . . simply saying—look, Jase, Julian goes about constantly calling Lady

Waine, 'love' and all other sorts of endearments. It is bound to be misconstrued. It has been mentioned to me that your brother is more taken with Lady Waine than he has been with any other woman of his acquaintance."

"Ah, now who is it that has been discussing both my brother and my wife in terms that I find most questionable?" asked Jason austerely.

Howard flushed. "I am afraid . . . I should not have let such a thing slip!"

"You will in the future request Miss Browne to refrain from such prattle. It is most unseemly for her to gossip about her betters!" said the Earl harshly.

"Jason!" objected Howard. "I take leave to inform you that Miss Browne and I are betrothed!"

It was Jason's turn to color. "Good Lord! I had no idea, man. It is *I* who should beg *your* pardon. I wish you every happiness."

Howard thanked him and apologized sheepishly. "I am afraid that I will not allow my afianced wife to continue working . . . though she will stay on until you can find proper supervision for the Wendall boys."

However, Jason's mind was back at the Castle and Howard found that he had to repeat this in order to get the Earl's response.

"Eh . . . oh yes, yes. Well, let's not worry about that now. On second thought, Howard, there is something at Waine that I really should attend to. Want to question that gardener."

The announcement of Howard's upcoming nuptials made the Earl think that perhaps he should give a bit more weight to Miss Browne's observations. Jason's jealousy flared up and he remembered that on Jenny's first morning she had walked hand in hand with his brother. There was that fellow Mac as well. For many reasons, Jason did not want Jenny alone with him. He waved to Howard and turned his horse homeward.

The Wendall boys charged through the woods. They knew something was wrong and they had to get to the Castle to get help. They had seen Mac pull Lady Waine roughly off her horse, and by the time they had reached the ground, had seen her backing away from him. Their young hearts heaved for air as they cut through untrodden ways toward the main road. They came shooting out of the thicket, nearly colliding with Jason's horse.

"Oh-ho!" exclaimed the Earl, grinning. "What have we here? You look as though you were being chased by the devil himself."

"Uncle Jason," breathed Jamie, grabbing at the Earl's gleaming boots.

The Earl's brows drew together. "What is it, lad? What is wrong?"

" 'Tis . . . 'tis Lady Waine." He gulped for air.

"What about Lady Waine? Speak up, boy," demanded the Earl, feeling his heart pounding in his throat.

"He's pulled her off her horse," managed Peter, squeaking nervously.

"Who has—where?" the Earl thundered.

"That man—Mr. McMillan. At the bridge."

The boys were left behind. No further explanations were required. The Earl's horse bounded forward beneath the Earl's urging, putting the woods behind him.

Mac had grabbed out and clutched Jenny's arm. She was struggling and sobbing. "Mac, give it up . . . for *my* sake, give it up. Can't you see. I will inform on you if you hurt Jason? I will be here to tell them."

Mac's eyes seemed to glow and he hissed. "Betrayal . . . you are speaking of betraying me, just as Johnny did." He shook his head. "I don't want to hurt you, but I see now this is really what I should have done. You must be with John. *He* mustn't be alone . . . without you!"

Jason had come to an abrupt halt at the fork. Somehow he had to get to Mac without being seen. His only chance was to ride hard and hope to startle him A moment later he had landed quickly and deftly upon the ground, bringing Mac's shoulders around. They lunged at each other and Jenny saw her husband felled. Mac was on him, and then, just as quickly, he was flung off. Jason rushed at him and settled his fist across Mac's face, sending him sideways. Jason threw his right into Mac's belly and then his fist came up hard across his chin. Mac fell backward onto the bridge and Jason grabbed him by his coat and pulled him to his feet so that another flush hit could be administered. Then suddenly Mac was falling ... and there was his scream, that long awful scream!

Jason saw him go down, saw the laths of wood folding in upon themselves, and he made a wild useless grab.

Jenny heard Mac's scream, the scream of a man falling and knowing he is falling to his death.

She saw her husband's face swim before her, heard him call her name, and then sank into the blissfulness of oblivion.

## Chapter Twenty-two

Ashley Grange had never before looked so peaceful, thought Jenny idly, leaning back upon her elbows among the buttercups. Day lillies were in bloom everywhere, throwing their tangerine robustness about defiantly. Jenny's chestnut hair twinkled copper lights as it fell down around her face and shoulders. She didn't think of Johnny ... or of her days at Waine ... she didn't think of Mac! She had put that behind her days ago.

At first she thought she would never get the terror, the disillusionment, the sadness out of her mind, and then quite suddenly she found she just could not be brought to think of it.

Jason Waine dropped down upon the buttercups beside her and took up her hand, putting it tenderly to his lips.

She ran her free hand through his black silken locks and dropped a kiss upon his nose.

Yes, it was over—all that had been keeping them apart. She remembered that first moment when she had come to ... there by the bridge with Jason calling her name. She had cried, cried all the way home on the saddle before him. She had heard him call out instructions about the

237

horses, about Mac, to the stable boys, and her heart had recoiled within her.

Questions were flung at them as he carried her into the house, past Lillian, past the servants, to her room upstairs. She had not been able to stop shaking . . . to stop her tears from falling . . . but he had stayed, soothing her, quieting her. Hours later he was still beside her, talking away her fears.

"Hush, darling. Hush, love . . . it is over," he said, holding her.

"He—he was trying to kill you . . . because of me. I nearly brought you death, Jason."

"My sweet life, you have brought me love. At least, I hope that is what you have brought me," he said teasingly.

She had flung her arms about him and said words she never thought her pride would allow. It flowed then, and each spoke of love and withered away each other's doubts.

Later they talked of Mac. She told him how Mac had broken beneath the strain of his terrors, how he had killed John, and why he had wanted to kill Jason.

Her husband sighed heavily. "It was because of him that I went to Dean last evening. I have a good friend living there—the Squire . . . we were at school together. We hatched a plan between us to trap my . . . er . . . ill-wisher by drawing him out. I always felt Mac was behind it, for I sensed something unhealthy in his solicitousness toward you."

Jenny had dived into her husband's arms. "Please Jason, take me home. Please, Jason."

He had stroked her head and told her not to fret, he would see his lawyers and somehow get a release from that particular requirement of his father's will. They had, in fact, discovered that while the will clearly specified that an uninterrupted month must be spent at Waine Castle after the wedding, it did not indicate *how soon* after the wedding.

Mr. McMillan's body had been retrieved and his remains were sent to his father in Cornwall, without telling that old gentleman the whole. The tale was set about that

Mac had met his untimely end by accident, and though speculation was rife, the story was not openly challenged.

Thus it was that the Squire and Aunt Beth joyously greeted their Jenny and her husband.

"I received an epistle from my cousin Howard," said Jason, grinning playfully.

"Oh . . . what does he say?"

"That, m' girl, he find life with Miss Browne far more enjoyable than you did."

She giggled. "How do the Wendall boys go on?"

He sighed. "As always, love. It's Harrow for them soon."

"And Julian?"

"He and Lillian have left for India, and I imagine they will be there quite some time."

She snuggled into his arms and he kissed her forehead. "What an affectionate little puss I have married. You gave me no hint of it when we met, you know."

"Odious man."

"And I thought you loved me?"

"Oh, Jason, I do," she said, suddenly grave.

He held her tightly to him. "Our sun shines, Jenny," he whispered lowering her to the ground, his lips warm against her own, and their hearts full with each other.

> *Thus with many a pretty oath,*
> *Yea, and nay and faith and troth,*
> *Love which had been long deluded,*
> *Was with kisses sweet concluded.*
>
> NICHOLAS BRETON, 1591

## ANOTHER REGENCY ROMANCE
## FROM CLAUDETTE WILLIAMS

**SPRING GAMBIT      2-3025-2      $1.50**

Nicole Beaumont was the joy and despair of every eligible London gentleman. Her first social season was a smashing success. The high-spirited beauty enchanted every young man she met, but she wanted only one—Adam Roth, Duke of Lyndham. When Nicky announced she was going to marry for love, unlike many in her set, Adam didn't know that he was her target.

SPRING GAMBIT—A joyous adventure in Regency England with a heroine who throws convention to the winds and her heart to the man she loves.